TIME ST PPERS

ESCAPE FROM THE BADLANDS

Also by Carrie Jones

The Time Stoppers series
Time Stoppers
Quest for the Golden Arrow

★

The Need series
Need
Captivate
Entice
Endure

★

With Steven E. Wedel
After Obsession

TIME STOPPERS

ESCAPE FROM THE BADLANDS

CARRIE JONES

BLOOMSBURY
CHILDREN'S BOOKS
NEW YORK   LONDON   OXFORD   NEW DELHI   SYDNEY

BLOOMSBURY CHILDREN'S BOOKS
Bloomsbury Publishing Inc., part of Bloomsbury Publishing Plc
1385 Broadway, New York, NY 10018

BLOOMSBURY, BLOOMSBURY CHILDREN'S BOOKS, and the Diana logo
are trademarks of Bloomsbury Publishing Plc

First published in the United States of America in August 2018
by Bloomsbury Children's Books

Bloomsbury books may be purchased for business or promotional use. For information on
bulk purchases please contact Macmillan Corporate and Premium Sales Department at
specialmarkets@macmillan.com

Library of Congress Cataloging-in-Publication Data
Names: Jones, Carrie, author.
Title: Escape from the Badlands / by Carrie Jones.
Description: New York : Bloomsbury, 2018. | Series: Time Stoppers ; 3
Summary: To save the enchanted town Aurora, Annie journeys deep into the Raiff's realm,
the Badlands, where she and her friends face everything from ruthless monsters
to their own deepest fears.
Identifiers: LCCN 2017034360 (print) • LCCN 2017045608 (e-book)
ISBN 978-1-61963-865-5 (hardcover) • ISBN 978-1-61963-866-2 (e-book)
Subjects: | CYAC: Fantasy. | Magic—Fiction.
Classification: LCC PZ7.J6817 Esc 2018 (print) | LCC PZ7.J6817 (e-book) | DDC [Fic]—dc23
LC record available at https://lccn.loc.gov/2017034360

Book design by John Candell
Typeset by Westchester Publishing Services
Printed and bound in the U.S.A. by Berryville Graphics Inc., Berryville, Virginia
2 4 6 8 10 9 7 5 3 1

All papers used by Bloomsbury Publishing Plc are natural, recyclable products made
from wood grown in well-managed forests. The manufacturing processes conform
to the environmental regulations of the country of origin.

To find out more about our authors and books visit www.bloomsbury.com
and sign up for our newsletters.

To everyone who needs magic and friends, this book is for you, and it is most especially dedicated to Emily, who began as Annie and ended up her own brilliant hero, and to Shaun, for believing in me enough to carry a giant gnome everywhere

Alexander wept when he heard Anaxarchus' discourse about an infinite number of worlds, and when his friends inquired what ailed him, "Is it not worthy of tears," he said, "that, when the number of worlds is infinite, we have not yet become lords of a single one?"

—PLUTARCH, *MORALIA*

TIME STOPPERS

ESCAPE FROM
THE BADLANDS

1

The Evil Statues of Evilness

Annie Nobody, the youngest Time Stopper in the world, tied her coat more tightly around her waist as the heat of the Badlands weighed against her skin, sweaty and oppressive. Her best friend, James Hephaistion Alexander, strode next to her, scratching at his shoulder blades. On her other side, Bloom, the last elf, scanned the dark landscape, searching for any trolls, vampires, or kelpies that might attack them while they tried to find the kidnapped elves. Behind them, Eva kept whipping her pigtails at SalGoud's stone-giant arms. They all knew they were out there—the elves were stationary, trapped, and dying as the Raiff drained their life forces to enhance his own power. And the monsters . . . Monsters could be anywhere, skulking through the shadows of the broken and burned trees, lurking behind boulders, crawling in the cracks of the crusty land.

Annie shivered despite the heat.

"Don't worry, Annie. We've got this," Jamie said before stepping back to check on Eva, who was walking behind them, her ax held ready in her small, sturdy hands.

They had no choice but to be successful. It wasn't very long ago that Eva, the pigtailed dwarf, had plucked Annie out of the winter woods, shoved her onto a hovering snowmobile, and whisked her away to the magical town of Aurora. But magical didn't mean safe, and they had to save the town from trolls sent by the Raiff, an evil demon. Then, he'd kidnapped Annie's time-stopping grandmother, Miss Cornelia, and brought her here, to the Badlands, hoping to get her to open a portal to bring him and all his minions back to Aurora, freeing them from this giant trap.

But the children had gone to Ireland, found the Golden Bow and Arrow, and saved Miss Cornelia. Now they would rescue the elves.

Annie just hadn't expected the Badlands to be so . . . dire? Hot? Horrible? Smelly?

And scary.

It was *so* scary. Black scorch marks marred all the tree trunks, fire had left them crooked and broken as they looked for respite from the heavy air. The red dirt of the ground was so dry that it seemed to crack with every step they took.

Tricking the Raiff and freeing Miss Cornelia had been the most frightening thing Annie had ever done—that any of them had ever done—and sending Miss Cornelia safely home to warn Aurora of the Raiff's return was even harder. Now the children were alone, trying to save the elves.

"I hope we find them, especially the grandmother," Bloom said, his voice breaking a tiny bit.

"The grandmother?" Annie asked, coughing from the heat. He hadn't mentioned her before.

His voice grew strong again. "We call her Seanmháthair. Cornelia told me all about her, and sometimes if I think hard enough I can almost remember her. When I was little, I would hear her voice just as I fell asleep, telling me she loved me, that all would be okay, that I wasn't alone." His voice broke, and he smiled as if trying to push away his sadness. "I thought it was just . . . that I was just imagining her voice. It gave me comfort."

Annie grabbed his hand and squeezed it. Bloom had thought for so long that he was the last elf living. He'd grown up the only one of his kind and now here he was trying to save the remaining elves.

She glanced over to Jamie, who was trying to convince Eva that drinking water was not for wimps, but an intelligent move to keep from dehydrating. Jamie's face looked hopeful despite the grim circumstances, the unrelenting heat, and their limited food supply. He was used to that, though, having grown up with trolls who kept him half-starved and always doing chores.

"'When angels visit us, we do not hear the rustle of wings, nor feel the feathery touch of the breast of a dove; but we know their presence by the love they create in our hearts.' Mary Baker Eddy," SalGoud, the stone giant, croaked out, readjusting his glasses on his long nose. "I don't know why I would think that. I think the heat is getting to me."

"It's a nice quote, but you seem hot. Your lips are cracked," Jamie answered, scratching his shoulder blades again. SalGoud was so tall, so kind, and so terribly fond of quotes and books that sometimes Annie and Jamie would fret together that he forgot how to live in the real world. "I'm worried you're too parched."

"Badge of a warrior!" Eva tossed back at him, latching and unlatching her ax on her belt for the fifteenth time in five minutes. "There's no time for water. No time for wasting. We have elves to save by breaking some evil demon machine with some dwarf treasure, a magic bow and arrow. We have to get those same elves to a portal back to the regular world, and away from this pixie-forsaken place; we have a demon and his minions to defeat and then . . ."

Her voice faltered.

"And then?" Jamie prodded.

"And then we have decades of listening to the songs in tribute to our glory!" Eva declared, beating her chest with her free fist and knocking the water bottle and its precious contents out of Jamie's grasp.

It flew through the air. Bloom caught it with one hand, righting it before more than one drop of water was spilled.

"Impressive!" SalGoud said.

Eva wiped the sweat off her forehead. "So, where is it we're supposed to go exactly?"

A bird cawed in the distance. They all jumped.

"Lichen said there is a Door of Descent at the base of the tallest mountain's west side, by the five trees that remain unscorched," SalGoud said, sounding almost as if he was reciting one of his famous inspirational quotes. Lichen, an elf who had escaped the Raiff's clutches and was now hidden with the hag Megan in Aurora, had told them the route to go, but there were so many details to remember.

Over and over, SalGoud had recited the checklist of steps that poor, possibly dying, Lichen had told them:

1. Go to the Badlands
2. Find the Door of Descent
3. Move through the Statues' Chamber
4. Get to Scot's Land
5. Find the Gate of Despair
6. Head toward the mountain range and the Pass of Sighs
7. Find the machine

8. Set the dwarfs' treasures—a diamond, a toy dragon plated with gold and stolen rubies, a sword, a dagger, and a shield—at five points of a star around the machine
9. Shoot the machine with the Golden Bow and Arrow
10. Bring elves back home

"Take care . . . ," Lichen had whispered. "The closer to the machine you come, the more you change."

Lichen had been so weak, hunkered in Megan the hag's closet, that it had been hard for him to even talk. The conversation seemed so long ago. Sometimes Annie couldn't believe that it had only been days.

Now, shoulders slumped from the dry heat, the group set off toward the tallest mountain. It wasn't long before they spotted the five trees, still blooming and green despite the constant heat and seemingly unrelenting sun.

"This is it!" Eva roared and started running toward the trees.

"She never runs." SalGoud shook his head and followed her. "She must be happy."

"She's never happy," Bloom muttered. "Unless she's boasting. Or talking about dwarfs and how awesome her family is."

Annie picked up her pace. "It's kind of the same thing."

Jamie smiled at her as Bloom began to jog, too. It seemed

unreal that they were here in the Badlands, so far from Aurora, Maine, the magical town they were trying to protect. He'd liked being far from the house where the Alexanders had pretended to be his family for years, all just so they could eventually eat him, or so he would turn troll. It was only a few days after his birthday, and he had less than a year to see if he'd turn troll, too.

His heart seemed to stop. He'd forgotten the risk for a moment, forgotten that he could become as horrible as the Alexanders. He had been so focused on trying to set things right and safe. It all seemed so big and impossible, but he and Annie had made promises to each other. They would be forever friends. They would never desert each other, no matter what.

Coughing from the heat, he tried to lift Annie's spirits and his own. "We can do this, you know."

She sucked her lips in toward her mouth. They were cracking from the dryness. "I know. We have to. There's no choice. Let's go find that door, okay, Jamie? You and me? No matter what."

He knew she meant, no matter if you turn troll. Bumping her with his hip, he made his voice braver for her. "Always."

———

Back in Aurora, two old friends soared across the sky, worrying about the children they'd left in the Badlands.

Finally, the dragon landed in the middle of a front lawn, scorching a giant circle of snow around him. The old woman hopped off his back, stepped across the steaming ground, and patted his muzzle.

"Well, old comrade," she said. "We're in quite a pickle, aren't we?"

"I should hope not." Grady O'Grady snorted and looked up at the Aquarius House looming at the top of the hill in front of him. "That would smell . . . quite vinegary. I can't stand that smell."

Miss Cornelia rolled her eyes and repressed a large smile. "You are such a literal dragon."

"Do you mean I am literally a dragon or that I am literal?" he asked.

Cornelia didn't have time to answer because a pale ghost had jettisoned herself out of the house right beside the left attic window and next to the widow's walk. She spiraled down toward the ground like an overambitious whirlpool and stopped suddenly to hover right above Grady O'Grady's nose.

"A DRAGON!" the Woman in White screeched. "Is it you, Grady O'Grady?"

Grady took one knee. "It is I. And I have brought you a long-lost Stopper."

The Woman in White's hand fluttered to her mouth and she squealed, before throwing herself into the other woman in an enthusiastic hug of nothingness. "Cornelia! I've been so worried! We've all been so worried! We thought you'd never get back! Oh, the Captain! Oh, you poor dear! DRAGON! You have brought her to us!"

Before either Grady or Cornelia could say anything, the Woman in White threw herself against Grady O'Grady, trying to hug him, too, and obviously still forgetting that ghosts can't quite hug.

The Woman in White flew straight up into the air and said in a hushed, horrified voice, "Where are the children? WHY AREN'T THE CHILDREN HERE?"

"The children have stayed. They—" Miss Cornelia said awkwardly, her eyes on the flame of light inside Grady O'Grady's pupils. "They have chosen to be brave and do something that they will not explain to me and we—I—we all have to trust them."

"Trust them?" The Woman in White shrieked and gave a great shudder. "They are children!"

"Exactly why we should!" Cornelia said clearly. "Children are much more trustworthy than adults. They haven't been sullied by life yet. And the Raiff can't read children's minds, which is why they are doing whatever it is they are doing there. They could not tell me, or the Raiff would read my mind and know."

Her eyes shifted to the group of people streaming out of the front doors of Aquarius House. Her best friends, Gramma

Doris and Ned the Doctor, fluttered out as Ned rattled off a quote about dragons being here. Helena, covered in powdered sugar, gasped and held on to Mr. Nate, who was tucking a book into his belt, the way librarians do. Several fairies stood in shock on the front porch. More villagers and forest creatures streamed up the hill, coming from the town.

"It's hard to be inconspicuous when you're a dragon." Grady O'Grady shrugged. "Please, no autographs. No requests for bonfire settings."

Gramma Doris shot forward to hug Miss Cornelia while Gran Pie the Big Foot fainted. Helena and Mr. Nate tried to resuscitate the Big Foot by tugging the hair between her toes and making her smell the chocolate mint croissant Helena conjured out of thin air.

Despite the commotion, Cornelia quickly explained all that had happened as more and more people joined them on the front lawn. "Grady O'Grady will fly back to the Badlands to scout things out, give us updates on the Raiff and his movements, and of course, protect the children."

"The children!" The Woman in White fluttered around in a frenzy, banging through several dwarfs and multiple werewolves until she finally settled against Leodora Lenci Leksi's fine furry arm. Leodora didn't seem to mind.

"Where exactly in the Badlands are the children, Corny?" Gramma Doris asked, hand over her chest as she scanned her friend's face.

"No questions!" The Woman in White spiraled off into the woods, barreling through Gran Pie who sputtered about dragons and quickly turned away.

"I don't know," Cornelia admitted. "I do hope they avoid Scot's Land. That's such a horrible place."

"It's *all* a horrible place," Canin growled.

"Indeed it is," Cornelia agreed, ushering the group inside the house as Grady took flight. "But some of it is worse than others."

As the mountain loomed over them, SalGoud and Annie scurried around between the five trees, prodding the ground with their weapons. Eva stomped this way and that, knocking at the ground, at tree trunks, and at SalGoud's back, which caused him to pick her up and move her away, which caused her to roar in anger, which caused Bloom to tell her to hush before the Raiff's minions found them.

But nobody had found the Door of Descent, and the mountain kept thumping like a giant heartbeat, which made everything seem even more urgent. It didn't help when a giant foot formed halfway up the mountain and wiggled its dirt toes at them, casting rocks and pieces of burned wood down all around them before disappearing.

"You're an elf," Eva sputtered at Bloom, twitching the dirt out of her left pigtail. "Can't you just sense it or something?"

Bloom raised an eyebrow, but didn't answer.

"This should be easier," SalGoud said. "Maybe these aren't the right trees."

"They are the only five normal trees we've seen," Annie said, surveying the wasteland around them, the burned-out bushes and broken trees. "I think this has to be it."

"Where are ya hiding, ya daft door!" Eva roared. She threw herself on the ground and pummeled it with her fists. "I can't avenge my mom's—" She broke off her sentence with a mortified roar of anger and plopped on the ground, snapping a broken tree branch with her fists.

"What are you talking about, Eva?" Annie asked, bending over the dwarf, whose eyes were squeezed tightly shut as she quaked with rage.

"Nothing!" Eva bellowed.

Annie backed away and looked to Jamie for help. She'd only been trying to care for her. She knew that this quest seemed impossible even for a dwarf, an elf, a giant, a maybe-human, and a Time Stopper. SalGoud was already mumbling random quotes about bravery and angels and perseverance, and Bloom leaned forward as he walked, almost as if the horrible land was draining his energy. She didn't know how to make it better, to make them believe that they could do this. Plus, the mountain had now formed two giant hands and was snapping its fingers at them and pointing. The Raiff and his monsters would surely notice soon. There might as well have been a sign that said CHILDREN ARE HERE! PLEASE COME EAT THEM!

"Everyone is giving up," Jamie whispered as he beckoned for Annie and Bloom to come closer.

Bloom's eyes widened. "We can't give up. The elves depend on us."

Annie placed a hand on his arm, trying to soothe him. "We aren't giving up, Bloom. We'll find the elves and the grandmother."

Jamie walked away from them. There had to be a clue—something they were missing. He inhaled the hot stale air and leaned up against the closest tree, trying to think. The tree was cold.

Cold?

That made no sense. Nothing here was cold.

"Guys?" he said, trying to get their attention as he turned around to feel the tree with his hands. It was absolutely cold, not as cold as an ice cube, more like the outside of the refrigerator. He tried again. "Guys?"

This time Annie heard him. A moment later she was by his side. "What is it, Jamie?"

He explained. She touched the tree, too, and gasped and ran around stroking the other trees. All were warm.

"Try to open it," she said.

"How?"

"I don't know."

"Maybe if I ask nicely?"

"Say please. It's always good to say please."

Jamie steeled himself and tried to make his voice sound as polite as possible. "Dear Miss Tree."

"Miss?"

"It feels like a girl." He cleared his throat. "Dear Miss Tree. Would you mind terribly showing us the door and letting us go through?"

Annie cleared her throat.

"Please?" Jamie quickly added. He couldn't believe he forgot.

For a moment nothing happened.

"Jamie . . ." Annie looked steadily at the bark of the tree trunk. It began to ripple and almost fold in on itself. And then, the tree opened, revealing a staircase made of roots and moss and lichen, spiraling down and down, farther into the ground, so deep that they couldn't see where it stopped. Annie was grateful they all had flashlights.

"Wow," Jamie whispered as Annie clutched his hand. "The Door of Descent."

Eva stomped over. "Good. Took you long enough."

And she started down the staircase without looking back. The others followed.

"One step closer," Annie told Bloom. "We'll get them."

"As long as it's not too late," he said as they began going down the staircase.

"It won't be," she said, but like Jamie she really wasn't sure. She was a Time Stopper, meant to use the strings to stop time and do magic, but she was so new at it all, and she wasn't 100 percent sure where the strings were. Usually, she could feel them, but the more they traveled into the Badlands, the harder they were to find. And if she couldn't find them, she couldn't use them. And then there was the cold. The more they traveled, the colder she got. That didn't make sense when the air was so hot and everyone else was so sweaty.

"It will be fine," she said, just like Jamie had said before. "We can do this. I can do this."

And she followed the others down the stairs.

The temperature had dropped a good twenty degrees as they'd descended the curving stone stairs, and the walls smelled wet and felt frosty beneath Jamie's hand.

It seemed as if they'd been walking down the stairs forever. With each step, Jamie's heart sank a bit deeper into sadness. He longed for Aurora, and Miss Cornelia's cozy house. For a minute, he wished that they could have brought an adult, Mr. Nate or even Ned the Doctor, someone to take charge, but if they had, the Raiff would have sensed the adult's thoughts and known what was happening. They couldn't risk that.

"I don't like it here," he muttered to himself.

"Nor do I," said Bloom behind him.

Jamie hadn't realized that he'd spoken aloud. Bloom put his hand on Jamie's shoulder. Cold. Bloom's hand was so cold against the warmth of Jamie's shoulder.

"I think we should slow down," Bloom whispered. It was a whisper that Jamie recognized immediately. It was the whisper of an elf focused on something. "Tell Eva."

Jamie hopped down two steps to catch up to Eva, who tromped along as loudly as an elephant. He tapped the dwarf on the shoulder. "Eva. Eva. Bloom says we should slow down and stop."

Eva grumped. "We gotta get there, don't we?"

Jamie sighed. "I think he hears something or senses something. It feels . . ."

Jamie struggled to find the words and couldn't quite get them. It felt, what? Cold? Scary? Ominous? He gulped.

"Elves are always listening and sensing and being all drama," Eva said disdainfully as she quickened her pace. "Maybe there's a fight waiting. I never get to fight. Even in the Badlands, all I do is walk, walk, walk. I'm sick of all these stupid stairs. How is a dwarf supposed to prove herself? To get her family name back into the *Rolls of Awesome Dwarfness*? How?"

"Eva—" Annie started, but the dwarf ignored her and ran down the stairs with her stocky little tree-trunk legs. They all had no choice but to sigh, grumble, and follow.

"I tried," Jamie said to Bloom, who had caught up to them. SalGoud panted behind him.

"Dwarfs don't listen." SalGoud wiped some sweat off his forehead, and used his shirttail to rub his glasses clean. "There's a T Swift lyric that begins, 'Like—'"

A bloodcurdling yell broke through the darkness below them.

"Eva!" SalGoud roared and smashed past Jamie, Annie, and Bloom, pushing them to the stone walls. Bloom followed, pulling out his bow and notching an arrow as he ran.

The stairs gave way to a flat room, also built of stone. Hazy orange light filled the chamber but Jamie didn't have time to determine its source. A giant statue of a cupid, the kind you find atop museum roofs, was attacking Eva. The stone angel's marble arms clutched Eva's waist, crushing her. Ten feet above the ground, she flailed, trying to get free from the smiling cupid. Eva's arms were pinned against her sides. She growled and kicked at the cupid with her boots.

But that wasn't the worst of it. All about the room were statues—horses, men carrying books, women holding babies, soldiers with spears, soldiers with swords, soldiers with guns—that stomped, shuffled, and ambled with definite purpose directly toward the children, determined, it seemed, to crush them.

"Stand back!" Bloom shot an arrow at the cupid's leg. It bounced off, harming nothing.

"Elf!!!" Eva bellowed.

"I'm trying, Eva!" Bloom stashed his bow in a rapid movement, searching for another option.

"I found the Statues' Chamber!" Eva declared, still trying to get her arms loose. "In the songs, make sure I get the glory for this! You can't take it."

SalGoud rushed the cupid and smashed its leg with the front of his head, like wrestlers do. The cupid twitched for a moment and kicked its stubby marble leg out, making impact with SalGoud's side and hurtling the young stone giant across the room.

Jamie gasped, sickened by the violence.

Annie raced to SalGoud, trying to help him to his feet.

Bloom ran up between two soldiers, scaled each of their legs as if he were scaling a tree, jumping between them, and wrenched a spear out of one's hand. He hurled the spear at the cupid and made a direct strike in the statue's neck. The arrow-shooting cherub stumbled for a second.

But only a second.

"Annie!" Bloom yelled, leaping off the soldier's shoulder and to the ground just as the statue tried to grab him in its marble hand. Bloom landed squarely on the floor and raced to Annie, gripping her by the waist.

"Stop time!" he yelled. "Stop it!"

Annie closed her eyes and tried to sense the resonance of the strings. It was so hard here. They seemed faint somehow.

What if she couldn't do it? She remembered her conversation with Miss Cornelia: sometimes the stop didn't work . . . and the strings . . . they didn't feel the same . . .

"Come on. Come on," she muttered, drawing the word in her mind, tracing it against her leg.

Eva hollered curses at the "little baby cupid and his stinky diaper."

Bloom's hands held strong about her waist. Annie reached out with her core, trying to touch the energy, trying to use Bloom's magic to help her own. She traced the word in the air, finding purpose in each letter.

Statues closed in.

Jamie ran toward them, reaching out his hand.

"Stop," she whispered. "Stop."

And suddenly the only thing Annie could hear was the sound of Bloom's breath mingling with her own. All the knots of tension in her body relaxed. And then he was gone. She opened her eyes. Bloom was already scaling the cupid, trying to squeeze Eva out of its arms.

All around the chamber, statues were frozen again like proper works of art; however, they were stuck in very non-museum-worthy poses. One soldier sniffed his armpit. A horse lifted his hind leg as if he was about to pee. The rest were in various threatening positions, all reaching toward the children. SalGoud's face was a mask of pain. Jamie was frozen, too, midstride, arm still outstretched toward her.

"Annie!" Bloom called. "I need help."

He was trying to pull Eva through the cupid's arms. Annie climbed up the statue's leg, using its diaper as a handhold as she stepped higher off its knee. She wedged herself in its elbow for balance, grabbed Eva beneath her armpit, and yanked on one side as Bloom yanked on the other.

Bloom grunted. "One more good tug."

They heaved Eva through. Annie kept hold of her while Bloom scrambled back to the floor. Annie dropped the dwarf into his arms, and he put her gently on the ground. Her face was frozen in a contorted expression of rage.

"Lovely." Bloom smiled.

"SalGoud?" Annie asked. "Do you think he's okay?"

They checked the stone giant.

"His eyes are open," Bloom said, leaning over his friend. "That's a good sign. Let's drag them all to the other side of the room. I've an idea."

At the other end of the room was a door, and Bloom rushed to it. "More stairs."

Annie tugged on SalGoud and didn't make much headway. The giant was a lot heavier than he looked because his bones were made of stone. Bloom came back to help and they worked together, dragging the boy across the floor. Jamie was easier, which broke Annie's heart. She knew he was so light because for years he'd barely been fed at all—for years. She wondered how he'd managed to survive so long. His bones seemed hollow like a bird's bones. And there . . . he'd somehow gotten a gold feather stuck in his hair.

Annie was close to crying.

Bloom's voice was encouraging. "You stopped time."

"You had to tell me to." Annie sighed, pretending that's what she had been upset about, but it was more about how much pain everyone had gone through and how she couldn't just magically make it better. That seemed too big to explain. So instead, she said, "I didn't even think of stopping time."

SalGoud's foot got caught up in the fin of a mermaid statue. Bloom went to detangle it. "But you did it. Sometimes we need help thinking of things. Leave yourself alone."

"It wasn't easy," she said, thinking about it all, trying to believe him. "I think something's wrong with the strings."

He checked for his Golden Arrow, making sure it was still safely stashed. "I know. Even my magic doesn't seem right. The farther we go into this land, the weaker it feels."

They left Jamie, SalGoud, and Eva in a heap just on the other side of the door's threshold by another set of descending stairs. Annie decided they should topple a few statues to block the way. They wrapped a rope around the neck of a kilted warrior and pulled him over in front of the door. As he fell, his arm hit the floor at a funny angle and broke off.

"Oh," Annie gasped. Bloom looked startled and then shrugged. They tumbled several more in front of the door and then slipped through the gaps.

"That should help," Bloom said as Annie grabbed his hand and whispered for time to start again.

Immediately the statues in the room behind them began stomping and running around in circles, searching for the children.

Jamie's breath came out in a rush. "Whoa . . ."

Eva sat up, glowering at Annie. "You ruined the fight. Do you always have to stop time just when things get good? I could have totally taken that cupid AND the rest of those crusty mossy statues."

Without missing a beat, she strode down the stairs again. Annie couldn't figure Eva out lately. Ever since they'd said goodbye to Johann, Eva's distant dwarf cousin, at the Dublin airport, the dwarf had been acting even grumpier than normal. She was always muttering things and was glaring more than usual. Maybe it was just stress.

Annie helped SalGoud to his feet. "Are you okay?"

He smiled sheepishly. "Just a little headache. It helps to be made of stone, you know."

He turned to pace after the dwarf. "Slow down, Eva. Be patient."

The statues were moaning behind them and trying to haul their bulky forms back up. Jamie fiddled with his ring and hung back with Annie as Bloom descended. They followed at a bit of a distance and he whispered, "I couldn't get to you in time before the stop."

"I'm so sorry," Annie said. "I hate freezing people like that."

"That's not it." The stairs turned to stone as they descended. Frost started to form on Jamie's eyelashes. "I hate the violence. I hate . . . I hate the fighting. It makes me hurt inside and it makes my shoulder blades itch."

Annie placed her hand on his arm. "I know."

But he wasn't sure that she did. When nobody else was looking, he peered at his skin, hoping against hope that it was still a nice, deep brown hue and not tinted the horrible green of a troll.

Annie noticed. "Jamie. We will always be friends. No matter what happens to you, even if you become a troll. You'll still be Jamie and we'll still be Jamie and Annie, friends forever, okay?"

He wanted to believe that, but he was so itchy and so scared of what he might become.

As the children continued down the Stairs of Descent and cold tunnels of the Underground, the thoughts that raced through everyone's head except Eva's were filled with doubts and fear. The way became even colder, and the children kept close.

And then in front of Eva was a door.

It was a rather unremarkable door, made of wooden

boards and with a curved top. A long black handle rested on its right side. It did not seem to be locked.

Eva reached for the handle.

"No," Annie yelled, surprising everyone and making Sal-Goud jump.

Eva's hand stopped.

"What is it?" SalGoud asked, his voice cracking.

Annie looked up into his face and noticed how scared he was. The flashlight's beam glinted off his glasses. She wondered how someone so big, so strong, could be scared. That wondering did not make her feel better.

"It feels dark behind it. It feels like horror," she whispered and then turned to Bloom.

He had laid his hand flat against the door.

"But the dark is not all that is there," he said in a low voice. He dropped his hand from the door. "And we are being followed."

Bloom's face was pale. They knew he meant business, and SalGoud glanced up the stairs from which they'd come. He rubbed his head in great sweeping motions with his oversize hands and said, "Statues?"

Bloom shook his head. "No. Something else."

He nodded at Eva and she pushed open the door.

2

The Headless Trunk

Darkness met them—a great, wide darkness more dense than badly made chocolate pudding, and, embedded in the darkness was a great cold feeling of despair, of bad things to come.

There was a long silence. Annie couldn't tell if her eyes were open or closed, and then the despair socked them in their stomachs.

"I'm so sad," SalGoud murmured. "This feels like that place in Ireland beneath Annie's grandparents' hotel where her grandmother made the sadness curse."

"There is no hope . . . No hope at all," Bloom added, rubbing at his face with his hands.

Eva grumbled. "Ach. Toughen up. It's just the dark."

Whatever the rest of them were feeling? Annie couldn't believe it, but Eva just ignored it, jumping right into the middle of the darkness.

Bloom grabbed Eva by the backpack, and pulled her to the relative safety of the wall. "You don't know what's out there, Eva. Don't be so rash."

"I'm not afraid!" Eva blustered, shrugging his hand off her. "I'm not afraid of anything."

"Nobody said you were," said Bloom quietly. "But stay with us."

"What is darkness? It is when a thousand voices that once praised beauty are silent. It is where a thousand eyes cannot see. It is a . . . what, a tangible terror," SalGoud whispered.

"Who said that?" Annie asked.

"Me," he quietly replied. "Do you think it's good enough to put in *SalGoud's Book of Self-Created Quotations*?"

Annie petted his long, hard arm in what she hoped was an encouraging manner. "Oh, absolutely."

It took another minute for their heart rates to go down. None of them could see much of anything. They didn't know whether or not to turn their flashlights on. The light could call attention to their position and attract ghouls or trolls, like a beacon that flashed the words GOOD EATS at a diner on the highway.

SalGoud hesitated and murmured in the overdramatic way he had when quoting, " 'We listened and looked sideways up! Fear at my heart, as at a cup, my life-blood seemed to sip.'"

"Who said that?" Annie whispered. "You?"

"Coleridge, 'The Rime of the Ancient Mariner.'"

"It's appropriate," Annie said, willing herself to step into the dark. One foot moved forward. Fear clutched her heart.

"Thank you," SalGoud murmured.

Jamie and SalGoud also stepped out into the night. The door slammed shut behind them with a heavy bang. Annie whirled around, patting down the wall, frantically trying to find a handle, but her hands just slid over cold stone. She couldn't see anything.

"The door's gone," Annie whispered as Jamie clutched her hand.

"Shhh." Bloom pulled out his bow and notched an arrow.

Annie's knees trembled. She pushed her backpack against the wall and clenched Jamie's hand even harder as she peered into the darkness.

A crunching, shuffling noise moved behind them. The air suddenly stank of hot metal. There was something out there.

SalGoud grabbed Annie's arm so hard that it hurt. She closed her eyes. What kind of thing was that, making its way through the dark, right at them? She wanted to run but knew that would be stupid. In the horror movies that her foster brother Walden watched the person who ran always died, didn't they? Of course, this was no horror movie; this was her life. Biting her lip, she willed her teeth not to chatter. Near her, Eva tensed and lifted her ax.

The great shuffling noise came closer and closer. A sniff here, and a swallow there.

Everything inside Annie begged her to run.

She refused.

Stay calm, stay calm, she told herself.

But calmness was out of the question. The rank whoosh of air from the shuffling thing hit her face. She imagined the teeth that would go with it. With her mind, she reached out for the strings, ready to stop time again, but she couldn't exactly feel them this time. It was as if they had moved from the place they always were. Another hot breath came from the thing in the dark. It pushed her hair back against the wall.

Eva's ax whacked through the air. There was the sickening sound of it striking into fur and bone. Then came an astonished sniff. Something large thudded onto the ground.

"Got it," Eva said. "Remember this part for the songs of glory, okay?"

The dwarf reached out her hand and grabbed Jamie's.

"We follow the wall. I lead," the dwarf whispered, pulling him along.

Jamie gulped. He was scared before, but even more now. Looking down at his hand in front of him, he shook. His skin was glowing, just the faintest of bits, giving off light.

He pushed SalGoud and Annie along. The fallen thing stirred on the ground and snuffed.

"It's not dead," Jamie said softly. He could feel the life of it, somehow, a darkness that was only the tip of the evil of this place.

"It wasn't dead?" Bloom whispered.

Eva ignored his question and urged everyone to move faster. The thing followed.

"What is it?" Annie murmured.

SalGoud's sharp intake of breath was louder than his quiet words, "Coluinn gun Cheann."

"Coluinn gun Cheann?" Jamie didn't even like the name.

"The Coluinn gun Cheann was a headless monster that used to roam the MacDonald lands in Scotland," SalGoud said. "I recognize it from my history books. The Mac-Donalds were constantly finding travelers mutilated by the horrible, headless creature. This wasn't any good because they enjoyed visitors, so one brave member of the family challenged the beast to a fight and won, though no one knows quite how, thereby earning the right to banish the immortal beast from their land forever. As a result, the beast romanced and spread its mutilating terror throughout the rest of the land."

"The Headless Trunk!" Eva bellowed. "He cannot hear, but he can smell. That's why we have to run."

Jamie wasn't about to argue.

They ran.

The part of the Badlands they now found themselves in felt different from the rest. It was no longer a landscape with scorched trees and dried-up ground, but a city with a dark cobblestone street. The children raced through it as a nasty brainless monster rumbled after them.

Wretched and seemingly empty, all the city's buildings were sideways or backward or upside down. It was like an artist had drawn it and kept turning the paper around and around, adding more and more buildings at all the wrong angles. And the buildings were old, made of cobblestone and brick, with dry, cracked wooden doors and gray stone.

But worse than that—it was as if someone had failed to draw in any details. No grass peeked out of the cracks in the street. No leaves sprouted from any bushes. No cats or dogs ran about. No business signs existed. No mailboxes peeked from the residences' walls.

Suddenly, as the children rushed away from the horrible monster that wanted nothing more than to annihilate them and possibly use their toes for Q-tips, there came a great multitude of noises from the windows all along the street and above their heads. Windows snapped opened into the darkness and dozens of children's voices shouted, "All clear. Poopy's here!"

Stunned, the travelers stopped running and peered up into the darkness. Then came the emptying of the chamber pots, a great splattering onto the cobblestone streets, and with it soared a stench so awful that it was all the children could do not to throw up.

"Ach!" SalGoud yelled, grabbing his nose. "What is it? It's worse than trolls."

"It's poop! Poop!" Eva screamed, waving her ax around with one hand while covering her mouth and nose with her other. "I'll kill them all. Death to all the poopers! Is it in my hair? Is it?"

Eva strutted back and forth in front of them, flinging her pigtails, panic clearly overwhelming her. "It is in my hair, isn't it?"

It wasn't. The smell, however, *was* in the air, giving the children a bit of a break and confusing the monster behind them, allowing them a few more seconds of a lead as the headless brute tried to sort out their smells from the smells of poop. Meanwhile, all the windows in all the houses and apartments quickly snapped shut.

"We could split up," SalGoud suggested.

"No," Annie and Jamie both yelled.

"We stay together," Bloom said, racing on and helping Eva, who had tripped on something brown and unfortunate.

The beast lumbered after them, having finally gained strength from the delicious smell of dwarf, elf, and giant with a little child thrown in. The Coluinn gun Cheann found it as intoxicating an odor as chocolate chip cookies were to Bloom.

That's what gave Jamie the idea.

"Everyone, quick," he yelled. "Take off a shirt or something and give it to me."

No one argued. They each struggled to strip off an item of clothing as they ran. It was especially hard for Eva, who had decided to remove a sock. They all hurriedly handed them to Jamie.

He took off before they could say anything. Deftly avoiding all the poop in the road, Jamie doubled back the way they came. He threw the sock and clothes all about, creating a confusing trail for the Headless Trunk, and ran back to the others.

They hurried ahead, feeling their way along. They came to the edge of a building and the corner of the road. They turned left. Jamie prayed that the monster would take the bait, become confused by the duplicate smells, and head toward the pile of clothes, which would buy them some time, maybe. He hoped it was a stupid monster.

Luckily, it was. Most monsters were. A good amount of their energy went to their muscles, their hunger, or their survival, and little went to their brains. Jamie knew that from living with the Alexanders.

Behind the children came the angry noises of a headless monster who had been fooled. Iron claws ripped apart clothes.

"My good sock," Eva moaned.

"This is a horrible place," Jamie announced. "I do not like this place at all."

They listened. The monster's noises had shifted.

"He's coming," Bloom breathed, setting off again and pushing them along the building's side. "Hurry."

But they weren't able to get far. Hands reached into the darkness and pulled each of them into the building. First went SalGoud, then Jamie and Annie, then Eva and Bloom. Once they were all inside, a door quietly shut behind them, and an iron bar swung down, and then three more behind it, keeping whatever was outside out and whatever was inside in.

The Grogans

Wherever they were, it was dark. Annie reached her hand out in the space in front of her and touched something hard and wooden, like a chair leg. Someone coughed.

"Ach, what kind of fool idiots are ya?" came the mutter of a low voice. "Running about at night like that? Bleedin' stupid, fer sure. Yer apt to be eaten or mutilated or sent to the Raiff."

Annie gulped. She didn't know how to answer. It was so good to be inside and warmer, and away from the headless beast. The angry lecture was kind of worth it.

"We are travelers," came Bloom's strong voice out of the darkness by Annie's right knee. "We do not know the rules of this place."

Annie smiled inwardly. He was even talking more like she imagined an elf would talk—all formal and confident and grown-up. She had been plopped unceremoniously onto some floorboards by the hands that dragged her in off the street. Sitting there, she listened to the breathing in the room. There was a lot of inhaling and exhaling going on. She didn't dare stand up yet, so she leaned toward Bloom's voice. She tapped his leg politely to let him know she was there. Outside, something terrifically large smashed against the door, rattling it.

"Well, travelers or no, ye should be smart enough to not be wanderin' when thar's a Coluinn gun Cheann afoot," said the voice, sounding slightly less exasperated but just as quiet. "Now, hush yerselves, or ye'll be wakin' up me masters."

No one said anything. Someone impatient tapped his tiny foot. Outside, the beast slammed against the door once more, but the strong oak held against it, most likely because of the multitude of iron bars reinforcing the wood.

Annie cleared her throat softly. "Thank you for saving us."

"Ah, well, as least one of ye has a wee bit of manners," said the voice. "Yer quite welcome, little lassie."

"Yes, thank you." Jamie tried to sound much more polite than he usually did, which was incredibly polite. He won "Most Courteous" in second grade. He still had the certificate hidden under the mattress in his old bedroom. "Would it be too much of a bother if we turned on a light?"

"Some light ye'll be wanting, is it?" The voice paused. "Just a wee bit, then, and if the masters rouse themselves then we'll have to be puttin' it off, right quick."

A candle flame in the middle of the room flickered, casting a soft glow onto a wooden table in the center of the room. Another candle nearer to the children also blinked, illuminating all of them in various sitting positions on the floor. Holding this candle above his head was a smallish man, dressed in brown. His forearms shot out from his tunic and were as big as his thighs. He gave Annie a wink.

"You're a brounie?" Eva asked, with so much disdain in her voice that Annie had to kick her, which was hard to do sitting down.

"A grogan, actually," he said, bowing and taking off his hat, causing the candle's flame to flicker about, casting shadows around the dark room, which seemed filled with wood and stone. "If you don't mind."

"But we're not in the Highlands of Scotland? Are we?" asked SalGoud, who knew a lot about where the fae, including brounies, lived. That's because Ned the Doctor was quite the teacher.

Jamie's ears perked up. "Scotland?"

"Yer in Scot's Land, of course, if that's what yer askin'. What sort of travelers do ye be when ya don't even know where ya are? Although I'm guessing since the Raiff and the Queen had their falling out, we're not in the Scotland true anymore but somewhere else entirely as part of the curse. But that gets me back to me original question—what sort of travelers do you be?"

The grogan set himself on the edge of the table and stared into SalGoud's eyes until the much, much larger boy blushed.

"Lost travelers?" SalGoud said, putting a finger in his shirt collar and pulling it out from his neck. "Um . . . sir?"

"Lost and with womenfolk?" the grogan harrumphed and began to smack a table knife against his thigh in a threatening manner.

Annie, annoyed with the "womenfolk" comment, looked to Eva for support in an instant eye rolling campaign, but the dwarf was oblivious. Eva had stood up and was wandering around, exploring a large fireplace, big enough for Annie to walk into. A black kettle hung from a rod.

"We're in a kitchen," Eva announced as if no one else had figured that out yet.

Then to accentuate the point, the dwarf's stomach gave a great gurgling growl. The grogan laughed.

"Hungry, are ya? I'll make ye's a deal. I'll get ye some food and ye will tell me where yer travelin' to and where yer been travelin' from. Ach, and I hope it's a good adventurin' tale ye'll be tellin'." The little man hopped across the rough plank that formed the table, rubbed his hands together, and watched the children eye one another trying to decide. "I've got bread and jam. Me name's Light of Nathan."

Outside, the Headless Trunk smashed into the door again and began to kick at it. Annie hugged her arms around herself, and then thought better of it. It didn't look brave, not like a Stopper, a traveler, an elf rescuer. She shrugged off her pack and set it down. Wooziness engulfed her head. She touched it with her hand.

I must be tired, she thought. *And hungry, like Eva.*

"We would love some food," she said, making the decision for all of them.

It had to be best to stay a bit in the cozy stone kitchen, have some bread and jam, and offer the grogan a little of the truth.

Jamie cautiously moved Annie back closer to the edge of the wall and announced for all of them, "Yes. We'll stay. Thank you."

After a while, the monster outside the door stopped attacking the building and thundered off to look for other travelers to eat. Travelers, as defined by the monster, were any creatures moving around outside from one place to another. It did not matter if that journey was only a few steps from the front door of the school to the back door of the library.

The grogan insisted the children get some rest. After what seemed like just a moment, Annie startled awake, her head resting on Eva's still-rumbling stomach. She heard voices right next to her cheek.

"Lordy. All I can find is a Golden Arrow. He must be a powerful elf indeed to have one of those. Look at it shine like sunbeams."

"I dunno. He canna be too smart being out after dark."

"It's 'cause he's a traveler."

Another voice came: "Maybe he's just so mighty he can be out and aboot in the night."

"Yeah, tha's why they was a'runnin' from the Headless Trunk."

"Well, he's bound to be caught by sumthin', soon. The Saltas will see him for an elf in a second. And the others, too. Thar jus' children, ya know."

"So, she'll be eating them or sending them to the Raiff. What a fate! All just to get back in the Raiff's good graces."

Annie cringed. Who would eat them? A troll?

"Well, the goofy-lookin' one has a strong look about 'im. He's some sort o' giant, he is?"

"And a dwarf, a 'uman boy, and a 'uman girl. Although, the 'uman girl isn't lookin' quite right, too pale by half. Ach, it's a motley crew."

"It's sad thinkin' that they'll soon be Queen food."

"Or his."

"Ach, I'd hate to see them go to him, the devil hisself, he is."

"Nah, but 'e serves 'im."

There was a bit of silence. "Well, I sure as don't wanna haf to cook them."

"She'll make us."

Who is this she? Annie wondered. *The Queen?*

Annie heard what seemed like a hundred sighs. She thought about whether they'd be served au gratin or with dumplings. She imagined Eva rolled up in white rice and a leaf of the algae-like nori used in sushi rolls. Then the roughest voice spoke again.

"Well, they'll be caught in a moment, sure enough, so I says we might as well be takin' the arrow. No use lettin' the Saltas 'ave it."

"How 'bout the ax?"

"That, too."

She'd had enough listening then. Annie jumped up and looked about the room. Eva's ax clanged to the floor.

"You. Will. Not," she steamed, staring into the shadows and the corners.

Bloom stirred slightly and Annie was sure he was just pretending to be asleep like she had been. She walked to where the ax vibrated on the floor, bent low, and picked it up. It was much heavier than she imagined.

"Give me the arrow, too," she insisted, looking about.

Silence.

"Right now."

The Golden Arrow flew through the air. From his pretend

sleeping position, Bloom sat up and caught it in his hand. Several of the grogans gasped from their hiding places and one of them said, "Aye, I told ya he was a mighty one."

Bloom's lips flattened in an angry line as he glared into the room. Annie wouldn't want him looking at her like that, that was for sure. Once more, she was glad he was on her side. The knowledge kept her strong. Friends will do that for you. She winked at him.

"Come out," Annie said to the voices of the men.

Light of Nathan, the same grogan who had let them inside the kitchen and fed them, appeared, stepping out of a shadowy chair leg by the snoring Eva's nose.

"No harm meant," he said, raising his hands in the air and attempting to look sheepish. "Jus' lookin'."

Bloom raised his eyebrows.

Annie wasn't having any of it. "The others come out, too."

Light of Nathan wrung his hands. "Wha' others?"

"The other grogans," Annie said, sighing and fiddling with the ax. Eva had carved her name on it and beneath it was the word DEATHS and then a little place for tally marks and another word, MAIMINGS. There weren't any marks on it.

The little man straightened his small brown fedora hat. He made like he was tying his shoe and set to whistling. He was a much worse whistler than SalGoud. Annie tapped her foot on the floor and the grogan looked up and sighed. "Very well, then."

He gave a long sharp whistle followed by three smaller toots, and all of a sudden there was a great bustle and commotion in the stone kitchen. Little men scrambled out of pots, from behind corners of chairs, and down out of the fireplace and the breadbox. Several scurried out of SalGoud's clothes and Jamie's shoes. In less than ten seconds, there were a hundred of the men standing about the room. Their skin ranged from deep black to pine tree green to pale pink.

"The grogan," announced Light of Nathan. He bowed, taking off his hat. The others followed suit.

"The grogan," Bloom repeated as if he were trying to remember something.

One of the grogan came toward Annie and began sniffing at the air around her knee. He had a set of bells strapped to his belt and his hair was a bit darker than the rest, more of a black than a chestnut brown. He looked at Annie with wide eyes.

"Ye have a bit of cold in ya," he said, cocking his head.

"Well, it's cold out," Annie said.

"Tha's na what I meant," he insisted. "It's yer blood."

Annie stepped away from him.

"Na offense meant. I smell things, ya see," he said, his hands flailing about as he explained. "Yer na quite 'uman, is all. Maybe a bit of elf in ya, but tha's not it. The rest of ye I've got straight figured. We've an elf, a dwarf, a giant one, and a young lad with too much goodness in his heart despite what smells like a long-time proximity to the trolling type, but ye—yer blood is cold tinged like a demon."

Bloom gave her a warning look, so she said nothing, but she shivered anyway.

He can smell the Raiff in me.

The Raiff is here, tainting me somehow.

Just thinking about it made her blood feel colder, and colder still, as if all of her were turning to ice, dark ice that could not break.

What if I become him somehow? What if I become evil and cold like my blood? What if I am just as evil as him?

The room began to spin and Annie watched it, wondering what was going on. But she only watched for a moment, because it was twirling about so fast, blurs of grogan men, and Bloom, the fireplace sweeping by . . .

Annie fainted dead away.

———

"We didn't mean ta make her pass out."

"Well, you did."

Annie recognized Bloom's voice. The back of her head throbbed and someone was lifting it. SalGoud. He smiled at her and announced, "She's awake."

Eva thumped her on the arm. "You faint too much. Fainting gets people killed! You can't faint when you get stressed, Annie!"

She rubbed at her head and agreed. It was true and it was embarrassing. But she also remembered Eva fainting a lot—especially when she saw trolls. It seemed a bit hypocritical.

Jamie stared at Annie, obviously worried. "You're freezing cold and you don't look right, Annie. You are as white as Tala, almost."

The little men all scurried about.

"She's not the hardiest thing," said Staggs, the grogan leader.

Ignoring them, Jamie scrutinized Annie's pupils. "How's your head?"

"Okay," Annie lied as SalGoud held up his fingers.

"How many?" he asked.

"Two."

"She can count. She's fine," Eva announced, shooing everyone away. "No thanks to you, grogans."

"Our apologies. We didn't mean ta make the wee lass fall. She's a frail thing."

"She ain't no frail thing. She's just different, that's all. Much better than the likes of you thieving little men. She's a Stopper," Eva grumped at them.

"Eva!" Bloom scolded.

The grogans all stood stock-still for a moment, their mouths agape showing sharp, broken teeth and deep throats. Then, they all started talking at once.

"A Stopper? Whadda ya mean, a Stopper?"

"Nay, not a Time Stopper? Such a frail, pale thing?"

"Crivens!"

"Let me ha' a look at 'er."

"Nay, dinna go too close."

One of them made a circular sign in front of his heart, meant to ward off evil spirits.

What if I am *an evil spirit?* Annie wondered and shook her head to keep the room from spinning again. She certainly didn't feel like herself. She hadn't since the Raiff had attacked her, turning her cold like him.

"Aw, get a grip!" Eva scowled at them and shooed several off a chair. "How 'bout some breakfast? My stomach's aching for food."

"Eva, that's hardly polite," SalGoud started.

And that resulted in Eva and SalGoud bickering for a while about food and the general protocols that make someone a polite person or dwarf, if there was such a thing. The grogans involved themselves in the exchange, with several pleas to Eva to "simmer down" so that she didn't wake the human occupants of the house. SalGoud made them all hush once he'd realized that he had actually (gasp!) gotten trapped in a "negative verbal interchange" with Eva.

"So much hostility," he muttered to himself. Then he managed through the force of sheer politeness to convince the grogans to sit cross-legged in rows on the table in front of him while he explained exactly what a Time Stopper was.

Annie closed her eyes and tried to listen but her head was still woozy, and before long Jamie sat next to her.

"You are not all right," he murmured low enough so that the others would not hear.

Annie shrugged. "I'm fine."

His hand touched her forehead, and she opened her eyes. "Your skin is cold, Annie. Like ice."

He stared her down, keeping his hand on her forehead. Warmth blossomed from the edges of his fingers. He said softly, "And you're weak like when people have the flu."

She gulped and closed her eyes again. "I still think it's the strings."

"You swear?"

"What else could it be?"

A small warmth drifted from Jamie's hand onto her forehead and spread down into her body. She wasn't warm now, but she wasn't shivering at least. He took his hand away and turned his attention to the table with the grogans, who had all taken up steak knives and forks and were preparing to march.

"You told them about the elves?" Bloom asked SalGoud, angry. He looked up at the giant and then down at the dwarf. "Can't you two keep anything a secret?"

"Have sum bread and simmer down, elfie. Ach, we don't have the brains of adult ones. Yer secret's safe with us," said Staggs, jabbing his knife into the air for emphasis. "We know all about the Raiff, anyhow. Know too much about him. We're comin' with ye. At least to get ya out of the city and away from the Queen. We're sick o' this place, anyhow. Too much quiet."

"We need some fightin'," Pagan of Joe said, pounding his fork onto the table.

"And maybe some warrin'," the tallest one, Farrar of Shaun, chimed in.

"And then maybe sum more fightin' and warrin'," Staggs yelled, stirring the entire group into an uproar. Upstairs they could hear the sounds of humans stirring out of bed.

"And then some hittin' and hoistin' and—and more fightin'."

Eva smiled and grabbed some bacon off the skillet, tearing it in two with her teeth. "These are my kind of folks."

Much to Eva's delight, they ate breakfast. Tala, Miss Cornelia's big white dog whom Annie loved so much, would have particularly enjoyed the bacon. There was no fruit, just bread, bacon, and eggs.

Angry bells rang throughout the house.

"Ach! No! Let's get a move on. Out! Out! Everyone out!" Staggs shrieked. The grogans started gathering up utensils and shoving them into bags. Nye of Alisa swished her hair around and started pushing the children toward the door.

"Hurry! Hurry!" said Spellacy of Sam. "But be quiet. Hi. I'm Spellacy of Sam, by the way. I cooked the bacon."

They all hurried out of the house. The bell clanged as Farrar of Shaun shut the door behind them.

"Lazy things," Farrar of Shaun muttered, as he scurried into Eva's backpack.

The children gaped at the house they'd slept in and realized that it was not a house at all, but a castle, huge and made of gray stones. The windows were small and barred.

"Who exactly are your masters?" Jamie asked the grogans, his eyes flinty. He felt like he'd been had, somehow.

Light of Nathan flushed, scratched his head, bit his lip, hemmed and hawed before finally announcing, "The Queen, the evil vixen herself. Thar you have it and she'll be sending the guards after us soon, once she's noticed we're gone."

Jamie groaned. His heart pounded with worry. They didn't need complications. They didn't need to be found out so soon. They had to save those elves and get back to Aurora. Nothing mattered more than that.

"You'll have to stay," Eva announced, sadly though, as if she understood how horrible the situation was for the grogans. "Look. I know ya want to prove yourself. I want that all the freaking time. You feel trapped there, right? And then you feel kind of broken like you're never going to be able to fix things or save elves or whatever, but we can't risk you coming. So you've got to stay there."

Nye of Alisa shook her fist. "Never! Ya don't know what it's like wi' 'er. She's evil and spoiled. Look over thar. See that?"

She pointed at a platform. A noose dangled above it.

"Tha's where she hangs those she suspects of witchery. Any whiff she gets of a magical human and she 'as 'er guards round 'em up. First they tie their fingers and toes together behind thar backs, then they throws 'em into a pond. If they rise, thar witches and get sent here ta hang. If they fail ta rise, they die beneath the water."

The children stared at the platform horrified. Jamie realized that the grogans lived like he did before, with the Alexanders. He couldn't let them stay like that.

"Ya can rest assured yer Annie would be taken fer a witch," Pagan of Joe announced.

"Well, I am, in a way . . . ," Annie mumbled, wiping the back of her hand against her pale forehead. "Sort of, depending on the definition . . ."

SalGoud pushed his glasses higher onto the bridge of his nose. "It's horrible! It's an atrocity! How could you help such a queen?"

"Keep yer eye up for the Saltas," Spellacy of Sam said loudly. "And make sure if ya see one, ya don't run. Thas a sure way to get their attention."

"I get it, but seriously, why do you help them at all?" Eva asked as they stepped into the street and the brisk morning air. The poop smell of the night before was just faint in the breeze. They walked quickly down the street.

Farrar of Shaun explained that the grogans had to help humans who ask them; it was part of some ancient code that also affected some brounies and other fae. "To ask a grogan for help, you have to touch us, which is pretty darn difficult since we're fast buggers, we are, and can go invisible at will, and then once you're touching one of us, ye have to ask us directly, see? Then the grogan is bound to ya and yer family until someone else catches us and asks for help. That's what releases us from our dreadful servitude."

"We're basically slaves," Grindoch, the one who seemed taken with Eva, grumbled. "Always stuck doing the washin' and the cookin' and the mendin' and the like."

"It's no life!" Eva bellowed. "A life without fighting and honor? It's horrible!"

"Tha' it is." Grindoch nodded. "Ach, but wait!"

He called to another, "Staggs, no one has asked us."

Staggs climbed out of SalGoud's hair, where he'd been riding peacefully. "Ach, right yer are. Crivens! Somebody ask us for our help, rescuing the elves, so we can get on with adventuring and leave this wretched house with all its cookin' and cleanin' behind us."

Jamie cleared his throat. "I, James Hephaistion Alexander, formally and respectfully ask the grogans' help in freeing the elves and bringing them back to Aurora."

It felt good inside his chest to say it. He remembered how he glowed a tiny bit outside and wondered if he should mention it to the others. Did it matter? It hadn't happened again, but right now the feeling in his chest felt just like that glow. It felt . . . good . . . There really was no other word for it but good. His shoulders started to itch terribly. It was all he could do not to ask Annie to scratch them for him.

Staggs nodded his approval. "Well done. Let's go adventurin', lads!"

"Blah, blah, blah," Eva grumbled.

The grogans all pulled out their swords and knives and forks and lifted them to the air. "Adventurin'!"

Then they all promptly disappeared, but a voice whispered into Annie's ear. "We're still here. It's just safer to be invisible now, ya know? Tha' way, no other beings can nab one of us and set us to housework again."

The children strode down the cobblestone streets, heading toward the outer gates. The buildings were still all askew and in the grayish light of day somehow looked even more wrong. They seemed like skeletons of buildings, wartorn and ravaged by time and neglect. Despair and hopelessness filled the children's hearts again. The magic here was a bad magic. It was the magic of loss, of things that should be put right, but were all terribly wrong. It was hopeless and sad.

"It won't be easy to pass through," Boucher of Steve, a

grogan, said. "We may have to fight our way out. No one leaves the city these days. Too much danger outside."

The grogans took the walking time to whisper instructions and advice about their surroundings.

The castle they'd just left dominated the entire city, lurking over it, standing tall on an ancient volcanic hill. The streets were close with the stone buildings, and a tall stone wall surrounded the entire area. Annie spotted the city's inhabitants, poking their heads and shoulders out of windows, standing in doorways, leaning against houses for support. Everyone looked so hungry; it made her heart hurt.

"They can't farm anymore, because of the dangers beyond the walls," Farrar of Shaun explained. "Farmers disappear. All we have is bread from flour saved, eggs, and bacon. The Queen's larders are fat with food, though. 'Course we are the ones that 'ave ta cook it."

The Queen, the grogans explained, had an arrangement with the Raiff. She sent him children.

"What do you mean, 'sends him children'?" Annie whispered, shivering again. Jamie's warmth had worn off.

"Ach, it's bad business. She rounds up the straggling children she finds, or her men do, and she sends them to the Raiff. He gives her food for them. It's a trade, like. And he doesn't let the trolls, the kelpies, the orcs, and the other nasties into the city—just the Headless Trunk. And he's only here because the Queen likes him. Thinks of him as a pet, she does." Staggs grimaced and shuddered. "Dinna worry. We'll keep ya safe."

They walked past a woman hurrying down the street, hugging a baby to her chest. No one they met seemed happy. They all seem scared.

"What does he do with the children?" Annie asked.

Jamie glanced at her, lips taut with tension.

Pagan of Joe's anger made his voice deep. "No one knows tha'. But, they never come back, the children don't. Some say he eats them or feeds them to the elves."

"Elves don't eat children!" Bloom yelled.

"Nay, but trolls do, and 'e 'as plenty of those working for 'im," Farrar of Shaun countered, sniffing as if he had a cold.

Eva smiled. "Well, we have nothing to worry about, then. I've my ax and it's hungry for a kill."

"Where is it you have to go again?" Staggs asked. "Out of the city and where?"

"Through the Gate of Despair and then to the Pass of Sighs," Bloom said, stepping over a pile of poop.

"Oh, that just . . . that sounds lovely . . . Not," Staggs said. "Don't look at me with those eyes, Farrar of Shaun. Grindoch, if you keep making that face, it'll freeze that way! West of Stuart, if you want to act like a child, I'll treat you like one. I dinna care how good ya are at baking upside-down cakes."

Bloom and SalGoud exchanged a glance.

"They are sticking their tongues out at me," Staggs said,

appearing again for a moment. "You all might not be able to see us when we're invisible, but we see one another and let me tell you, they are acting horrible. Taylor of Davis, as long as you're under my roof, ya live by my rules."

"We are not technically under a roof," said a logical voice that sounded as if it was balanced on Bloom's right shoulder. Annie assumed that was Taylor of Davis.

"Ack!" Staggs shook his fist in that direction and disappeared again.

They continued walking through the desolate streets, sticking closer to the buildings than the middle of the road. The windows and doors that hung above them, sometimes not even connected to structures, seemed dangerous. Anything could be watching. According to Staggs, deadly fields and forests encircled the city; beyond that lay more mountains and the Raiff and the elves. It was there that the children had to journey to.

With the grogans whispering directions in their ears, they made significant time through the city's streets. The sun rose higher in the sky, showing more of the city to the children, the decaying stone, the crumbling walkways. It seemed old but harmless enough. Annie had a hard time imagining children rounded up to be eaten, or witches hanged before the castle.

It's all so quiet, she thought. She thought too soon.

From above their heads came a great swooping noise that

reminded Annie of dragons and that awful beast they had encountered in Ireland. She huddled into Jamie and Sal-Goud. Suddenly, the grogans turned visible and surrounded the children. They raised their swords, knives, and forks above their heads, ready for battle.

"Salta!" bellowed the grogans. "Look grown-up!"

"Look grown-up?" Jamie asked. "How do we do that?"

"Act boring and grumpy," Eva said, standing on tiptoe and holding her ax, ready to swing.

Soaring through the air above them was a large reptilian being with a lion's head, scorpion tail, and six stumpy legs. Below it was another winged creature, draped in white robes that seemed to be both transparent and glowing.

"Angels," SalGoud said, and quoted Shakespeare, " 'Fling away ambition.' "

"It's no angel. It's a Tarasque . . . they are real . . . ," Bloom whispered as he pointed at the white-robed creature. "It's flying off . . . but the other creature . . . what is it?"

"That scaly thing is a Salta, and they are hateful creatures and the Queen's beasties and if they think yer easy prey they'll sooner snatch ye away than bat an eye. Devils they are," Taylor of Davis growled.

It seemed that everyone else on the street had run inside. Everything was horribly quiet.

The Salta swooped down and hovered just out of their reach, examining them. His face was cleanly cut like a statue's, all his features sharp and perfect. His eyes scanned the group. Annie stood on tiptoe. Bloom's carriage was erect. The Salta's eyes centered on Eva for a moment longer than everyone else. Jamie gasped.

"He's going for the dwarf lass! Ready, boys!" Farrar of Shaun yelled.

Grindoch growled and the Salta dived down, arms outstretched for Eva.

"Attack!"

The little men leaped up and grabbed the Salta by his robes, jabbing him with their knives and forks and swords. Grindoch and Pagan of Joe made it up to the Salta's head and pulled his scaly hair.

Horror twisted Jamie's insides. Every time anyone yelled at someone, he felt like he'd been punched, but this violence—it was so much worse.

"Run!" Levesque of Jon screamed after pausing from his biting campaign on the Salta's knee. "Get to the gates. We'll catch up."

The children rushed forward through the streets. Eva couldn't keep up, and stumbled. SalGoud doubled back and tucked her beneath his arm, carrying her. Eva bashed her fists against his arm.

"Nobody carries a dwarf!" she yelled because dwarfs often yell that. It did no good. She was too slow. SalGoud had no choice but to carry her. "I am not my mother! Let me fight!"

"What are you even talking about, Eva?' SalGoud asked, shifting away from her fists.

"Nothing."

"You just said something about your moth—"

"I said, 'Nothing'!" she roared, and SalGoud gave up trying to talk to her and focused on getting away.

There were odd enchanted carvings on the stone houses that they raced past, but no one could take the time to examine them. They ran toward the gate. Turning a corner, gasping for breath, looking over their shoulders, they nearly ran into a tiny girl in shabby clothes who was standing in the middle of the road.

Her voice came out small and clear. "Have you come to save us?"

She may have been five years old, if anything. She planted her feet directly in the middle of the road in front of Bloom. Her lip trembled. She looked about to cry. Bloom held the tiny girl by her shoulders. Her big puppy dog eyes stared up into his face.

"Save you from who?" he asked steadily.

"We need to hurry," Eva grumbled, still dangling from her undignified spot at SalGoud's side. SalGoud put her down.

"Me mam says that it'll be an elf who saves us, but he's stolen the elves," the little girl said quietly. "He stole 'em and then he got locked up here and we did, too. But the elves.

That's who is supposed to make this right. But they're dying. All of them except you."

Bloom said nothing, but his eyes seemed wounded like it hurt him to listen.

"Even the grandmother elf." The girl's lip trembled and she rubbed her hands on her grubby dress. "And they're dying . . . all of them . . . And we will, too. And you . . . Unless you save us."

"The grandmother elf?" Bloom asked, stepping back as if the thought was too much to bear or maybe too much to hope for. Annie wasn't sure.

Behind them came the noises of the grogans' battling. There were several cries of "Take that, ya mutated dragon ghostie thing."

The little girl bit her lip and didn't answer Bloom's question.

Annie knelt down to her level.

"We will be back to save you," she said quietly.

The girl did not look at her, but kept her gaze fastened on Bloom. "Swear?"

He stood straighter. "I swear."

Shooting Annie a look, the girl stepped back. "Me mam says the elves don't break promises. Not like demons."

She turned on her heel and ran off toward a building, slipping through a crack in a door, which promptly slammed behind her.

Bloom rubbed his hand against the side of his face. He gulped.

"The last elf will not stand alone," the dwarf announced, hip checking him. "Now, let's get out of this foul place and rescue some elves and then we can get on with the saving of everybody else. Saving . . . saving . . . saving . . . It never stops, I tell ya. A dwarf's hero work is never done."

SalGoud snatched Eva up again, running with her. Jamie followed, but Bloom hesitated, staring at the home the little girl entered.

Annie's hand went to his arm.

"We will be back," she said softly.

He nodded. "We will."

4

Going Without

The friends ran to the end of the street and straight to the dark purple gates, which stretched upward hundreds of feet like the biggest skyscrapers in the largest of cities.

"What does it say?" Eva demanded, hands on her hips. None of them instantly recognized the golden, glowing writing.

Bloom shook his head. "It's not Elvish."

"Ain't dwarf. Keep watch for Saltas," Eva grumbled and straightened out her overalls. SalGoud had set her down and she looked more crumpled than normal.

Striding over to the plaques, SalGoud took off his glasses and squinted. He repositioned his glasses back on his long nose, turned around, and announced, "I believe it's Angelic."

"What's it say?" Eva demanded.

SalGoud cleared his throat. "It says, 'Prepare to be shamed.' Then, it's signed 'H and A,' or maybe that's just 'Ha'?"

"That's friendly," Annie said sarcastically as she turned toward Bloom, who nodded but took a step forward anyway, touching the writing with his fingers. "Shouldn't angels be nice?"

"It's a new curse," he said, pulling his fingers away from the stone. "Less than fifty years old."

"Ach, what sort of curse is that at all?" Eva made her voice into a mocking tone. "Prepare to be shamed. Soooo scary. Angels . . . Blah . . . You know you switch one letter in the word 'angels' and it's 'angles'? How pixie poopy is that? Angels are what? Tall cherubs with harps and wings? I don't even think they exist."

With a loud poo-pooing noise, Eva raised her ax and with a mighty downward arc sliced the blade through the gate's golden chains and lock. The gate gave a terrific creaking noise and slowly opened outward. A crow sitting at the top flew away with an angry cackle. Eva stomped through the opening.

"Eva!" SalGoud grabbed her by the shoulder, stopping her. "You do not *always* have to go first."

"Excuse me. Dwarfs *always* go first," she said, threatening him with her ax. "Right, elf?"

"Right, Eva." Bloom sighed.

Annie checked behind her. "But what about the grogans?"

"They'll catch up once they're done with their battling," Eva grumbled, and she set down the cobblestone path outside the gate. The others followed in a line, side by side, close behind. The moment they crossed, a great mist engulfed them. They could barely see one another through the gloom.

"It's sunny out, though," Jamie observed, scratching at his shoulders again. "Where did the sun go?"

Bloom motioned for quiet and notched his bow. Eva held her ax above her head. Annie tried to feel the strings.

"Why is it even harder to feel them now?" she wondered aloud.

"Maybe because we're getting closer to the machine," Jamie suggested. "If the machine is what the Raiff is using to hurt the elves, to sap their energy and twist the strings so that he can use them, then it only makes sense that the closer we get to it, the harder it will be for you to feel them? Or maybe it's not even about how close we are? Maybe it's just that the machine is getting so powerful the strings are already different."

Something slimy and fluid streaked past them and was gone.

Jamie grabbed Annie's hand just as voices emerged out of the mist.

"It sounds like someone turned on the TV," Jamie whispered.

"And they are turning up the volume." SalGoud pointed. "Look, something is coming into focus."

The mist rolled to the side revealing someone in one of Aquarius House's bedrooms.

It was a blond boy, a younger version of Bloom. He was in a bed, face red with fever. He whimpered.

Bloom groaned. Throwing his hands up in the air, he pleaded, "Nobody watch this. Nobody look."

"Is that you?" Annie asked.

"Yes . . . It's embarrassing . . . Just . . . please don't look," Bloom begged.

But they all did.

The younger Bloom sat up straight in bed, pulled back the sheets to reveal Superman pajamas. He jumped to the floor and there was a giant wet spot on the bottom of his pj's. He began pulling the sheets off the bed when Miss Cornelia walked in.

"What are you doing, Bloom?"

"Nothing." He tried to hide the sheets behind his back. "I was dreaming of my father . . . of his death."

"Your father died bravely fighting a hundred monsters. He killed every last one of them before succumbing to his wounds. He is buried on the beach." The younger version of Miss Cornelia snapped her fingers and the sheets flew up into the air and out the door. Another finger snap and new sheets and new pajamas were on the bed, and on Bloom, respectively. The new pajamas were Care Bears. Miss Cornelia didn't have much fashion sense.

"Can we please not look at this?" the current Bloom moaned. Eva snorted, and he punched her on the arm. "I was really sick then. Elves do not wet beds, you know. I had a fever. Let's just not look. Shut up, Eva."

"Care Bears," Eva snickered.

The vision faded away.

Then the sound of a young girl hysterically sobbing rushed toward them with a great wind, and it whipped their hair from their faces. SalGoud had to clutch at his glasses to keep them from being swept off. The noise settled in a spot just to the front and right of them. Shapes and shadows materialized out of the darkness. It was a dwarf, Jamie realized, a young dwarf girl. With her was her mother, and it looked as if they were in a room.

"It's an illusion," Jamie said quietly to the others. "Just like with Bloom. It isn't really there."

It *was* an illusion, but a good one, three-dimensional and solid. It even smelled like a dwarf's home, like pine needles and mildew and the sharp, metallic tang of recently worked gold and copper.

Eva gasped, stepped back toward the group, and grabbed Annie's arm so tightly that Annie knew she'd have a bruise. She didn't care. The scene unfolding in front of them seemed far more important.

The dwarf mother was holding an ax above a sweet brown teddy bear's head. The teddy bear sprawled across a nightstand, as if it were an executioner's block.

"His head is off, unless you stop sleeping with him," the mother threatened. Her raw red fingers twitched on the ax handle.

The little dwarf girl had her own hands covering her face. "No. Not teddy. Not teddy's head."

"Are you going to sleep with him anymore?"

"No," younger Eva sobbed. "No. Don't hurt him."

"And why not?" asked the mother, her ax still threatening the teddy's chubby little neck.

"Because." The girl hiccupped and then her voice grew flat, as emotionless as someone reciting their multiplication tables. "Because dwarfs don't sleep with baby things. Dwarfs are brave and need nothing but their ax to keep them safe at night."

"Good," said the mother, her ax coming down. She took the teddy and tossed it headfirst out a window. The little dwarf screamed and raced after her mother, pummeling at her with her fists.

"Good," the mother gruffed at the hysterical young dwarf. "Anger is good."

And the vision disappeared into the mist.

Eva's face had drained of color.

"I was weak then," she muttered. She started stammering,

kicking at the fog. "She was weak, too. That was when she left. It wasn't 'cause of me, though. I always thought it was, but it wasn't. It was 'cause of what she did."

Jamie put his hand on Eva's shoulder, but Eva shrugged it off. "What did she do, Eva?"

Eva didn't answer. She stomped around in a circle. Then she said, "Stop scratching, Jamie! It's like you've got fleas. AND NOBODY ask about my mother ever again? Got it? Got it? Good!"

Please not me. Please not me, Annie prayed as the mist began to take shape.

Out loud, she said, "Maybe we should walk forward, try to get beyond this."

"It's the curse. The gates are trying to shame us," SalGoud said, taking a cautious step forward.

"Well, they're doing a good job." Bloom slouched and stared at the ground.

"It doesn't matter," Annie said. "It doesn't matter what it shows us because we're friends."

"Right." Jamie nodded fiercely.

Despite her words, Annie began worrying what the mist would show from her life. The time when Walden sat on her and shoved his dirty underwear in her face? All those times girls at school had called her Weenie Roast or Charity Girl and laughed at her raggedy clothes? The time she passed a little gas during gymnastics at school right when she was doing a back handspring?

Oh no, she sighed in her head. She could feel all the shame coming off Bloom and Eva in waves. *We have to get out of here.*

They'd barely gone a few steps when another vision came. This time it was SalGoud and somewhat more recent; he was running around the outside of the school completely naked, holding a soccer ball in front of his most private parts. His ribs stuck out like giant planks against his skin.

"Odham did that to me. He stole my clothes," SalGoud said, sighing. "I wasn't naked on purpose or anything."

"You're too skinny," Eva grumped. "All bones."

"Thanks, Eva. That helps." SalGoud cringed. He tried to sound nonchalant but it came off fake. "Not many people saw."

The naked version of SalGoud ran smack into the principal, who opened his mouth, horrified, and then started laughing hysterically while pointing at the soccer ball. SalGoud tried to quote something and simply stammered, no words coming out. The principal laughed so much that his bow tie fell off and he began rolling around on the sidewalk in front of the school. The naked SalGoud crept by him and then sprinted up the stairs toward the boys' locker room.

The vision vanished. SalGoud was bright red.

"Annie's turn," said Eva. "Or Jamie's."

It was a winter night. A girl lay on a snow-covered blueberry barren, and above her hovered a man with short blond hair and a sinister face. The Raiff.

The girl was just waking up. She was wearing the same clothes Annie was wearing.

"This didn't happen!" Annie blurted. "I never fell asleep near the Raiff."

The man cut his wrist with Annie's phurba and then put his wrist to her mouth, held her head as she drank.

"Oh, Holy Gods of Thunder," Eva cursed beside her in the mist. Annie didn't hear, she was too enthralled, too horrified at herself, blindly sucking at the demon's blood.

"Annie?" Bloom's voice beside her was a big question.

Tears started to form and leak onto her cheek. "That didn't happen. I don't remember that happening."

In the vision, she was too weak to even keep her head steady on her neck. It kept drooping forward as if she was a cloth doll propped against a headboard.

The Raiff watched her struggle and petted her hair like she was some sort of puppy dog.

"What does it mean?" she asked. "What does it mean that I have your blood?"

He used his free hand to fix his hair.

"No!!" the Annie of now screamed.

She couldn't watch this vision anymore. She sobbed and ran through the middle of it, stepping on her other self and pushing past the Raiff, running blindly forward for half a minute. The mist suddenly gave way in front of her and she found herself on top of a hill looking down on a green valley. Behind her, Bloom broke through the fog with Jamie.

"Annie . . . ," Jamie started.

"Don't say anything," she said, heading down the hill.

"You didn't tell me."

"How could I tell you when it hasn't happened?" she gasped, tripping on a rock. She stumbled and slowed to a power walk.

Bloom said nothing, just elegantly ran a pace behind her. Jamie followed.

"Wait for us," Eva yelled from the top of the hill.

But Annie didn't want to wait. She kept walking, arms pumping at her sides. If she walked fast enough maybe she could just get away from the vision, get away from the coldness inside her, get away from the worries that she wouldn't be able to save the elves.

Bloom caught up again. "Annie . . . what if that isn't the past? What if that's the future?"

Jamie had caught up to them, too, and answered before Annie could even open her mouth. "It won't be. We won't let that happen to Annie. Not ever."

———

By unspoken agreement, the children decided that they wouldn't mention anything about what happened, but Eva kept casting sideways glances at Annie. They marched across the rolling hills that were covered with standing stones, sheep, and cows with huge horns and great, long brown hair like magazine models. It sounded pretty, but the hills themselves were made of rusty metal, and barbed wire would occasionally jut out of them, dangerous and deadly. They had to get to the Pass of Sighs next, and they wanted to be there before night. The grogans caught up to them quickly, each of them relating the mass vision they all had at the Gate of Shame. It involved the Queen and kissing her toes. None of them could tell the story without breaking down, and Annie spent a good hour comforting them before they refused to talk any more.

"There was no vision of me," Jamie said, breaking the new silence.

"You're lucky," Eva grumbled, but Jamie didn't feel lucky. It mattered somehow that everyone else saw something and he didn't. He just didn't know how.

In Aurora it was winter, and spring flowers were distant dreams; cold and mud ruled the day. The buds on the trees had not yet incarnated. In the Badlands, it was even worse than winter, because there was nothing lurking under the rusty metal hills. There were no flowers blooming. Even the tiny tufts of grass that managed to break through the metal ground seemed to be foul, smelling of old eggs and broccoli.

In the distance, a row of blackish purple mountains jutted out, high above the rest of the landscape. The children headed to the mountains, with the now invisible grogans scattered among them, hitching rides after their battle with the Salta, a battle they could not stop talking about.

"Ach, it was glorious, I tell ye," an invisible Staggs murmured into Eva's ear. "Ye should have seen Farrar of Shaun smack the he-devil with his head, right on the Salta's nose. Then Levesque of Jon bit his ear, just latched on like a dog, he did, and daren't let go."

"It was like poetry," Pagan of Joe said.

"Better than poetry. Like a good root beer," Staggs announced.

"Better than root beer. Like a good battle."

The grogans all started cheering. It was hard for the children to hang on to their shame when the grogans were so happy.

"To battle!" Bench of John yelled.

And for a moment they all became visible, raised their forks, knives, swords, and one spoon into the air and shouted, "To battle!"

Eva walked on, jealous.

"Ach, ye'll get yerself a battle, Eva," said Farrar of Shaun who was near her ear. "A fine fightin' machine like yerself. Ye mark me words."

Eva harrumphed.

5

Hidden Dangers

The children hurried toward the mountains, taking occasional bathroom breaks behind obliging cows. In his haste to get to the elves, SalGoud stepped in a large cow patty, not once but twice.

The grogans emphatically tried to explain that there were real dangers in the fields despite the relative calm. The children, soothed by the endless movement of their feet, had a hard time believing it.

"The Raiff's lulling us into a false sense of safety," Levesque of Jon said. "We should hurry before we really believe it."

The grogans talked nonstop about all of their adventurin' and fightin' and would sometimes materialize to reenact scenes from their past.

"I'll be wearing that demon's horn as a necklace soon enough," Staggs boasted.

SalGoud periodically poked his ribs, obviously wondering if he really was too skinny like Eva had said. Again, he went through the checklist of steps that Lichen had told them, fretting to Jamie that they had possibly skipped one.

Ten steps in all, but they seemed a bit stuck at six (the Pass of Sighs), and also there seemed to be a big gap between steps nine and ten, shooting the machine and bringing the elves home.

"I wonder how many little steps are between those two," he said.

Jamie could tell that the heat of the world, the hard metal feel of the ground was getting to him. SalGoud was always an optimist, ready to see hope and the best of things, but now he just felt . . . His glasses burned little marks onto his face.

Jamie watched and worried and waited.

Eva drooled over the grogans' tales of adventures and kept her eye on Annie, "just in case she was possessed or something."

"I'm not evil, you know!" said Annie. She stomped off ahead of the dwarf after Eva muttered something about "demon blood."

Eva threw her hands up the air. "I didn't say you were."

"Well, then stop looking at me like that," Annie fumed, kicking a rock. It hit a boulder and cracked in half.

"Looking at you like what?" Eva said, glancing at Annie sideways.

"Like that."

"Like what?"

"Like I'm a demon."

"If I thought you were a demon, I'd 've killed you already," Eva muttered. "Maybe Megan was right."

Annie didn't hear her but Jamie did. He wasn't sure what to do. Megan was the hag girl who was trying to nurse Lichen the elf back to health, hiding him in her closet. She had said Annie would "fall with evil," which wasn't the best kind of prophecy to have about someone. She didn't seem to like Annie much. Jamie knew the prophecy hurt Annie's feelings and Eva did, too.

"You okay, Annie?" he asked, catching up.

She sighed. "Eva is so . . ."

"Eva?" he suggested.

She smiled weakly. "Pretty much."

"But you're okay?"

"I'm okay."

He wouldn't have worried about Annie usually, but she still didn't look all that well, and despite the warm air her lips were blue and she shivered. She didn't seem as hardy as she had before all the troubles with the Raiff—braver, yes, but less healthy. And Eva, well, Eva was obviously running out of steam. She huffed and puffed with each footfall. Dwarfs didn't have the best cardiovascular systems. They weren't the type that ran marathons.

Bloom announced that they had to find a ride. He couldn't locate any horses, or even a donkey, couldn't sniff one in the air.

Jamie thought of Lichen making this journey by himself, the weight of all the elves on his shoulders. If Lichen could do it, so could they. Couldn't they? He went back to help Eva, who refused his help, of course.

He sneaked a peek at Annie. Her lips were tightly clenched and her hands in fists.

"Annie?" Bloom moved to Annie's side and they walked a bit ahead of the others. A shard of metallic dirt danced in front of them.

Annie tilted her head toward Bloom and said out of the side of her mouth, "What is it?"

"It's . . . It's Jamie. He's staring at his skin and scratching a lot." The words didn't feel good to say.

Annie stumbled on a particularly spiky patch of metallic grass. Her hands were deep in her pants pockets. When she finally spoke, she looked directly at Bloom's beautiful, sweaty face. His hair hung limply in a tight ponytail and he had dirt smudged on his left cheek. "I don't care if he turns troll."

Bloom winced as if he didn't want to think the thoughts he was thinking or say the words he didn't want to say. "What if he does? What if he can't control himself?"

Annie's face crumpled. "He won't. And if he does? He will still be good. He will still be my friend, *our* friend. He's Jamie, Bloom." She whispered the words emphatically and grabbed the edge of Bloom's hand in her own, pulling his fingers into hers and squeezing. "Jamie is the kindest of all of us. You know it. I know it. We can't abandon him just because he changes."

"It isn't just a change, Annie."

"If he becomes a troll, he'll still be good."

"I think those are mutually exclusive."

"Not for Jamie," Annie insisted so vehemently that she started shivering. "He can't. He won't."

Bloom stared at her, and she knew he was feeling badly but she wasn't sure why.

"You're right, it will be okay," he said finally, squeezing her hand in what was obviously meant to be a reassuring way. "We'll all be okay." He focused on the mountains ahead. "We need to find something to ride. Eva can't walk much longer."

Bloom spotted the two cows on the crest of the hill.

He pointed and announced, "Our rides."

———

"Woo-hoo," yelled Boucher of Steve, one of the younger grogans. "Look a' me. I'm a'swingin' like a wee ape beastie, I am."

He clung to one of the long hairs that fell downward from

the highland cow's neck. With a kick of his feet he swung back and forth on the fur.

Willey of Thom climbed up the cow's antlers and sat on one end. "It's a splendid view, it is."

Eva grumped from her perch on top of the cow, "I was just fine walking. Dwarfs do not ride cows. My family is—"

"Cattle," SalGoud corrected.

"Cows," Eva insisted.

SalGoud smiled. "How about heifers?"

The ground had shifted from metal to a brittle, thick grass with pointy, sharp ends. Annie contented herself to braid the long hairs of the smelly cow, whose back was not as comfortable as you would imagine, and all in all was more difficult to ride than a dragon. The back was too broad to sit with her legs around, and a cow didn't have a nice smooth gait, which caused Jamie, Eva, and Annie to bobble back and forth a bit. Bloom strapped them and the packs on the two cattle. He and SalGoud walked alongside.

"It's shameful," Eva grumbled. "Riding this foul beast."

Annie leaned down to kiss the cow's head. "Eva, it's a nice cow. It isn't fowl."

"It's cattle," SalGoud said. "Fowl are domesticated birds. Cattle are the large animals with cloven hooves and more kissable, apparently."

"Do not tell me you are kissing the cow." Eva rolled her eyes.

Annie stroked the cow's back and spoke in a smoothing tone. "It's a sweet little cowie-wowie, isn't it? And what matters is that we get to the elves as quickly as possible, before it's too late."

Eva groaned and turned around as if the sight and sound of so much lovey dovey-ness was too much to handle. She rode backward. Her pigtails bounced with every step the beleaguered bleating cow took. Jamie offered to thumb wrestle. His thumb instantly regretted it. They walked this way for a while, and then the grogans stopped talking and became very still, which was quite an unusual state for grogans.

Bloom stopped abruptly.

SalGoud adjusted his glasses. "What is it?"

The elf scanned the forest ahead of them for signs of movement and saw nothing. His brow lowered. "I do not know."

On the top of Bloom's head, Levesque of Jon materialized. He always saw the worst of every situation, but Jamie had quickly learned that as far as grogans were concerned the worst is really another's best, given that their priorities are adventuring and fighting and then fighting some more.

Levesque of Jon pulled on his purpling hair and said, "Ach, I bet it's nothing. No good-size kelpie. No scheming satyr. No Tarasque to swoop us up in its nasty claws. Probably jus' a souther' wind blowin' in . . . nothing, again." He crossed his arms grumpily in front of his chest. "We'll never get any adventurin' done a' this rate."

No sooner did he make an obnoxious noise involving his hand and the pit of his arm, than the ground beneath them rumbled. For a second, Jamie believed this was the noise of the grogan's armpit.

"That was quite the noise, wasn't—ahhh!" SalGoud started to say. His scream obliterated his words.

Two large, green tentacles broke through the soil, spewing rock, dirt, and metal in all directions. Spinning razor pinwheels chewed through the air. The tentacles wrapped around SalGoud's bony ankles and big calves. They sucked him down beneath the ground. All that was left on the surface were his glasses.

"SalGoud!" Eva screamed and started to jump off the cow. Her ankle got stuck in the knapsack strap somehow. Rather than valiantly vaulting to the ground to rescue her friend, she merely flipped upside down, dangling in a very unheroic manner, her face turning red like a valentine heart. "Ach, this freakin' milk maker . . ."

Jamie's heart lurched in his chest and he jumped to his feet, balancing on the panicking cow.

The grogan had all turned visible. They leaped off fur and heads and cow tails to raise their kitchen utensils and shout, "To battle!"

"No! Don't!" Jamie yelled.

The moment they jumped down to the dirt, the tentacles sucked them beneath the ground. Bloom pulled out his bow. Within seconds he was sucked beneath the ground, too.

Eva flipped herself back up into standing position, panting.

Annie stared, shocked. The ground seemed normal again. Nothing moved. Nothing rumbled. Her friends were gone. It was almost like a time stop. The only sound was that of Eva cursing and the cows' frightened breath. Annie glared at the land, anger rising within her throat, taking away any chance fear had.

"Annie?" Jamie whispered. "Why didn't it take the cows?"

"I don't know," Annie whispered back. "But I think if we get off the cow, it'll take us, too."

"Let it try," Eva growled, whipping out her ax.

Annie pulled out her bow and bit her lip. Jamie took out his sword, stomach clenching.

Annie drew back the string with the arrow and sent it singing into the earth.

Nothing happened.

Hands strong and cold, she notched another one.

Zz-zing.

This one made contact with something. A grogan flew up out of the turf, covered with bits of metal and rocks.

"Ach, it's a nasty beastie, it is!" he yelled before a tentacle sucked him back down under the ground. "Keep shootin'."

The cow bleated.

Eva pulled herself underneath the cow, clinging to it with a mighty roar. Her face had turned so red it looked as if a three-year-old had taken a crayon to it. With one hand she held on to the cow's upper leg and dangled there, ax ready.

"Send your ax in," Annie told her, letting fly another arrow.

"No way. A dwarf doesn't part with her ax."

Annie rolled her eyes. Her voice was firm. "Just do it."

Eva pulled herself back up onto the cow's back.

"I hate to do this to ya," she said and kissed the handle, pulled the ax behind her head with both hands, and whipped it forward with great momentum, so much momentum that she nearly lost her balance. The ax sliced into the ground and disappeared. A second later, SalGoud's fist appeared above the surface.

"SalGoud!" Eva yelled.

Annie tied a rope around her waist. SalGoud's fingers were fluttering about, wiggling. He was obviously still alive.

Annie handed the end of the rope to Jamie. "Hold me, Jamie. Don't let me touch the surface."

Jamie gave Eva his knife and grabbed the rope.

Annie jumped arms-first off the cow and grabbed Sal-Goud's hand. His fingers wrapped around her wrist.

"Pull!" she yelled.

Eva stashed the knife and with Jamie yanked at the rope, and Annie yanked at SalGoud's hand with both of hers. It burned terribly hot, too warm to touch almost, and the skin was bright red. When Annie grabbed it, the mix of her freezing skin and his heat sent steam into the air.

Annie yanked him up till his head, glowing red, popped through the surface.

"It's boiling," he gasped, spitting out dirt. "There's a cavern. The monster is so hot. And horribly ugly. All arms and . . . and . . . The grogans are jabbing her, but she's looking to eat Bloom."

"Pull, Eva!" Annie screamed and the little dwarf yanked the two of them back up. A tentacle followed out of the ground after the limp body of the exhausted SalGoud. It grabbed for him. Not thinking, Annie slapped it away from SalGoud's feet, as they heaved him onto the cow. She grabbed the writhing tentacle between her two hands, ignored the scorching heat of it between her fingers, focused all her energy, and yelled, "Cold!"

"What are you doing?" Eva yelled at her. "Shoot more arrows."

Eva turned to SalGoud, who lay sprawled across the cow's back. "Did you see my ax down there?"

SalGoud sneezed some hot metal shards out of his nose.

"Someone shoot arrows!" Eva bellowed.

Annie paid no attention. The tentacle shrank beneath her hand. It grew brittle and struggled to get away.

"Cold," she ordered. "Cold . . ."

"Annie?" Jamie whispered.

Ice covered the tentacle's tip, then spread down, down to where she couldn't see the creature's arm anymore. The ice spread beneath the ground, a crackling noise that grew louder and louder. The tentacle pulled and pulled, slapped against her cheek, but Annie would not let go. The beast beneath the ground gave a great growling noise, the tentacle in Annie's grasp shuddered and then broke into a million pieces. From beneath the earth came a sound like ice on a pond cracking beneath the weight of a tractor-trailer truck.

A moment later, the grogans began appearing, one after the other, shaking from cold, but looking no worse for the wear.

"A lovely battle!" Taylor of Davis cried, brushing dirt out of his beard. "Wrong again, weren't ye, Levesque of Jon?"

"Glad ta say I was." Levesque of Jon adjusted his ample stomach, pushing it back inside his shirt. "What a beast. Wi' those tentacles and razors, mighty set o' teeth on 'er, too. The elf sure ga' her the business."

"Tha' he did," Taylor of Davis agreed. "Did she eat 'im?"

SalGoud sat up on the cow, blood clogging from a wound on his ankle. His eyes were wild with sorrow. "Oh, no . . . not Bloom . . ."

"Bloom?" His name became part sob as Annie said it.

Jamie stared at the ground. There was no sign of their friend.

6

What She's Become

Annie didn't know what to do.

Bloom was gone.

The rest of them were just sitting on the cow, staring at the ground.

One of her best friends was beneath the dirt somewhere, possibly wounded, possibly frozen, possibly dead.

Dead.

That can't be, she thought. *That* won't *be.* She sprang off the cow, landing softly on the earth. She jumped on it, testing how solid it was.

"It seems solid," she told them, thumping around in different places. The piercing grass was covered with frost now, even though it was midday and somewhat warm. The frost crackled when she stepped on it. "We have to get through."

Eva hopped off the cow and landed with a thud, falling on her stomach. She bounced back up without comment or hesitation and started whacking away at the hard ground with a stick.

"If I had my ax, I'd get us through. Whack. Just like that," she muttered.

The grogans turned visible again and started attacking the earth with steak knives and salad forks.

"Take that, ye bloody ground."

"Are ya lookin' a' me, grass? Eh? Are ya?"

There was no progress.

Jamie cleared his throat. "This isn't working."

Nobody paid attention. Every moment that passed brought Bloom closer to death.

"We aren't doing this the right way," Jamie said, wiping bits of dirt and grass off his face. "Force isn't working. We have to think. SalGoud, how do we get down there?"

SalGoud wrapped a bandage around his ankle. "The monster took us down."

"But how did it do that?" Jamie asked, pacing across the grass.

Taylor of Davis accidentally stabbed himself in the foot and fell over.

"The monster made the ground like water I guess, made it soft."

Jamie and Annie exchanged a look.

"Water," Jamie said, thinking aloud. "Water is made up of

molecules like everything else. But in water the molecules sort of float, they are looser, not like a tree trunk or the ground."

Annie stopped stabbing the ground. "Strings are what make up molecules."

Eva groaned. "No science!"

"The strings make up everything in every world, everything in every universe," Annie said, her voice getting stronger as she got excited about Jamie's idea. "And they can be moved. They can vibrate and bend, stretch out like ribbons, or turn inward like thoughts. What I need to do is make space between the ones that make up the ground, make enough space so that I can squish between them and get to Bloom."

Eva's eyes bugged out. She had a piece of metal stuck in her teeth. "What?"

"I get it," SalGoud said, gingerly slipping off the cow and testing his ankle. "You need to change the ground from solid to liquid by resonating the strings enough to make space between them or the molecules. I guess they are kind of the same thing."

"Sort of. Right, Jamie?" Annie asked.

"Exactly," Jamie said.

SalGoud clapped his hands together, startling the cow into pooping on the field right there. Luckily, it missed the closest grogan. "So . . . How do you do that?"

Annie shook her head. "I don't know. Maybe just think it."

Eva scoffed and muttered about how thinking was pointless. Action was what mattered.

Annie squatted down, closed her eyes, reached out her hand. "Just think it."

Her fingers nudged the cold grass. The frost was beginning to melt in the sun. She smelled the wetness of it, and then unfortunately smelled the cow pie behind her.

Concentrate, she thought.

"Nothing's happening," Eva muttered. "If I had my ax . . ."

"Eva, will you just be quiet," SalGoud said. "Your ax is not the answer to everything."

"Are you insulting my ax?" Eva yelled.

The cow bleated.

"No," SalGoud moaned, exasperated, "What I'm saying is that . . ."

Jamie put his hand on Annie's shoulder for support, and Annie stopped listening to the bickering. His touch was warm, comforting, good. A raven cawed in the distance. She imagined the strings that made up the ground. She imagined they were like little earthworms. She asked them to move aside. Her fingers slowly reached through the earth, and then her hand was gone. Then her forearm reached through and she shifted so that she lay flat on her belly and her whole arm to the shoulder was inside the ground.

Above her Eva shouted, but it sounded terribly distant,

like in another room. "Enough! You keep nagging and look. She's got her arm in."

Annie wiggled her fingers around. Her hand was definitely not in the ground like the rest of her arm, but in someplace open. She snapped her fingers, hoping that Bloom would see her and the snapping would get his attention.

"Nothing's coming," she told Jamie, who was now holding her other arm in case something tried to pull her through.

A grogan hopped on her head, Nye of Alisa. Annie recognized her voice. "Keep concentratin', lassie."

"It's hard to concentrate with you on her head," Eva barked.

Nye of Alisa jumped off.

Annie ignored them and wiggled her fingers again, snapped them. Then she tapped . . . something. Something hard in the dirt, but not rock-hard. It moved. She reached through the dirt and there—What was that? A wrist?

"Come on, Bloom," she whispered. "Come on. You can't leave us now."

Fingers circled around her lower arm.

"I've got him!" Annie yelled triumphantly. "I've got him! I can't pull him up, though."

SalGoud whooped.

He, Jamie, and Eva began to dig the brittle grass by her, scooping up the dirt with their hands. The grogans joined in, stabbing their utensils into the ground as if they were farmers tilling the land with hoes and shovels. Annie grunted. Bloom was slipping. His other hand grabbed her wrist. She tried to scurry backward, but when she did, it just made her lose her grasp. She had no idea what would happen to Bloom if she let go, if he'd fall into the monster, if the ground would turn solid again and she wouldn't be able to make it shift. She just knew she couldn't drop Bloom and she was certain that she wasn't strong enough to pull him up by herself.

"SalGoud, try to stick your arm in next to mine," she suggested.

The giant sprawled out so that the top of his head was touching hers, sending several sputtering grogans scooting out of the way. No one wants to be crushed by a stone giant. SalGoud milled his teeth together and tried to thrust his hands down through the ground by Annie's shoulders.

Dirt and pebbles scattered.

"It's no good," he grunted. His hands were only in to their wrists.

Annie groaned. "Okay. Let me try to spread it out."

SalGoud's hair brushed against Annie's. "You mean make the displacement of the molecules bigger?"

"What are you two talking about?" Eva asked, stomping her foot on the ground, but not stopping her pounding stick throws. She was slowly chopping through the earth and making some headway. "Stop speaking science and speak English."

"Annie's going to try to make the earth so that she can move her arms through, big enough so that SalGoud can get his arms through, too," Jamie explained.

Below the ground, Bloom's fingers squeezed. Annie forced the thoughts out of her head and focused on the ground, on moving the molecules, on increasing the spaces between them.

Ah, but she was so cold.

"Almost through, Annie," SalGoud said. She couldn't see him because her own face was against the ground, but he had indeed reached both arms into the supposed-to-be-solid earth and now was sticking his head in as well, leaning forward. Next, his shoulders disappeared. "Almost through . . ."

Bloom let go of her fingers. She screamed.

Swallowing dirt and grass, Annie began to frantically scrape at the soil in front of her, pawing it, crying, "Bloom . . . Bloom! SalGoud, I lost Bloom!"

The stone giant's legs scrambled backward along the ground, his head and shoulders still beneath the earth. He looked stuck.

"Pull him!" Eva shouted. Annie, Jamie, and the grogans scrambled to positions on SalGoud's legs. They heaved as Eva counted.

"One, two, three," she bellowed.

Pull.

"One, two, three!"

Pull.

Out came SalGoud's back and shoulders, and then out popped his head, and finally his arms.

SalGoud's grass-stained lips quivered with fear. Bloom's limp, unmoving body dangled from SalGoud's arms.

Hanging from Bloom's belt was Eva's ax, but even Eva didn't really notice it thud against the ground as SalGoud rested Bloom by the cow. The elf's face burned red.

The children huddled around his body. SalGoud wiped some dirt off Bloom's cut and muddy face, then arranged the elf's cloak around him. Annie, no longer able to hold herself back, threw herself on top of Bloom's chest, weeping.

"My fault . . . all my fault . . . ," she whispered, horrified.

Light of Nathan ordered, "Hats off, boys. Show yer respect fer a great warrior."

The grogan obeyed. Ravens circled overhead and Eva, mad with rage, waved her ax at them, jumping up and leaping at the birds. The birds shouted at her, angrily cawing.

Annie talked into the fabric of Bloom's cloak. "Oh, Bloom, I'm so sorry."

Her cold hand touched his cheek. The redness faded. His hands where they had held on to each other were their normal golden color, too. But the rest of him . . .

Annie gulped and listened to the birds' voices and realized that she heard something else as well, a rhythmic thumping. Were trolls coming?

"I hear something!" she said quietly.

The grogans put their hats on and looked to the deep woods before them.

"No, not from there." She bit her lip. "It's Bloom. It's his heart."

A raven dropped a piece of paper from its talons. It fluttered to the ground. Levesque of Jon snatched it up, and stuffed it in his pocket.

Annie stared into SalGoud's watery eyes, joy overwhelming her. And she said again, "It's Bloom's heart. He lives."

She smoothed her cold hands across the boy's steaming face, and couldn't resist the urge to kiss his nose. "He lives."

"Ew . . . don't kiss his nose like he's a puppy . . . ew . . . ," Eva spat out, but she smiled and lifted Jamie up in a big bear hug, twirling him, she was so happy. Jamie coughed from the pressure.

They were all still alive, but for how long?

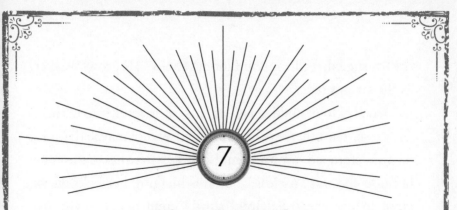

The Attack

There was no way the children could keep walking with Bloom in such a state, so they made camp in the field, covering Bloom with blankets and tending to his needs. SalGoud wandered about making potions and medicines from the herbs he found.

"Dr. Ned says pine needles work for fever. Let's hope he's right," he said as he mashed some into a paste. "Let's hope these actually are pine needles. Everything here is so strange, twisted . . ."

Every hour that went by, it seemed like the strings were weakening, growing more distant, and that meant the Raiff's machine was succeeding. And if the machine succeeded . . .

"We have to find the elves," Annie told Bench of John, as

she brushed dirt clumps off Bloom's shoes. "He grows weaker as the strings fade."

Bench of John nodded and put his battle spork into his belt. "As do ye. The others are na as affected, except maybe the lad."

Eva stomped around, muttering how angry she was because she was "useless," but still hugging her beloved ax close to her chest. SalGoud slowly crept about, trying to make medicine, looking much worse for the wear with all his cuts. Jamie scratched at his back.

"Elves are more attached, ya know. Perhaps, that other boy might ha' a bit o' elf in him. He sure enough doesn't seem troll no matter who he was raised by." Bench of John scratched his beard with a dessert fork and tried to act casual. A bit of barbeque sauce stuck to his whiskers.

"Every time anyone talks about fighting, Jamie looks like he's going to puke," Eva grumped.

Spellacy of Sam pulled at Bench of John's beard. "You have barbeque sauce in there. So. Hey. Night comes soon."

Annie shivered. "We'll set watches."

She touched Bloom's blond hair, whisking a lock of it from his forehead. He was so good at hearing things, at knowing when danger was lurching toward them. Bench of John turned toward the forest, listing the evil beasts that might be lurking there. Annie just stared at her friend, heart lost in worry, as the night came rushing in.

Jamie and Annie took first watch. The others fell to sleep after loading themselves on cookies and carrots and the other provisions that the children snuck out of Miss Cornelia's house and Gramma Doris's kitchen. It seemed so long ago. Eva patted her own belly and smiled for the first time that day, then winked at Annie before thinking better of it and snuggling next to the cow to sleep.

Annie and Jamie sat atop the other cow, back-to-back with their weapons out. Jamie faced the woods, while Annie faced the way from which they'd come. The lights of the castle city were just tiny dots in the distance. More dots decorated the sky. A cold wind came with the night. They'd walked a long way that day, and the battle with the underground monster had made them all weary in both body and mind.

Annie strained her ears, listening for noises, for the clicking of troll heels, for the swoop of air that signaled bloodthirsty vampires, for noises that indicated some sort of something was out there, some sort of something that she had never even imagined before. It was hard to believe how little she knew about horrible things. She hadn't known that the tentacled monster even existed.

She could just make out Bloom's features in the starlight.

"You'll be okay," she whispered to him. "We'll take care of you."

Bloom still hadn't woken up.

"Jamie," she said into the darkness.

Jamie's back muscles tightened. She let the back of her head rest against his.

"What?"

"Do you think Bloom will be okay?"

Above them, a star shot across the sky. In the distance, a twig might have snapped.

"I hope so." Jamie scratched at his back again, wedging his hand in between them.

"Are you scared? I mean, I don't know how we can do this without Bloom. What if he doesn't wake up?"

"We'll carry him," Jamie said with his warm, practical voice. "Or find a way to have the cows carry him. Maybe lash him on so he doesn't fall off."

"Okay."

They were silent for a minute and then Jamie admitted, "Yeah, I'm scared."

"Me, too."

Jamie brushed his hand against the cow's fur and sighed, "But we don't have any choice now, do we?"

"I don't think so."

Staring up at the stars, Annie pulled her coat around her tighter and settled back into a cross-legged position on the cow.

"I think it's bigger than us," Jamie said.

"What do you mean?" Annie couldn't get comfortable. Cow's backs were not like sofas. They bumped in all the wrong places and smelled.

"I think..." Jamie paused. He scanned the night. "I think... I don't know. I think this is about more than the elves. I think it's about the strings and the nature of everything. It feels as if we could lose it all. Aurora. Each other. It feels like the Raiff is trying to twist it up and rearrange the order of things."

Annie searched for things in the dark, ready to nab them. "I wish Bloom would wake up. It feels wrong without him talking to us, leading us, you know?"

Below them, Eva began to snore, a deep rustling bark.

Annie sighed and then summoned up the courage to say the thing that really was bothering her, other than whether or not Bloom would be okay, or if they would find the elves.

"I don't think Eva likes me anymore."

There, she'd said it.

Jamie cleared his throat. He didn't disagree.

Annie's heart sank. She was losing everyone. She sniffled.

Jamie turned his body a bit so that he was facing Annie. "Eva kind of likes things simple. Black and white. Night and day. You know? I think that maybe she just doesn't understand what's going on with you. All of a sudden you seem weaker and you did that cold thing with the tentacle monster, and you've had some trouble stopping time. No offense. And I think the vision we saw with the Raiff giving you blood unsettled her—even though it wasn't real."

A cloud drifted across the moon.

"I get it," Annie lied. She knew how hard it was for Jamie to say anything negative, but that didn't make it hurt her feelings any less. "I'm not sure exactly *how* I stop time. I just know it has to do with the strings and changing how they move and that the strings are the basis of everything." She sighed. Again. "That doesn't make a lot of sense. I wish I were smarter. I wish I could be like, 'Okay, that's how it works. Accept it and move on.'"

"You're really smart, Annie." Jamie plucked a cow hair off his wrist. "Albert Einstein said, 'Once you can accept the universe as matter expanding into nothing that is something, wearing stripes with plaid comes easy.'"

Annie giggled. "You sound like SalGoud. You really like science, don't you?"

"Yep. I'm not sure if that's really an Einstein quote, but it was on a poster at my school." Jamie turned enough so that he could look at Annie's eyes. They glistened in the starlight, but hollows had formed beneath them and her skin was so pale. Her back next to him was as cold as an ice cube. He was worried. He was really worried. "How did you do that freezing thing? Was that because of the Raiff?"

"I don't know." Annie shifted uncomfortably on the cow.

Jamie kept on. "But, in the castle fortress when we were captured. He touched your face and made you cold . . ."

"Demon blood is cold, right? Yes, and . . ." Annie's voice lacked any emotion whatsoever, and that's what bothered

Jamie the most. "So, if I'm so cold, then maybe I'm a demon. That's what we're all wondering, isn't it?"

Jamie stuttered, "Well, um, no—no, it's just . . ."

He felt like a complete heel, but it *was* what everyone was wondering, wasn't it? Just like they were wondering if he'd turn troll.

Annie scooted away from him and said nothing more, instead choosing to stare into the black, black night.

"I know what's it like for everyone to expect you to go bad, Annie. Everyone's been expecting me to turn troll since they met me," he finally said into the darkness. "It's like all of a sudden who you are has nothing to do with who you actually are, but it's about who you are expected to be. And who you are expected to be has nothing to do with your actions or your heart. It's about physical characteristics or your genes or who raised you. But that's not you. That's never you."

After a moment, Annie scooted back toward him, rested her head against the back of his again, and said, "You could never be bad, James Hephaistion Alexander. Even if you were ever a troll, you'd manage to be a nice one."

"And you'd be a nice demon," he said.

She laughed. "We'll be the nicest troll-and-demon team ever. Maybe my grandfather will write a book about us."

"And the dwarfs will sing tales of our glory," Jamie added, laughing softly.

"Oh . . . that would be asking too much," Annie giggled. "Dwarfs only like to sing of their own glory, you know."

"True." Jamie fist-bumped Annie. "But we would be the best troll/demon matchup ever, right?"

Annie made exploding fingers after their fist bump. "Right."

When their watch was over, Jamie and Annie stretched out beside Bloom, flanking him, protecting him.

Turning over, Annie listened to Bloom's breathing. She was so afraid he'd die. She touched the zipper of his sleeping bag and held on to it.

"SalGoud," she whispered across Bloom's unmoving form toward where SalGoud lay beyond the already sleeping Jamie. "Do you think we'll be okay?"

SalGoud stared up at the stars. "We've been through worse, Annie."

"I know, but do you think *he'll* be okay?"

SalGoud heaved his bulk up onto an elbow and looked past Jamie, unconscious Bloom, and right at Annie. She reminded him of a first grader, so young and scared.

"Elves are resilient, Annie. They heal well. They recover from things that would kill others three times over," he said, obviously trying to put a lot of conviction into his deep voice.

Annie thought that over as she fell into her exhausted sleep: *Elves are resilient.* But, it wasn't elves that she dreamed about. She dreamed about Tala falling into a dark hole and not being able to catch him, about Jamie turning green, about her heart turning into an ice cube as the mayor stood in front of her, making a speech. The traitor-giant pulled out a knife—her own knife—and lunged . . .

She startled awake. Grogans stood on her face. Spellacy of Sam made a "come with me" motion with her hand. Annie slipped out of the sleeping bag and looked around. Bloom was still beside her, fortunately not looking like he'd been snuggled, but unfortunately still looking quite unconscious. She bent down to check his pulse. It seemed stronger. She placed her hand on his forehead and willed him to be safe. "Protect. Heal."

For a moment, her hands warmed, but the heat faded and she stood and woke up Jamie, putting a finger to her lips to keep him quiet.

Beyond Bloom, SalGoud stood still as the standing stones of Stonehenge. Eva was crouched with her ax held ready in her hands, and the grogans were all in battle positions.

SalGoud motioned toward the woods with a quick jerk of his head.

Annie squinted through the darkness. Large, iron-clad figures shuffled in a line toward them. How many? Oh, maybe one hundred.

She gasped. One hundred.

"Do they see us?" she whispered.

SalGoud nodded. He tried not to look scared. It wasn't working.

Levesque of Jon appeared on SalGoud's shoulder. "It'll be a lovely battle, it will, and ta die fightin' orcs is ta die a happy grogan."

Jamie joined them.

I am not a grogan, Jamie thought, stomach cramping, *and I do not want to die and I don't want to make anyone else die either.*

Still he took his sword. He bit his lip. Annie scooted down and got her bow, notching it, knowing that she was nowhere near as good with it as Bloom, knowing she had no real chance of killing many. Dread filled her. She counted her arrows. She had maybe three dozen. Not nearly enough. She glanced down at Bloom, sleeping like a baby.

"Light of Nathan, turn invisible, sneak up, and attack the ends of the lines so they can't circle around," Annie told him.

Light of Nathan vanished and so did the rest of the grogans.

SalGoud turned to Annie for instructions as she pulled out an arrow.

"Behind me, SalGoud. Jamie, guard Bloom."

As one, the advancing orcs pulled out their swords. They shone hideous in the moonlight, the dried red crust of blood tarnishing the blades of their swords. Each blade was finely honed to a sharp point.

For a moment Annie's bravado faded. "The Raiff sent them. He sent them to kill us."

Eva whispered, eyes gleaming from adrenaline, "The devil himself can't take us."

Annie closed her eyes and tried to feel the strings. There was nothing. She couldn't find them.

Tentatively she whispered, "Stop."

SalGoud's eyes widened. Eva growled.

"I can't stop time," Annie said, panicked. "I can't find the strings."

Eva grunted. "Then we do this the old-fashioned way."

She raised her ax over her head and rushed the orcs.

"Eva! No! Hold the line!" SalGoud yelled, racing after her little mighty body, his steps long and lanky. They reached the orcs at the same time and were quickly surrounded.

Eva hacked at an orc's strong, greasy legs while another one lifted her bodily from the ground. She kept her ax swinging. The nasty beast roared in her face, pelting her with its foul breath.

"NO!!!" SalGoud screamed, knocking the orc aside. He stared at what he'd done. "Sorry."

"SalGoud. Do not apologize to orcs. Kill the orcs," Eva huffed out, punctuating each word with an ax sweep.

Eva growled, slicing at the air with her ax. She and Sal-Goud stood back-to-back, and the orcs watched them with amused expressions.

"You don't think we're a match for you?" Eva demanded. "We have fought worse than you icky fleabags!"

SalGoud held his sword in front of him. His glasses fogged up. He announced, "Winston Churchill said, 'When you have to kill a man, it costs nothing to be polite.'"

"These aren't men."

The orcs leered at them. Then they actually smiled.

"I'll give you that," SalGoud said. "Get ready. They're about to attack. Annie?!"

"Coming!" Annie let fly an arrow and then another. They bounced off the orcs' armor.

The orcs rushed in, grabbing Eva and tossing her into the air like a hot potato as she bellowed threats.

"It's fun. Toss the dwarf before we kill her!" one orc yelled. "Best game ever!"

Eva bellowed as an orc launched her back into the air. "I am not meant to be tossed!"

The grogan were doing a better job with their attack, materializing on top of the orcs in a massive group, prying off their armor with barbeque tools and kitchen utensils before attacking them and then disappearing again, but Eva and SalGoud . . .

"NO!!!!" Annie screamed, still rushing them, stashing her bow behind her and pulling out her knife. "NO!!!! Don't hurt them!"

She dashed headfirst toward the fray, heard the battle

cries of the grogans, and reached her hands out before her, trembling in the night. Birds' wings fluttered close behind her.

"COLD!" Annie yelled, even though she wasn't sure why she said it. "COLD!!!"

And a ball of ice shot out from her right arm and smashed into five of the orcs, freezing them in place. Another ball bulleted out from her left hand and shattered as it struck five more orcs, pelting them with ice as strong as gunshots.

Something screamed.

It may have been her.

The orcs that were taunting SalGoud with his own sword let him go and turned toward her. They gnashed their teeth. SalGoud lurched away, struggling to maintain his balance. He had no weapon.

Annie looked up her coat sleeve. Where had that ice come from? What even was she? A Stopper? A demon? Stopping didn't do this, didn't make ice.

The orcs' anger thumped against the air. Annie froze in place as they rushed her, thirty of them at least, screaming something she didn't quite understand, but she knew it wasn't good. Their muscles bulged beneath their armor. Their mouths twisted in blood rage. She held her ground. SalGoud screamed her name.

The birds began to sing battle songs, racing across the sky, as if they were cheering her on.

The monster warriors came closer, sprinting at her now. Fifty feet. Thirty. She raised her hands and the energy ricocheted between them. But where was it coming from? She couldn't even feel the strings.

"Please work . . . please, please work . . . ," she mumbled, desperate to stop the orcs.

SalGoud yanked a sword from a fallen orc's hand. Annie was still against the sky, silhouetted by an icy blue light that came from a giant ball of whiteness, hovering above her head between her hands. To his right, Eva cursed as she hacked at an orc.

"That'll teach you for tossing me!" she yelled.

The coldness stung Annie's hands. It didn't matter. She had to save Eva somehow. She had to.

———

Jamie couldn't take his eyes away from Annie. She looked so fierce, so little, so *cold*, like the ache of a million ghosts had been laid upon her soul. The orcs were almost on her. His stomach burned as if fire was spinning inside of it, trying to get out.

"Annie!" he yelled and, despite the pain in his stomach, started running toward her, knowing he'd be too late, too late to stop the orcs from slicing her to pieces, too late to do anything at all. "Annie!"

Behind her, another figure was running forward, moving

to help. *Bloom. Was that Bloom?* An arrow flew through the air and downed one of the orcs closest to Annie. Bloom could get hurt. Annie could get hurt. His friends.

Something twisted inside Jamie and it was all he could do not to throw up. He loved them—all his friends— He had to keep them safe. Something wiggled inside him. His stomach exploded in pain.

"Annie!" Jamie yelled again. His yell echoed across the field.

The battle cries and clanking dinnerware of the grogans were just distant noise in his mind. The stars blacked out as thousands of birds came streaming into the battle; shrieking and with talons out, they lurched at the orcs that the grogans fought, ripping one near Eva to pieces.

Jamie ran forward, struggling past the birds that beat their wings around him. He had to help Annie—who looked like she was about to turn into an ice cube as she bounced the giant ice ball between her hands trying to control it—had to protect them all.

They weren't strong enough. The birds couldn't possibly hold the monsters off. And his friends were trying hard, but they were so tired and weak. The orcs were only ten feet from her now, swords reaching forward.

"No! Safe! Be safe!" Mist seemed to explode out of Jamie and the world flashed, full of brightness and light for one moment and another. Power spilled over everything.

Jamie gasped, not sure what he'd just done. "Annie! Now!"

The ball between Annie's hands moved, spinning forward in perfect precision. It knocked the orcs down like bowling pins, freezing them as it struck.

"What the heck—" Eva bellowed.

Annie's entire body shook from effort. Tears streamed down her face, turning to ice.

The ice ball mowed across the field, spinning a freezing path of destruction as it hit one orc after another. SalGoud and Jamie smashed themselves flat against the ground as the ball lifted itself over them, not touching them at all. The grogans turned invisible. Eva stood and gaped, mouth wide open, ax still over her head. The ball of ice zigzagged around her and the boys. The birds flew safely out of the way as the ice approached.

And then it was over.

The ice vanished. The birds perched on trees. The orcs lay sprawled out across the field in various positions. None of them moved.

They were all dead. Every single one of them.

Eva let out a bloodcurdling victory yell and scrambled up to SalGoud.

"Where's Annie? Where's Annie? That was some battle trick, wasn't it? Whoa! Was that the demon in her? Because, I can't tell you how freaking awesome that was. I mean, what the heck?" Eva was nearly popping out of her corduroys in excitement. "Where is she?"

SalGoud pointed to the girl, halfway between them and the cows. Her arms were wrapped around her and she was shivering. A green boy stood beside her, leaning on her. Actually, they were leaning on each other. SalGoud gasped. It was Bloom.

"Eva. It's Bloom," he said. "It's Bloom! He is a strange shade of green."

Eva rolled her eyes. "Duh. Obviously. Where's Jamie? Staggering about? Did he puke again?"

Bloom took Annie's hands in his own, turning them over. Green coils covered the elf's hands like tattoos, but that wasn't what he was studying. He was studying Annie's bluish fingers. They were colder than ice cubes.

"How did you do that, Annie?" he asked.

"The ice ball?" She stared at the frozen orcs, put her face in her hands, and sat on the ground. Between her fingers, her voice came out in a whisper. "I don't know." She gulped. "I don't know what I've become."

He sat down with her.

"It's okay, Annie," Bloom said, watching Jamie, SalGoud, and Eva walk toward them, looking at the strangeness of his own skin. The green markings faded now. He pressed his lips together.

Jamie reached them and, crouching down, wrapped his arms around both elf and Stopper and announced, "It's over, guys. That part is over. Everything will be okay."

"Is this group hug time?" Eva yelled. "Because honestly, I'm totally okay with a group hug right this second even though I normally wouldn't be. This hug part does not go down in the songs of glory. Got it? Got it? Good."

And with that, she yanked SalGoud down with her and they all hugged one another. For a moment, Annie felt warm.

Night continued and the children kept watch, sitting on the cows, each facing a different direction. After the initial burst of enthusiasm caused by the fact that Bloom had finally woken up, they stayed quiet mostly, intent with watching the night, intent on listening to their own thoughts—although SalGoud would occasionally startle them with voicing a question unexpectedly.

"Why did the birds help us?" he asked.

No one knew.

"How did you do that freezing thing, Annie?" he asked.

Annie didn't know.

"Why did you finally wake up, Bloom?"

Bloom didn't know.

"Why were there green markings all over your skin? It was pretty, like vines and leaves."

Nobody knew.

"You're like some pesky two-year-old who can't stay quiet," Eva grunted and started carving two notches into her ax for the orcs she'd killed. SalGoud watched her out of one eye. He took off his glasses, wiped them on his coat, and then stuck them back onto his nose, where they hung a bit crooked.

"Don't you feel bad for killing?" he asked Eva.

"Bad? Bad!" she was nearly yelling and she stood up on the cow's back, which made the bovine shuffle and moo. Bloom hissed at her to be quiet, and she lowered her voice. "Those monsters were going to kill us. I feel good." Eva harrumphed and sat back down. "You aren't asking Annie if she feels bad."

SalGoud looked at Annie. She was shivering and her teeth chattered. "I know she feels bad, I don't have to ask."

Annie, truthfully, didn't quite know how she felt. She didn't think she had a choice with the orcs, but she didn't really know what she'd done, exactly. She'd frozen them somehow. She shuddered. Bloom took his cloak and wrapped it around her shoulders. Everyone else was wearing as little clothes as possible and yet she was shivering.

"Annie did what she had to do," Bloom said.

"And it was so cool," Eva said, all excited again. "That big ice ball thing. I mean, man . . . If you were here during the Purge and weren't a baby . . . Wow. I mean, something like that? Maybe we could have won. Bloom's dad wouldn't have died. Your parents wouldn't either. There would have been so many songs of glory about you that the dwarfs would have such a hate for you . . ."

She kept carrying on and reenacted the fight, jumping about and smiling, thrashing her ax in midair. SalGoud laughed watching her.

Annie watched Eva scamper about for a moment and then whispered to Bloom, "I still can't feel the strings."

He adjusted the cloak on her shaking shoulders. "Neither can I."

They sat in silence for a while.

Annie asked him, "Are you feeling okay?"

"Yeah, I'm fine," Bloom lied. "The green coils are gone."

Annie could tell by his tone that he was not exactly telling the truth. She stared at the dark outlines of the trees in front of her. To her left, the ravens slept in the grass. The world smelled cold. She smelled cold.

"We'll find them," she said. "We'll find the elves and the grandmother, all of them."

Bloom sighed. "I slowed us down."

She could feel the sadness in him descend.

"Bloom," she whispered as the sun rose, spreading light on the frozen orcs and the reality of what she'd done. The ravens flew as one with the sun's first rays, flocking to the forest, turning the sky into a moving black carpet. The freedom of their flight looked majestic and surreal.

Bloom looked at Annie. She had frost covering her nose. He wiped it off. "What?"

She blushed. "If we fail, maybe Megan will come. Lichen

will be okay and the grandmother elf will come home and be safe and the rest of the elves, too. I know Megan's a jerk, but she'll think of something."

He shook his head. "We won't fail."

"If we do, then I'm glad you were my friend."

He smiled and stood up. The blood from his wounds stained his clothes, but his smile made him seem like the old Bloom.

"We will always be friends, Annie. All of us. Always. No matter what any of us become or don't become."

The ravens flew back and a white piece of paper fell from the blackness that they created. The whiteness stood out against their feathers. SalGoud snatched it up and stared at it. The children crowded around him.

"What's it say?" Eva asked.

SalGoud showed them the word written in scratchy pencil:

WELCOME

They ate breakfast. Eva insisted. It was cookies and carrots, again, with bread. The grogans reappeared and feasted as well. Then Levesque of Jon remembered the paper he'd found yesterday and showed it to them. It, too, said **WELCOME**.

The children tried to figure out exactly what that meant and then gave up. They rolled up their sleeping bags, packed their gear, and set off again. They headed to the forest and then the mountain. Lichen's directions were vague, but their path seemed right. The cows suddenly bolted, no longer following behind them.

"I don't like the look of the forest," Jamie said, adjusting his pack.

"Wimp," Eva muttered.

"Eva!" Annie scolded, blowing on her hands to warm them up. "That's not nice."

Eva laughed and then stared at Annie's mouth. "Your lips are blue."

"I'm cold."

Eva unwrapped her scarf and gave it to Annie. "I'm hot. Take this."

"Thanks." Annie shrugged it around her neck and the girls followed behind Jamie, SalGoud, and Bloom.

After a couple of moments, Eva cleared her throat.

"Look, you may end up being some freaky, cold, demon thing, but you kicked some major orc butt last night and I respect you for it. I'm sorry I was hard on you and didn't trust you." Eva poked her in the arm. "And don't go telling anyone I apologized. Got it?"

Annie smiled but didn't answer.

They walked past the orcs, who were still frozen in place. Some dead ravens scattered the ground as well. Eva looked at the destruction.

"This is worth admiring," she announced. Taking off her jacket, she gave it to Annie. It was small, so Eva tied it around Annie's head like a hood. So far, Annie had her own jacket, Bloom's cloak, Eva's scarf and jacket, and still she was cold. It felt like her veins had liquid nitrogen in them.

They walked across the grass and through the battle site and then Eva announced to the air, "Any grogans, stop listening. Annie and I are going to have some girl talk."

"Erk, girl talk, na that," Staggs complained loudly, turning visible and then quickly disappearing again.

Eva rolled her eyes. "They think girls are poison or something, like if they hear us talk it'll make them put their beard hair in rollers and wax their eyebrows. It's so stupid."

Annie laughed. She liked the thought of beard rollers or the image of a grogan perming his mustache.

Eva fingered the notches in her ax and cleared her throat again as they kept walking. When she finally spoke, her words came out in an excited rush. "I saw something on Bloom . . . on his skin. It looked like green knots and coils, like the inside of a jeweled heart. Did you see it?"

"It vanished."

"Do you know what it is?" Eva whispered.

"I think Jamie did it somehow. I looked up and Bloom was running toward me and this mist seemed to explode out of Jamie and . . . and it hit Bloom." Annie forced herself to think about what she'd seen on Bloom's skin. She wasn't sure what it was, but she had an idea. She might have seen it in a book. "Do you know?"

"No clue." Eva plucked up a pebble and threw it as hard as she could.

It bounced off SalGoud's bottom. Jumping straight into the air, he grabbed his rear and yelled, "EVA! Behave."

"He thinks I'm such a baby." Eva sulked.

A brilliant blue butterfly had landed on Annie's nose, tickling it.

For a moment, she thought she heard it say, *Danger ahead.*

Butterflies do not talk, Annie thought. *The cold is making me crazy. Maybe I have the flu.*

Something harrumphed and the insect fluttered off.

Eva glanced at the boys striding in front of them, getting more and more distant the farther they walked with their long legs.

"Think they'll ever stop?" the dwarf asked.

"Not unless they fall down."

Eva laughed. "Or some tentacles grab them again."

In the field behind them, something pounced on a mouse, ate it in one gulp, and continued to follow their tracks.

"Look, when we were leaving Ireland, my cousin Johann told me something. It's . . . It's . . . about my mother and yours," Eva said. She swallowed hard, obviously having a hard time talking about whatever it was. Then she blurted, "Your mom was facing the Raiff and my mom . . . She had a chance to kill him. He was all focused on your mother, and my mom snuck up behind him. It was just them. Your dad was running along the beach and then . . . Well, my mom passed out. She didn't kill him and she could have. When my mom passed out, your mom got distracted and that's when . . . that's when . . ."

"When the Raiff killed her?" Annie said. She made it a question, but she knew. Sadness filled her heart, but she wasn't angry, not at Eva, not even at Eva's mother. Her own mother had been dead so long that she couldn't even imagine her, couldn't remember her, couldn't . . . It hurt to know how she died, but she couldn't blame anyone except the Raiff. *He* was the one who killed her. *Only him.* And he had killed her father, too, she figured. Nobody seemed to know exactly what had happened to him.

"That weakness . . ." Eva's voice was softer than Annie had ever heard it before. "It's inside me, too. I faint all the time."

"You never do anymore," Annie insisted. She touched Eva's shoulder and surprisingly, Eva didn't flinch away.

"But I might . . . I could . . . I could let you down." The dwarf's voice broke, overcome with emotion. She wiped at her eyes with the back of her hand.

"You haven't yet and you won't," Annie told her. "Look, everyone has a weakness. Bloom is bossy and hasn't been super confident until recently. SalGoud is afraid to act and speak for himself. He'd rather hide in quotes. Jamie is . . ." She had to think for a moment. "Jamie is worried that who people think he is *is* who he is. And he's afraid of never being loved. And I'm . . . I'm cranky all the time right now, and scared . . . I'm always scared of messing up, of getting kicked out of where I'm living, of not being good enough. But the thing is, you love people anyways, even though they have weakness."

Eva harrumphed and kicked a rock.

"You love them for their strengths or because they try, or because they have a rocking ax and pigtails." Annie smiled and bumped Eva with her hip.

Eva smiled back. "You better not be saying you love me."

"I lovey love love you," Annie teased and made big eyes.

Eva harrumphed again and hip-bumped her back, but managed to say through gritted teeth, "I love you, too, Stopper. I love you, too. I like you better cranky, anyways."

Annie wiggled her eyebrows. "Of course you do."

She linked her arm in Eva's, and much to her surprise and delight, Eva actually let her.

The Forest

It was already midmorning when they reached the forest. The massive cedars, firs, and maple trees were easily three times the size of any the children had ever seen in Maine, a state known for its forests. There was something so sad and lonely about the trees, as if they were mourning nature. Their leaves were black from the heat and brittle looking. Their trunks were a sooty gray. Their branches hung like human skeleton arms and hands. Sometimes the twigs seemed like fingers, waving, beckoning.

SalGoud stretched, and his bones made popping sounds. "I swear, the more we walk, the stiffer I feel." He motioned toward the trees. "The trees look like they can think."

Bloom stared up at the long, sweeping limbs, the thick

trunks. The lines of the trees that seemed to spread deeper and deeper into the land.

"Maybe they can."

Before they entered the forest, the children had a snack, each eating alone. They found a pathway through the trees, taking care not to step on roots. There were no saplings, no bushes along the ground, just leaves and brown needles that had said goodbye to their hosts and settled to the ground.

The wind had gone. No branches shifted. No leaves crackled with the wind. It was so silent that even the children's breaths seemed loud. Still, there was a great, ugly feeling of being watched. The unease grew bigger until Eva was constantly looking over her shoulder, growling, hand ready on her ax.

"Simmer down, Eva," Bloom said, voice calm. "Your growls will not make it better."

"I so don't like this place," she grunted, tripping on a tree root and falling sprawled across the forest floor.

"And it seems it doesn't like you." SalGoud reached down and helped her up. She didn't bother to wipe the pine needles and dirt off the front of her overalls.

The land began to slope up and Bloom stopped to look around and get his bearings. He pointed forward, the steepest part.

"This is the path," he said. "We go this way."

Their route wandered straight up steep slopes and down into a gully or two.

"The trees get bigger." Eva wiped her brow. She was hot from the walking. Yet Annie shivered as if it were a winter day with a full blizzard and she was standing outside in her bathing suit.

They stopped for another snack because Eva kept complaining that she would soon die from hunger. They sat on the forest floor munching away on apples and crackers. The grogans agreed.

"Snacks make the world better," Taylor of Davis shouted.

"And barbeque," Bench of John added. "What I'd do for a nice cedar-smoked salmon . . ."

As the grogans went on about their favorite foods, Annie turned to Bloom, who had stood up and was looking ahead into the forest. For a moment, she thought she saw something green flare on the bare skin of his right hand, but she shook her head and decided she was imagining it.

"Do you think Lichen is okay?" she asked instead.

Bloom ate the rest of his cracker.

He turned to her. "We will all be fine, Annie."

The food raised their spirits a bit and brought up their energy levels.

Still, for Jamie, Annie, and Bloom, there was a horrible feeling of being watched. This was not true for SalGoud.

The food had made him cheerful and he began to toss about his hat as he walked, laughing at his own foolishness.

A giant is a giant is he
Especially when he has a dwarf for company.

He kept making up silly rhymes and sang them in a sing-song voice, driving Eva to threaten him with her ax and curse all his descendants and all stone giants for three billion years.

The grogans and Jamie thought it was great fun and joined in on some of his more spirited verses.

A Stopper, a giant, a dwarf, and an elf
Which one is too full of themself?

"Better not be me," Eva grumbled, stomping along through the trees following Bloom but turning around to send a fiery glare SalGoud's way.

They passed by ruins of gigantic statues that had been felled centuries ago, the features of their faces worn smooth by weather. Hundreds of spiders covered some of them.

Annie's feeling very chilly.
I, of course, feel rather silly.

Jamie knew that SalGoud's merriment was driving Eva crazy, and his rhymes were horrible, but he took hope from it in a way. The giant seemed so full of warmth and life and optimism despite the ominous forest.

"Why are you so happy, SalGoud?" he asked, catching up and grabbing his arm.

SalGoud peered down at Jamie and shrugged. "Because I'm alive, I guess. Because we have something we're meant to do. A mission." He hesitated and continued, "I guess, because yesterday, with that beast and with the orcs, I was brave. I didn't know I could be brave."

Jamie glanced over his shoulder, stomach tightening again, and said, "You will have plenty more chances to be brave, SalGoud."

It was not a threat. It was not a warning. It was a fact.

From behind them, something heavy snapped a twig. They froze.

Bloom motioned for them to be quiet. Eva didn't listen.

"Who dares follow us!" she roared, running ax-first toward the sound, her small but heavy feet thundering through the woods.

"Eva!" Annie shouted, running after her. The trees muffled her shout. "Eva!"

"There is no stopping a dwarf heading toward battle at a sprint, ax raised and blood hot!" Bloom said, exasperation raising his voice.

They all watched helplessly as Eva galloped straight for the thing that had snapped the twig.

Eva screamed into the woods, waving her ax in circles around her head. Her pigtails flopped to her shoulders. Her eyes glared and darted, looking for something moving beyond the tree trunks.

"I know you're there, you stinking, skulking coward. Come out and meet my ax!"

Nothing happened.

She roared with fury. The leaves on the trees shook. She swung her ax into the ground, insulting the forest. Several nearby trees creaked in protest.

"You are upsetting ze trees," came a warm voice with a ridiculously fake-sounding French accent.

Annie and Jamie exchanged glances as Eva hauled her ax out of the ground. A root grabbed her by the ankle and made her trip. She sat on the forest floor without a sound, just breathing and feeling stupid.

A short-haired calico cat sprang out from behind a tree. He had a sword in his hand and a sheepish look on his face. "Yes, it is I. Purcee!"

Eva raised her ax. "And we know you how?"

"Have you not been searching ze wretched Badlands for me? I am Purcee, long-lost cat from Tasha's Tavern in Aurora. I was accidentally sucked over here during ze Purge. I had trailed ze Raiff and bitten into his leg only to be caught in a whirlwind of magic and then—poof! Here I was. Trapped. Have you not heard of me? Honestly? Tell me ze truth."

Annie swallowed hard and reached her hand out to shake his little paw. "I'm so sorry. I've only just arrived at Aurora really and haven't heard of a lot of people and ... um ... cats. I'm Annie."

He trotted to her and bowed and stood up again. "My Annie, you are so old now, and beautiful! No longer a baby, no? You look so much like your father. Oh, to think of you out here in this—this—world without anyone to protect you from the dangers that exist beneath the earth and in ze sky and in ze mind."

His kitty tongue licked her hand, a sandpaper texture scraping across her skin. Annie blushed. Jamie, however, was thinking of other things.

"Purcee, how did you find us?" he asked, squatting down to the cat's level.

The cat stood up straight on two hind legs, exposing his white belly. "Ah. Ze nose. I followed ze nose to my Annie. I remember her smell well from ze time before. Only she smelled a bit more like diapers then. And I saw ze dragon . . . Grady O'Grady . . . He came back on a scouting mission. But he is all caught up in a fight with a Tarasque at ze moment."

Annie's mouth dropped open. "Is he okay?"

"He was . . ." Purcee shrugged his right shoulder and preened his whiskers. "They careened off toward Scot's Land, but it was a battle, yes. He was holding his own, yes."

Jamie bit his lip and panicked. "But Purcee, this is an important question. Ready? You have to be completely honest. Tell me, for your species, are you mature?"

The cat appeared insulted. He looked away and licked his paw. "Why, yes, of course, can you not tell that I am a superior specimen of my species, fully grown and powered. I have fathered many cats. They are all great protectors and haters of ze trolls."

Bloom plopped down on the ground and put his head in his hands. He moaned. "This ruins everything. We'll never find the grandmother elf and the others."

Annie recoiled and whispered, "Oh no . . . Oh no . . ."

Purcee sat back on his haunches and held up his front paws, "What? What is wrong?"

"Only everything," Eva grumped.

Jamie was the one who explained the whole thing. He explained that they had a quest, but they couldn't tell him exactly what the quest was because the Raiff would know if anyone with a mature mind knew.

"And now you are here with your muddling muck mature mind." Eva coughed and looked up at the darkening sky. Was it going to rain? "And everything is ruined."

SalGoud wiped his glasses. "No offense. It is like they say, 'the best laid plans of mice and men often go astray . . .' Who said that? Oh no . . . I can't remember."

SalGoud began to mutter to himself. Eva had her arm around Bloom's shoulders. The elf looked devastated, as if he might cry. Annie couldn't handle that. She looked with pleading eyes at Purcee's sweet kitty face.

"Maybe, if you go now," she whispered. "That way we won't have to worry about accidentally saying anything about what we're doing."

But Purcee shook his head. "No, no, I have a better idea."

———

His better idea was to become a kitten.

"When I am in zat form, I am young, see? I think no mature thoughts, of no grown-up things." He sleeked back his whiskers, "But I must warn you I become quite, em, how do you say, kittenish."

He leaned against a tree trunk thinking; the children gathered around. The tree reached down and scratched behind Purcee's ear.

Bloom shook his head. "Do it now, before it's too late."

Purcee closed his eyes. "Farewell, Annie. Remember, I may scratch. But only in play."

Annie stroked his head, eliciting a purr, and she kissed his cheek.

He changed as she kissed him, shuddering once, then twice, until he was a young kitten's size. He looked up at her and meowed.

"Purcee?" she asked.

"Meow." He butted his head against her cheek, sliding it along her skin, the way kittens will when they try to mark you, claim you as theirs.

Annie held him out at arm's length, inspecting him. "I don't think he can talk anymore."

"Great," Eva grumbled, slapping her pack back onto her shoulders, getting ready to walk some more. "Fat lot of good he'll do for us now."

Annie snuggled him in between her coat and sweater, kissing the top of his kitty head. She could feel him purring. "I think he's cute."

Eva rolled her eyes, but Bloom smiled. "No, Annie's right. I like him much better now that he can't talk."

"True, no more 'Oh, Annieee, you glow with the light of a thousand night-lights,'" Eva said, following after Bloom, mocking Purcee's accent.

"'To go like a cat upon a hot bakestone,'" SalGoud quoted, taking Annie's pack and slipping it over one of his own shoulders. "That's John Ray, 1627 to 1705."

Eva turned around to glare at him. "What does that have to do with anything? Annie's hardly a hot bakestone. She's freezing cold. You are such a freak, SalGoud."

SalGoud bristled. "'Misery loves company.' Ray again."

Eva almost screamed out of frustration, but instead decided to head off after Bloom into the fog, which had quickly descended upon the woods.

SalGoud, walking next to Annie, finally noticed the fog, too, and muttered, "'The fog comes on little cat feet. It sits looking . . .' Carl Sandburg."

Eva didn't even bother to turn her head. Instead she just yelled, "I hear you!"

Annie patted SalGoud's arm and they walked on in silence, a giant, a boy, an elf, a dwarf, a girl, and one now sleeping kitten.

We Learn How Evil the Raiff Is

The Raiff was not pleased.

"How could you have failed to kill them?" He snapped his fingers at an orc.

The orc muttered that they were distracted, that the children had gone to the city, that they followed but the Headless Trunk interfered. The Tarasque spotted them again but was distracted by an Aurora-based dragon, and then when the orcs located the children again, the girl . . . The girl did something with ice. They had never seen anyone do anything with ice besides the Raiff.

"What are they even doing? If only I could track them . . ." The Raiff glanced up at the mayor, who was hemming and hawing next to the orc, obviously wanting to say something. "What?"

"Maybe they know about the elves," the mayor suggested.

"Impossible!" the Raiff barked, ice shooting out of his fingertips and hitting the ground before bouncing off around the orc's toes and knees.

The mayor and the orc exchanged a glance.

"Torture the elf." The Raiff seemed bored, flittering away the thoughts and words with a slight wave of his hand. "Until she tells us their location. The elf should be able to feel her kin."

"I can't see them," the elf, Aster, said. She was tall and thin from the torture of living in the Badlands. She smiled, brave and strong despite her tired face. "And if I could, I would never tell you." She turned her attention to the mayor. "Or you. Traitor."

The whip cracked against Aster again and again and still her smile did not break.

The Raiff roared at the insult of her smile. Horns sprouted out of his hair.

An older elf, another woman, shouted for the demon to stop. Aster lifted her head.

"Grandmother . . . ," she whispered.

Though weak from years of torture, the older elf began to utter words of power. Within seconds, energy emanated from her, as if she'd been saving it up all this time, for just this moment. Her skin began to shine and lines of green encircled her wrists, edging up her arms. The orc turned on her, venting rage with a whip crack around the neck.

"Strength to all," she whispered and within a moment, Aster's defender slumped forward, dead.

Aster screamed and tried to lurch toward the older elf, but the mayor restrained her.

As the grandmother died, a pain hit the hearts of every elf left alive, slicing their hearts with loss and sorrow until there was just a hole, a deep, dark hole where the grandmother should have been.

Aster's knees buckled. There was a loud moan and then the strong smell of flowers filled the air. The world shuddered, and Aster tried to break free, tried to clutch the older elf despite her own restraints, to somehow keep her from falling. The grandmother's body dropped, motionless, at the Raiff's feet.

"Oh. Sigh." The Raiff prodded her lifeless body with his toe. "I could have drained her energy a bit more. She was such a strong one."

The elf had been the oldest of them all, a source of strength to them throughout the ordeal. They had called her Seanmháthair, the grandmother, and now she was gone. None of them thought they could survive another day without her.

In the foggy woods, a horrible pain smashed into Annie's, Jamie's, and Bloom's hearts. Simultaneously, they crumpled.

Annie collapsed like a sack of rocks. Bloom dropped to his knees. Jamie doubled over and staggered into a sitting position.

SalGoud stiffly crouched to Annie's level and then yelled up to Eva and the grogans, "What's happening?"

He picked Annie's head off the ground. The kitten woke up and mewed, licking her face, which grimaced with pain.

Eva shook her head, panicked. She clutched her ax and then dropped it to stoop over Bloom. "I don't know. He's just all curled up and shaking."

"Annie, too," SalGoud called. He and Eva looked at each other, their eyes filled with fear. "I bet it's happening to all the elves. What about Lichen?"

"It'll kill him." Eva resisted the urge to stomp in a circle, instead cradling Bloom's head.

"And the wee boy, Jamie," gasped Nye of Alisa. "It's like they've been hit straight to the soul."

Eva gasped and released Bloom's head, scurrying away backward, her hands over her mouth.

"What?" SalGoud demanded, looking at Eva, then at the writhing Annie and back at Eva again. He was trying to smooth Annie's hair off her face, but he wasn't doing a good job because she kept moving. Frantic, he tried to figure out what Ned the Doctor would do and he couldn't. He couldn't figure it out and it was annoying him that Eva was standing there making a scene.

"What?" he asked again, stuffing a sleeping bag under Annie's cold head.

Eva just pointed.

SalGoud was in no mood. Annie's head flopped off the sleeping bag and landed on a rock, cutting her ear, and there was his best friend Eva acting very un-Eva like, and his voice came out terribly rude, "What, Eva? What?"

Her voice sounded like a little girl's, high and clear. For a moment, SalGoud wondered if that was her real voice and she made a pretend gruff voice because she thought that was how a dwarf was supposed to sound.

"His skin—Bloom's skin," she squeaked.

The grogans shrieked and vanished.

Annie was tightly clutching SalGoud's hand. He slowly pulled his fingers away and said to Eva, "Take care of Annie and Jamie."

Eva scuttled down.

Two long-legged strides brought SalGoud to Bloom's side, and it was his turn to gasp. His friend's face was scrunched up in pain just as Annie's was, but his skin . . . Green markings had appeared on it again, coiling and shifting in patterns that were as beautiful as any SalGoud could imagine. There were knots in it and crosses, twining like ivy vines. The markings seemed to be a part of Bloom, but also protecting him. It was like what had happened when they fought the orcs, only much more vibrant.

"Bloom?" SalGoud brought his finger out to touch Bloom's hand. He traced the pattern there. It was hard to touch and hard to the touch. "Bloom? Can you speak?"

The elf nodded and his voice sounded hoarse, "I think . . ."

"Eva, get some water!" SalGoud ordered. Eva hustled over with a bottle, not even complaining about SalGoud's bossiness. She cringed and lifted Bloom's head as SalGoud brought the bottle to his lips. The markings were even on his face and neck. They were everywhere.

Bloom swallowed the water and his body shook. The green markings started to fade. Eva rested his head in her lap.

"What is it?" Eva asked. "What's happening?"

Bloom shook his head and looked up at the sky, now completely gray with low clouds. "A death. It is a death."

"An elf has died," Jamie said, lifting his head from his hands. "It's like—it's like the universe just lost so much goodness. It's like the elves are even more vulnerable. She had been protecting them with her energy. And now . . ."

The giant's mouth dropped open. He tilted his head the way a puppy will when she tries to figure something out. The grogans began to materialize one by one, wiping tears from their cheeks.

Bloom raised his hand and struggled to sit up. "No. Jamie's right. An elf has died. I fell because we are all connected, all the elves. Like parts of the same tree, we are each a limb. It was a strong elf, a leader. Seanmháthair."

"The grandmother?" SalGoud whispered.

Jamie sat up, too. "I'm not an elf, though. Annie isn't either. Why are we affected?"

Eva shuffled off toward Annie, who was also struggling to sit up. "How do you know that? The death part."

"I felt her death. It was as if someone took a knife inside my chest and cut out a piece of my heart," Bloom explained, running a hand across his forehead. He stopped when he gently touched the armor and peered curiously at his own skin, examining the green lines and swirls. "I am marked."

Annie limped over, supported by Eva. She stared at Bloom's skin. The markings were almost gone. She stumbled into a sitting position next to him. Purcee put his head in her lap. "I felt it, too."

Bloom turned his hand over and over, staring at it. "Because you are Stopper. Stopper and elf magic is linked. I'm more intrigued by Jamie. An elvish leader's death shouldn't hurt a human or especially a troll."

"Jamie ain't no freaking troll!" Eva bellowed, and the grogans shouted their agreement. Jamie gave them all an appreciative glance.

Annie touched Bloom's palm. "You're marked again."

"I'm not sure what it is. Do you know, SalGoud?"

The stone giant creaked into a squatting position and took off his glasses to squint at the markings. He shook his head.

"I do," Annie said, gulping. "I think I do. I think that, um . . . I think that maybe Jamie did this to you. At least the first time."

"What?" Jamie scuttled backward through the pine needles.

Eva's head jerked up. "You?"

"I saw something come from him when we battled the orcs. Let me show you." She snapped her fingers and ordered, "Purcee, bite Bloom's hand!"

Bloom's eyes grew big and he shuffled backward on his bottom. "Annie, what are you—?"

He tried to reach for his arrow.

"Purcee, bite Bloom!" she said more frantically and the kitten leaped forward.

From his platform on top of the machine, the Raiff sniffed through his nose as he watched the werewolves drag the lifeless form of Seanmháthair through the valley.

"Useless elf," he muttered and then smiled. He liked the way the werewolves' muscles strained as they pulled Seanmháthair's body along the paths, liked the way they let her head bump against rocks and things. He was glad to have some of the werewolves on his side. He smiled again and lifted his hands up to the sun.

There was fog on the other side of the mountain but not

here, not where he kept the elves enslaved, not where his happy machine buzzed with life. He lifted his arms up again and yelled, "I can feel the strings!"

And indeed he could. It had been so long.

"But look who's here now," the Raiff gloated. "Look who is here."

He surveyed the scene, the pitiful-looking elves tied to the walls of the canyon, wires connected to them. The wires fed into the machine. The machine gave off a burning smell, like metal and gasoline and acid. The demon sniffed it in and let it touch his lungs. He could already feel the power growing. Soon, the machine would be ready; then he could kill the useless elves or maybe keep some of the prettier ones, like Aster, as pets. He could let her live, make her feed him. Then, once the elves were gone, and the strings' retuned, all the power would be his. He would never have to worry about elves or Stoppers again.

He let his mind reach out and feel the pain of the elves, the newly changing resonance of the strings, beyond the mountains to where the stupid Queen fretted over losing some servants, toward the other worlds, beyond . . . and then his mind jerked and centered on a little town called Aurora. He closed his eyes. Black birds circled above his head.

"They know . . . ," he murmured. "They know . . ."

He snapped his fingers. "Orcs! It appears that the children

are coming. I have a mission for you. Someone else—anyone—go fetch the Queen. I'm trusting her to take care of this—and them—while I go back to my fortress and prepare for my triumphant return to Aurora, my home."

10

Bloom's Armor

Purcee's sharp teeth and strong jaw clamped around Bloom's wrist.

"No!" Eva cried, lunging forward as all the grogans suddenly became visible and also rushed toward the cat. "Not his shooting wrist. Bite his nose at least, you evil kitten!"

Eva grabbed Purcee's midsection, yanking him backward as he squealed and let go of Bloom's arm. Bloom held up his wrist. It was covered in the green coils, all now tightly bound together like a thick bracelet.

"Purcee's teeth bounced right off," he said. "I'm unhurt."

Eva lifted up his wrist, examining it openmouthed. There wasn't a single mark on it.

"I've never seen such a bloody thing," muttered Pagan of Joe. "Can I have sum o' it?"

Bloom stared at Annie. "You knew that would happen, that I wouldn't be hurt."

She nodded and stood up, looking down on her friends. "I thought it would protect you like it did the other night when we battled the orcs. You glowed green with it."

"Jamie gave it to me? How?"

Annie didn't answer, but SalGoud said, "When he said, 'Safe. Be safe' during the battle, and then when Jamie created the mist. It gave you the armor somehow. Whatever it is, or whatever he is, it's probably connected to why he felt the grandmother die, why he doesn't want to fight. Do not say anything, Eva," he said to the dwarf who started to grumble that everyone should always want to fight, "because now is not the time to judge people for their non-violent tendencies."

Jamie stared at Bloom's wrist. He wasn't sure how to feel or what to think.

"An elf hasn't had armor like this for hundreds of years," said Bloom.

Annie turned her face to look at him. Her nose was red. "It's happened before?"

"It grew more powerful when . . . when the grand-mother . . ." It was like he couldn't say it. He began again, voice a little stronger. "Maybe her death increased its power."

Bloom, too, stared at the fading bracelet. "I've heard of it in legends. It's a powerful gift. I hope it lasts."

Eva pulled a grogan off Jamie's shoulder and demanded, "Aren't you going to say something?"

"Do . . . do trolls do that?" he gasped. "The protection thing. I mean, it *is* green. Trolls are green."

"Heck no." Eva laughed. "No way in a vampire's butt."

He met Annie's eyes. "Did you make me magic?"

"No," she whispered. "I think . . . I don't . . . I don't really know how any of this works, Jamie. I'm sorry. I just—?"

"Maybe trolls protect other trolls like that," Jamie said, doubting himself.

Annie yanked him and Eva into a hug. "What matters is that we're alive. That we are sort of safe for another minute. Not this . . . this . . . green thing."

"Ew! Hugs!" Eva bellowed, breaking free.

Jamie held Annie a second longer. Her eyes met his and he figured that maybe he didn't have to explain how he was feeling, how confused about the magic he was, or how much what was happening scared him and excited him all at once. She just knew.

"You hugged all of us after the battle, Eva. You can't pretend you don't like hugs." Bloom ruffed up the fur on Purcee's head and rubbed his ear. "No hard feelings."

The cat rubbed against Bloom's fingers.

"There ain't nothing like a hug," said Staggs, pulling at

his ear before attacking Bloom's leg with a hug so fierce the boy almost went off-balance. "It's good therapy, it is."

Next to them, the oak tree stretched its limbs toward the sky and smiled.

Across the mountains, the Raiff called together the werewolves, cursing the fact that it was daytime and he couldn't use the vampires, orcs, or trolls. No matter. He knew the party was small, an elf, an injured Stopper, a boy raised by trolls, a stone giant, and a dwarf. They would be no match for twenty of his strongest werewolves, who could turn from wolf to human in the flick of an eye.

The werewolves paced, howled, gnashed their teeth, thought of the blood and joy that comes from a fresh kill, thought of hunting their prey, of ripping flesh. Still, they waited for their master to release them. They'd been whipped too many times to leave without his command.

The Raiff was ready to give it.

He pointed toward the Pass of Sighs. "Take no prisoners except the Stopper. Go!"

Eventually, the hugging stopped. The children, Purcee, and the grogans looked toward the mountains, or where they thought the mountains would be. It was hard to tell, the fog was so great.

"It would be nice to just go home," Eva said, picking up her backpack and her ax, "and maybe beat up on my brothers a little."

"I didn't even know you had brothers," Jamie said.

"Eight," Eva boasted. "I have eight. There's a lot you don't know about me."

"I could see Miss Cornelia and Gramma Doris, and sit by a great fire and finally get totally warm and make them explain everything about my parents to me," Annie murmured, wrapping her arms around herself to ward off the chill. "And maybe they could tell me why I'm so cold. And maybe we could—"

"Eat some of Gramma Doris's pies," SalGoud suggested. "And talk about philosophy or quotes and work on my book with Ned the Doctor."

"Or eat Helena's doughnuts," Jamie suggested as his stomach growled.

Purcee meowed and Annie picked the little kitten up, stuffing him back inside her jacket. She checked on her phurba, still sheathed. She slung her bow across her back and put her quiver on her shoulder. She'd let SalGoud handle her backpack again, since he didn't mind.

"I would like to feel the wind of the woods against my face, to see the animals of the forest I love, the sun shining down on us, not like this cursed place, and to do it all with other elves," Bloom announced, surprising them all. Bloom was always so gung-ho; now he looked tired, a little beaten.

The others seemed stunned. "The fog grows thicker, and I fear it does not hide friends but foes."

They were all silent and then Levesque of Jon growled, "He's speaking like an elf again."

"Well, he *is* an elf," Jamie said defending him.

"But he doesn't have to talk like one," Eva complained.

Then they were silent, all staring ahead of them at the thick fog.

Finally, after a great many moments Light of Nathan said what they'd all been thinking, at least with some little part of their minds, "Maybe we shouldn't go."

Jamie's head jerked toward him. Purcee purred against Annie's chest. Jamie said, "Not go? What about all the adventurin' and fightin' and more adventurin'?"

The grogans didn't answer, just fiddled with their kitchen utensils.

Bloom sighed. "I can feel a great danger racing toward us."

"We've been through danger before," Eva barked, swishing her ax through the air so fast that Jamie had to jump out of its way.

Shaking his head, Bloom said, "It is bigger than that. I cannot ask any of you to go any farther. I can barely ask myself."

"But the elves!" Eva said, blowing hot air out her nose, angry and annoyed. "You expect us to turn our back on the elves. Jeez, Bloom, I thought you were smart, but you're acting like such an idiot."

He bristled. "I can go alone. It is my burden."

SalGoud shook his head, shrugged on his pack and Annie's. "It is not even close to yours alone. That's not how friends work."

Bloom was too overcome with emotion to say anything.

SalGoud smacked Bloom's shoulder. "Let's walk with our weapons out and our hearts ready to fight."

Eva yelped with joy, "Now we're talking!"

"But—" Bloom shook his head again.

SalGoud began walking. "We have not voyaged all this way past portals, past a wicked city, past fields and monsters, past our own fears because we are made of mashed potatoes. We are made of stronger stuff than that. All of us. We are the elves' only hope. We must go on."

"Mashed potatoes?" Jamie whispered, trotting behind SalGoud.

The stone giant blushed. "It's hard to come up with a good motivating quote like that on the spot. Mashed potatoes were the best I could come up with."

Reaching up, Jamie petted SalGoud's shoulder. "It's good."

"You think so?" Relief flooded SalGoud's face as he stepped around burned ground.

"It should go in your book."

SalGoud smiled. "I think it will."

Ned the Doctor Makes a House Call

Back at Aquarius House in Aurora, Miss Cornelia gasped. Her hand flew to her heart and she staggered against the wall of the front foyer where she'd been talking tactics with some of the townspeople.

Mr. Nate and Canin rushed to her side, each grabbing an elbow. "What is it?"

She slowly raised her head and looked past them to Gramma Doris, who was gathering weapons. "The grandmother . . . She was alive and she just left. She is dead now."

"The Seanmháthair?" Doris whispered.

Mr. Nate gulped, stepping back. His hands went to his chest.

"That's why . . . That's why the children are doing this?"

Canin growled, settling Cornelia in a chair by the mermaid fountain. "There were elves still alive? In the Badlands?"

"How could they have been alive? How could they have survived?" Cornelia spoke slowly. Her voice was weak with worry and shock. Her hands shook in her lap. "They must be trying to rescue them."

"Well, it doesn't look as if they're doing a very good job if the grandmother just died," Canin grumbled.

The door to the house flew open. Megan, the young hag, stood there, snow wetting down her hair, breathing hard and heavy. "Miss Cornelia! You have to come! It's Lichen! He's dying! I can't—I can't— Something has happened."

Miss Cornelia snapped her fingers and coats flew out of the closet and onto everyone's backs. "Lichen? Who is Lichen?"

"An elf!" Megan cried, running back out of the house and into the snow. "And he's dying. He's gotten so much worse, crying about his grandmother and now not speaking at all. Please! Come! Come!"

"Corny . . ." Canin grabbed her arm before she headed out the door. "It's not safe for you to be outside. If the Raiff comes— It could be a trap."

She petted his hand quickly. "It is an elf, Canin. I must help him."

And she was gone, following Megan through the woods.

"Doris!" she called back. "Keep preparing for war. And

make a nice healing pie in case Lichen survives. Have Helena help you! The two of you can cook anyone back to health."

"I don't need help," Doris muttered, pulling off her coat and putting on her apron. "What I need is some salted caramel tea, pierogi of the cheese kind, some rest, and an end to all of this evil."

Miss Cornelia rushed to the hags' house, running down the long front hill of her own home and across the town, her skirts whipping behind her, her hair flying out straight. Behind her, Ned the Doctor, the dwarfs, and most of the rest of the entourage struggled to keep up.

They raced through the barren streets, causing a bit of commotion as they passed houses and buildings. Children burst out the doors to see what was going on. Mothers cautiously peeked out of windows. Fathers snored away in the living rooms. Whisperings of what was going on quickly spread.

"An elf, I heard . . ."

"No, it couldn't be."

"The elves are dead."

"No, they are alive, and Bloom and Annie have gone to rescue them."

Soon, most of the town was straggling behind Miss Cornelia to see what was going on. Miss Cornelia was oblivious to it all. She stormed into the hags' little house, an old-fashioned place with weathered white clapboards on the back side and white stone walls on all others. Once inside the hallway, she sniffed the air and headed directly for Megan's room. She didn't look at the posters of teen idols on the walls, or the fluffy purple lamp. She went straight to the closet and flung open the door.

She gasped.

Inside was a pale, pale boy, all skin and bones. Beneath his eyes were dark red hollows. His hair hung limp. He had none of the golden glow that elves normally have.

Miss Cornelia pulled his blanket up over his chest, tucking it in. Her hand smoothed the hair from his face, touching his fevered brow. She placed a nice teddy bear beside him and kissed his nose. Then she stepped aside so that Ned the Doctor could do doctor things. He had his gigantic black bag, which held his medicines and herbs, a talking stethoscope, and a thermometer.

The stethoscope kept murmuring as Ned the Doctor listened to Lichen's thin chest, all his ribs jutting out against paper-like skin.

"Oh, this is bad. Oh, this is terrible," the talking stethoscope mumbled. "Oh dear. Oh dear. Oh dear."

"Shh," Ned the Doctor hushed him. Lichen did not wake up.

Ned sighed, straightened his long back, and tugged on the end of his navy blue wool sweater, which was threadbare at the elbows and fraying at the neck.

Just like SalGoud, he pushed his glasses up his nose to give Miss Cornelia the news. "I'm afraid the young elf is quite bad off."

"He's dying!" squawked the stethoscope, so annoying Ned the Doctor that he smashed it into his bag, catching the earpiece in the latch. The stethoscope squealed in pain and Ned opened the bag and pushed it back in.

"Sorry, so sorry," he murmured.

Miss Cornelia could hear the stethoscope's muffled swearing, and raised her eyebrows. Like Gramma Doris, Miss Cornelia did not believe in swearing.

She turned to Ned the Doctor. "Can we do anything?"

Ned the Doctor sighed. "I will do all I can, but, man, I think his fate doesn't depend on me. This is bigger than me, Corny."

She nodded. "It is bigger than all of us."

Miss Cornelia gave a short, low whistle and the Woman in White appeared floating above Megan's Barbie collection.

"Would you look at this," the Woman in White said, holding up a Ken doll. "Our dolls were made of rags pulled off potato sacks . . . This looks like, well, like a real man."

She stared at Ken adoringly. "He's so handsome."

She floated him up toward her face and had him pivot around in midair. "Do you think Megan would let me borrow him for a while? Just to keep me company?"

Ned the Doctor awkwardly stepped back.

"I'm sure she would," Miss Cornelia said, trying not to sound impatient or do anything to spook the very easily spooked spook. "I need a favor from you, if you please."

The Woman in White clapped her hands together, delighted. "Anything!"

Miss Cornelia pointed to the closet. "There is a young elf in the closet. He is terribly ill. We need to move him to my house, preferably to the safari room, where it is warm. We can't have him jostled, and I knew no one can levitate things as beautifully as you do, my dear."

The Woman in White blushed, which looked very strange on a transparent face, just two red circles upon faded features. "Oh, that's too kind, sweet Cornelia."

"You are lovely at it," Ned the Doctor said, pouring on the charm. The Woman in White fluttered her eyes. All women fell for Ned the Doctor because he was so nice. It didn't matter about his sweater or his granite fingernails or his white hair. "You'll have to stay focused, though, because one drop could kill him."

The Woman in White looked stricken. "Oh, dear . . . I don't know . . . You know how I am."

The Woman in White was notorious for fluttering off in a tizzy whenever anyone mentioned her lost Captain or she looked out at sea or if someone asked a question.

"Couldn't you do it?" she asked Miss Cornelia.

Miss Cornelia sighed. "Normally, I could. But I grow weaker by the minute. I just don't think I'm strong enough, but I know that you are. Levitating is easy for most ghosts, but you, my dear, are a pro."

The Woman in White flew over to Lichen and touched his cheek. "He looks so sweet—to think, another elf! Bloom must be so excited. Oh, but do you think I can do it?"

"I am sure you can do it," Miss Cornelia proclaimed, clapping her hands together. "I have every faith. So let's go."

The Woman in White bit her nonexistent lip, raised her arms, and began.

It was a rather strange parade that marched through Aurora's main street. A young boy floated at the head of the group, closely followed by a ghost in flowing white skirts. Then came a hairy creature known as a Big Foot, holding the hand of an old woman with rainbow stockings. Behind them marched an extremely tall man, an extremely hairy man, and an assortment of dwarfs.

The town's librarian with her snake hair and a large panther-like cat walked side by side. Fluttering fairies and pixies flittered about.

The procession weaved its way slowly through the town and up the hill toward Miss Cornelia's large Victorian house. The sky was clear. There was no wind. Where it showed through the snow, grass was starting to turn green. Winter was over, but spring had not yet begun.

"You are doing wonderfully," Miss Cornelia praised the Woman in White.

The ghost nodded, her teeth gritted. She kept her hands upraised and her eyes on the boy.

Behind them, the mutterings of the other townspeople became excited outbursts that grew louder and louder.

"It really is an elf."

"Oh my word."

"I hope that ghost doesn't drop him."

"What can this mean?"

"The prophecy has come true."

"Dang, I left a cake in the oven."

"Don't drop him."

"Don't drop him."

"Don't . . ."

"Mommy, I gotta pee."

They rounded up Miss Cornelia's curve and above their heads a lone seagull flapped its wings.

"Almost there now," Miss Cornelia said in as calm a voice as she could muster. "Almost there."

But the Woman in White spotted the seagull soaring to their right, and just beyond it was the ocean, the great wide grayness of the Northern Atlantic on a winter day.

"Oh, no . . . ," Gran Pie muttered, lunging forward.

"Ghost! What are you staring at that seagull for?" demanded a dwarf.

"QUESTIONS!" The Woman in White stopped walking. "Oh, the sea . . . It is the sea . . . My Captain . . . My Captain, he calls me . . ."

As one, the entire crowd gasped.

The Woman in White dropped her arms down and drifted away toward the sea, completely forgetting about the elf hovering above the ground.

It was the hags who saved Lichen.

As he began to fall the three older women reached out their own arms, and a great calmness swept the crowd. The smell of cinnamon and apples seemed to drift from the women's fingers. A pink ray of light caught Lichen just three inches from the ground. The hags shook with the effort, but they raised him another half foot and slowly pushed him toward the house.

All the creatures held their breaths.

"Oh, good show," Ned the Doctor whispered excitedly. "Good show."

Megan ran to open the door of Aquarius House, her face still tearstained. She gasped as she saw the women of her family helping her charge.

Lichen floated past her, followed by the hags. The tallest

darted a glance at Megan as she passed and said, "I'd ground you, but I'm too proud."

The shortest one muttered, "I say you're still grounded."

Megan sighed, leaning against the doorframe. Perhaps now, Lichen would get better. She crossed her fingers and tiptoed after them, not bothering to shut the door.

12

Something Wolfy
This Way Comes

Jamie knew they were walking toward danger. They all did. Still they walked, somber and oppressed, except for the sleeping kitten. The woods seemed to hurry them along. The lower limbs pushed them ahead and skeleton finger twigs brushed against their backs.

"We will be heroes when we rescue the elves," Eva boasted, hunched forward as she strode through the forest, her ax ready in front of her. "They will toast us. They will make up ballads. Our names will be whispered on young children's lips!"

SalGoud stopped midstride, causing Jamie to have to skirt around him just to avoid bumping into him.

"Eva," he scolded. "You are absolutely ridiculous."

"I am not." Eva stuck her tongue out at SalGoud. "And try to keep up, giant. You are so slow and ungainly."

"We can do this," Jamie said, even though he wasn't sure how anyone was actually surviving.

Compared to the others, Jamie couldn't help thinking that he was a small, goofy wimp.

I'm not like a typical hero at all. I don't like swords or killing like the grogans. I am not terribly brave. I don't want any songs written about me, how embarrassing, he thought, blushing just to think about it, and then he realized. *I am just me. Jamie. Maybe that's all I'm supposed to be.* But he had done something to Bloom . . . He wasn't normal. That was for sure.

He glanced at his friends. Bloom's face was determined and ashen. He had rips in his sweater from the monster. Annie still wore his cloak along with Eva's scarf and all the extra clothes and coats. Her lips were gritted so that her teeth wouldn't chatter; her hair that leaked out past her hat became a twisted, tangled mess against her face. The kitten's ear peeked out of her jacket.

Eva trod in front of him through the white fog. She seemed fierce and waddled a little as she walked. He could see her bare ankle from when she'd forfeited a good sock to that Headless Trunk.

SalGoud walked as if every muscle hurt him. The grogans had gone invisible again and even they were quiet. Nobody seemed well, and it worried Jamie. He decided to cheer them up.

"What do you call people who are afraid of Santa Claus?" Jamie asked.

No one answered.

Then Eva said, "Stupid."

"No." Jamie made his voice merry and light. "Claustrophobic. Get it? Claustrophobic. Hee. Hee."

"Kill me now," Eva grumbled, but Annie and Bloom started giggling, too. SalGoud gave Jamie a slow-moving thumbs-up.

"Fine, then," SalGoud said and announced in a loud joke-telling voice, "A dwarf went to WalMart and looked around and asked a saleswoman, 'How much for the TV?' The saleswoman said, 'Sorry, we don't sell to dwarfs.'"

"I already do not like this joke," Eva grumbled, smacking her ax handle with her hand.

SalGoud smiled and continued the telling, "The next day she came back all covered in fur like a Big Foot. She asked the saleswoman about the TV. She said, 'Sorry, we don't sell to dwarfs.'"

Eva growled.

"The next day she comes back with fairy wings and sparkles in her hair and in a tutu and she asked the saleswoman how much the TV costs. She said, 'Sorry, we still don't sell to dwarfs.'" SalGoud paused. "So, the dwarf goes, 'I came here looking like a Big Foot and looking like a fairy. How do you know I'm a dwarf?' And the saleswoman sighs and says simply, 'Because that TV you want to buy is a microwave.'"

Bloom started laughing so hard he clutched his stomach. Annie tried not to giggle and insult Eva, but it was hard. Eva growled. The grogans fell down and rolled in the pine needles, guffawing.

The fog didn't seem quite so scary anymore to any of them, at least not as scary as Eva. She stepped in a hole and twisted her ankle, hopping right back out and hoping no one noticed. Everyone did.

Spellacy of Sam slapped her thigh, twisting in mirth. "Tell us another. Tell another."

Bloom straightened up. "We have to keep moving, though. I think I hear something."

SalGoud cleared his throat. "Okay. Um. Oh, here's one . . . Two dwarfs were driving to Sugarloaf, you know, the ski area, when they got to a fork in the road. The sign read: 'Sugarloaf Left.' So they went home."

"Oh that is too much!" Eva screamed, and she lunged at SalGoud, tackling him. He held her at arm's length—which is quite long since he is a stone giant—giggling as she flailed at him.

"Bigoted, evil stone giant . . . Not rude, huh? Stone giants are so good, eh? I'm going to shove your glasses up your nose and pull 'em out yer freakin' ear!" she shouted.

"Eva!" Annie scolded.

"Fight! Fight!" the grogans started chanting. "I've got odds on the dwarf."

"Ten ta one for the dwarf."

"I'll bet on the giant."

"Are ya daft?"

Bloom yanked Eva off SalGoud and roared, "There will be no fight."

His face was stone white. Annie had never heard him yell before. She didn't know elves ever yelled. Jamie clutched his stomach. The pain returned. The kitten woke up, mewed, and scrambled up to Annie's shoulder. SalGoud struggled to his feet, wiped needles from his butt and the backs of his legs. "I'm sorry, Eva. Everyone seemed so serious . . ."

"It *is* serious," Eva grunted.

Bloom raised his hand for silence and crouched down, touching the earth. Purcee growled, teeth back and lips curled.

"What is it?" Annie said, but Bloom did not answer. Instead, he whipped his bow out and motioned for them to fall behind him. "Bloom?"

The kitten lunged out into the woods. Teeth clashed with fang. Fur and skin tore. The noises panicked her.

"Purcee!" she screamed, starting to run after him, but Eva caught her arm and pushed her down. Just in time, too, because the biggest wolf Annie had ever seen leaped at the space where her head once was, jaws gnashing.

Eva whirled around with her ax. "Come and get me."

The wolf snarled but stayed put. Its eyes glowed yellow.

"There are more," Bloom said, sending two arrows through the woods. Something yelped.

The children and the grogans stood with weapons raised and backs to one another. They could hear the sounds of Purcee fighting in the woods. A moment later, more wolves emerged. Bloom shot one in the chest. It staggered but kept coming.

"These are not ordinary wolves," he said, letting fly another arrow.

"What are they?" Annie whispered.

"Werewolves," said Taylor of Davis, his utensil raised high. "Canna be killed by mere arrows."

The wolves circled around the children, snarling. Annie knew it was only a matter of time before they struck. Bloom shot another arrow directly into the wolf's heart. It did nothing except make the wolf growl.

"Light of Nathan, give Bloom your fork," Annie insisted.

Light of Nathan glared at her and hissed out the side of his mouth, "Are ya crazy?"

Annie snatched it out of his hand and gave it to Bloom. "I'll buy you a set of dessert forks when we get back, okay? I promise."

Bloom looked at the fork and sudden realization dawned. He smiled and notched the fork in his arrow, letting it fly. It sliced through the air, hitting the closest wolf in the chest. The wolf yelped and backed away.

"Silver!" Eva yelled. "Freakin' genius, Annie! Freakin' genius."

She grabbed Bench of John's extra-long barbeque fork knife and threw it with such force that it stuck in a wolf's muzzle. It growled and stepped back a pace or two.

Purcee skittered through the wolves' feet, covered in blood. Annie scooped him up into her arms, searching for wounds.

The wolves growled and prepared to spring.

Annie stuffed the kitten back in her shirt. She raised her sword and screamed, ready to fight, wondering if her sword was silver, thinking that she'd never hug Miss Cornelia again, never have another Gramma Doris pie. She braced for the impact of the wolf's body against her own, preparing for the pain that comes from teeth and claws.

SalGoud let out a bloodcurdling cry, and Bloom shot off as many forks as he could in that moment that the wolves leaped. Annie knew it was for no purpose. There were too many.

She gritted her teeth and prepared to fight anyway.

13

Wolves Can Be Wicked

The wolves leaped. But before they could reach the children, the great pines and firs reached down with their strong bottom limbs, twisted and grabbing. The trees bashed the wolves out of the air. The forest was a mess of bodies and fur, and some wolves turned back into men in the rumble, but in less than a minute every single one of the werewolves was lifted thirty feet high and caught in the limbs of the trees.

The children craned their necks to see the wolves hanging there. The white underbellies of the wolves wiggled above them. The animals struggled to be free from the limbs, but the trees held fast.

"I knew these trees were not just trees!" Eva declared, fixing the elastic of her pigtail in a very casual manner, considering what just happened. "I knew they were watching. Although, I have to say, we totally coulda took them wolves, trees! I was totally ready for another battle! Ya denied us a battle!"

The trees ignored her.

Annie couldn't believe it. She closed her eyes, stepped away from the circle and to the nearest tree. For as long as she could remember, trees were the only real friends she'd ever had, the only things that let her hug them before that feeling of terrible loneliness almost swallowed her up whole. Small tears of thankfulness crept out of the corners of her eyes. She placed her palms against the rough bark of the spruce that was closest. Two wolves whimpered above her head.

The tree warmed her hands and she whispered, "Thank you."

Annie wrapped her arms around it in a hug, and the tree brought down two of its free limbs and for a moment hugged her back. Then they both let go.

Annie nodded to the others. They set off again. This time they ran and neither SalGoud nor Jamie told any jokes. They knew the sun would set soon. The elves were running out of time, and so were they.

The sun already sent long shadows across the land. The rivers flowed more slowly now and their color changed to something even less clear, something even more murky. The grass had changed, too. It was more yellow, less green, harder in texture. The sky showed less blue, less vibrant. The strings were already changing, and with the strings' change, so changed the world.

The squirrels that gathered in the trees of the forests mourned in high, shrill chiding voices. They looked at their own fur and cried over its manginess. Their cries grew and then faded as if they couldn't believe the shrieking sounds they were making themselves.

Distant, but deep, came the noise of a thousand beings surprised and sorrowed at the slight changes in their nature wrought by the Raiff and his machine.

Annie grabbed Jamie's elbow as they hurried. "Things are getting worse. He's getting more powerful."

Jamie gulped. "We will fight him together, always friends, Annie. Remember?"

She remembered. She just didn't want to lose him the way they almost lost Bloom. She didn't want him to get hurt.

14

The Pass of Sighs

It was almost night and the children's leg muscles burned from running through the foggy woods for so long. The land kept rising steeper and higher, and after an hour or so Bloom noticed that Eva needed to catch her breath. SalGoud kept moving more and more slowly as if his joints needed to be oiled.

In a place where the trees grew thin, the children gulped the last of their water. Eva wiped the sweat from her brow with the end of her pigtail and pointed to the sky.

Above them, hundreds of dark birds circled and soared, cutting through the fog. A white piece of paper dropped from one's talons. Bloom snatched it out of the air and read it aloud. It said **THEY COME**.

Pulling out their weapons, the children bundled closer together peering into the fog. There weren't enough trees to help them here.

"Will it be wolves again?" Jamie asked.

"Hope so," Eva said, just as Annie said, "I hope not."

"I don't hear anything," Bloom whispered. "Do you?"

Fear took their voices.

Another bird flew low and dropped another note, written in the same scratchy writing. SalGoud read it. It said **TROLLS NEXT**.

"Trolls," Annie whispered. "It's not night yet. We have time."

Bloom nodded; they sheathed their weapons and ran.

———

Following Bloom's quick steps, they found themselves beside the mountain. Two rock walls surged before them, and beyond there was no fog, merely the pinks and purples of a setting sun.

"The Pass of Sighs," Bloom said. The words seemed important, monumental. SalGoud went through his list of steps again and nobody shushed him.

"We've made it to step six," the giant confirmed.

"We haven't made it until we're through," Jamie said.

The tunnel in front of them seemed colder than the rest of the Badlands. A spider or thirty-five clung to the sides of the entrance, but there were no webs to slash through.

"We have made it this far," Bloom announced. "Past Headless Trunks, Saltas, our own shame, tentacled monsters, lack of hope, self-doubt, werewolves, and orcs. We have made it together, but if anyone wants to stay here, I'd think no less of them."

"You could say you're guarding the pass," Annie suggested.

There was a sudden deafening roar from Eva. Annie staggered backward as the dwarf lifted Bloom up in the air. "Don't you dare make like we're not all going. You ain't robbing me of the final steps of this quest."

The grogans all materialized, holding their silverware in the air, yelling "YAH!" and a few choice curses. Then Eva let Bloom back down to the ground and winked. "You first."

"You *always* say that dwarfs go first." He rolled his eyes, straightened his cloak, and headed into the pass first anyway.

They followed him in. The pass was high and reached up eight hundred feet. Behind them, the fog of the forest seemed so much safer.

"If we're ambushed, we'll be trapped," Eva said, her eyes darting this way and that. Her knuckles whitened as her fingers grabbed the ax handle. "We'll be butchered like pigs."

"Not with your ax," SalGoud said.

Eva grunted in acknowledgment.

"It's not night," Annie said, walking behind Bloom and Jamie. "The trolls won't come yet."

"That's if the birds were telling the truth." Eva scowled, whipping around to fend off an attack from the rear. There was nothing there. She plodded on behind them, obviously still nervous.

"You don't trust the birds?" Annie asked.

"I trust my friends."

Jamie leaned forward, a feeling of menace overcoming him. He tapped Bloom's back and said, "Death. There's death up ahead. I don't know how I know, but I know."

Bloom nodded and kept going, his feet disturbing the pebbles on the trail. Annie ran her hand along the cold, dark rock that made the mountain.

A hundred feet more and Bloom stopped suddenly and said, his voice a ragged whisper, "Jamie, don't look."

"What?" Annie asked, pushing forward behind him.

She gasped. The rest of the passage was decorated with severed heads hanging off chains. She clutched Bloom's arm.

SalGoud bumped into them. "Why did we stop? What . . . oh?"

He made no more noise, just stared at the hideous line of heads stretching toward the sunset. Then he murmured, as if to comfort himself, a quote, " 'A dirge for the most lovely dead that ever died so young,' Poe."

"They're elves." Annie burrowed her head into the back of Bloom's shoulder.

"Yes. They've died one by one over the years. I didn't feel

their deaths. Just the grandmother's. They were too weak and far away."

Slowly, Bloom moved forward and they followed him, Annie still clutching his arm. Jamie clutched hers. SalGoud and Eva, too, took hands. By each head, Bloom murmured a name, stopping to feel the souls of the dead elves as they walked. Jamie's heart shook inside his chest, filling with sorrow.

"This is Robin. She sang sweet songs to me as a baby when my parents were gone. This is Oak. He stood strong for Miss Cornelia. This is Juniper. She liked to play with the squirrels, would make them acorn strings."

As the children made the solemn and grisly procession through the Pass of Sighs, sadness burrowed its way deeper and deeper into their hearts. But at the same time, Annie, Bloom, and Jamie sensed that they were gathering more strength with each elf they passed.

"I will kill that demon," Eva muttered between gritted teeth. "I will take his teeth and make 'em into a necklace. I'll turn his eyeballs into Ping-Pong balls. I'll—"

They reached the last elf. Her hair was whiter than new clouds in a clear blue sky. Bloom reached up and touched her forehead with his two fingers. "Grandmother."

SalGoud took off his glasses in respect. "The Seanmháthair."

Even in death, she was beautiful. Her dark skin shone in the sinking sun's light.

Annie bowed and murmured, "Seanmháthair."

The elf queen's hair blew in a slight breeze and both Annie and Bloom heard her whisper in it. She said one word, "Vengeance."

Bloom turned to study Annie for a moment. She nodded, and as if ordered by an unseen voice they rejoined their hands and raised them toward Seanmháthair's head. A golden light surrounded them, a beautiful light full of warmth and power.

"Holy!" SalGoud said, stumbling backward.

"What is it?" Eva stood petrified.

Jamie swallowed and said in a hushed, focused voice, almost as if he were praying, "There's nothing wrong with the light. It's a gift from the Seanmháthair. It's like she's protecting them, giving them strength. I think."

"How do you know?" Eva whispered. As she asked, the light changed, taking the shape of a tall woman bending over Annie and Bloom in a long hug. Then it shifted, glided past Jamie and then around his belly and back, and then soared up to meet the setting sun as it sank beneath the sky's line.

It was gone. She was gone.

The color returned to Bloom's face. The green armor bracelet flashed solid around his arm and then up toward his shoulders, stretching across his cheeks and chin before vanishing.

"I feel good." He turned to Annie, eyes wide with wonder. "Strong. Nothing hurts anymore. How do you feel?"

She squeezed his hand before letting it go and said, "I feel . . . I feel warm. Jamie? How about you?"

Jamie poked his stomach with a thin finger and then reached around toward a slightly itchy place in his back. "Me, too. I feel strong, too."

He didn't tell them that he still felt itchy, but as SalGoud returned his glasses to his nose, Jamie thought the stone giant was looking at him curiously, as if he knew somehow. Jamie resisted the urge to scratch.

With great effort, the children left the Pass of Sighs and headed on to step seven: Find the machine.

"This is a horrible place," Annie said as they stepped out of the pass and to the side of the mountain.

Below her, the valley had been stripped of all things good and green. The mountains were black as if the earth had been charred and then burned again. The children leaned forward to see what was down there, shielding their eyes against the setting sun, and then as one, they leaned backward as if stepping away from what was before their eyes.

Devastation. Disgust. Evil.

In the middle of the valley below them hulked a silver machine as big as any Maine library. It was made of three or so squares stuck together and covered with conduits and electrical gizmos that Annie knew nothing about. They hadn't gotten to electricity in science yet. But she recognized the wires coming out, the sparks crackling between circuits, the horrendous humming noise of it, like a broken refrigerator turned up so loud the entire town could hear it, even with the doors closed. There was a platform near it and some sort of shacks.

"Are those . . . elves?" SalGoud asked, squinting, taking off his glasses again, rubbing them on his shirt, and then placing them back on his nose, but in an incredibly crooked way.

Eva grabbed Annie's hand, and they both gulped. Along the sides of the valley were human shapes, their heads hung low, their clothes tattered. They were all tied to the hideous mountainside, great long wires attaching them to the machine.

"This is more of a valley than a pit," Eva whispered. "And I thought there were cages, but they . . . they . . . they are chained and exposed to the elements."

"The Raiff must have moved them," Annie whispered back. "Maybe to make them suffer more? Maybe because he's closer to being done?"

The grogans turned visible and as one swept off their hats and bowed their heads as if they were at a funeral, and all the elves were dead.

Anger welled up in Bloom. He started to run down there but Eva headed him off and made him trip. He jumped back up, drawing out his bow, but SalGoud caught up to him in three strides and pulled him to a stop with a firm grab around the arm.

Bloom tried to rip his arm free, but SalGoud would not let go.

"I have to save them," Bloom hissed. "Let me go."

The stone giant shook his head. "Not like this. The sun is setting. You will stumble in and be caught."

"I can't stand to see it," Bloom mumbled.

Jamie didn't think he had ever heard him mumble before.

SalGoud tightened his grip on Bloom, looking to the others for help. They took a step closer, but Eva was unable to wrench her eyes free from the horrible valley below.

SalGoud muttered, "No, Bloom. Remember what Lichen said? We have to dismantle the machine, break it so it can't be used."

Bloom's back straightened. "With the dwarfs' things."

Jamie found his voice. "In a star shape around the machine. It will break their chains and the machine."

"Lichen *thinks*," said the ever-doubtful Eva.

"It will," said Annie, voice strong and sure. "I know it. Come on, we have to hurry. It's getting late. We'll have to split up."

Just saying it made her shiver.

SalGoud's head jerked. "Oh, I don't know . . ."

"Annie's right. It will take too long any other way. We will be quiet. We will be like wolves in the night," Bloom said, suddenly focused again. He pulled off his backpack to take some items out of it.

"It's the wolves in the night that scare me, and also the vampires, and also the trolls," SalGoud said, sulking a little. Still, he pulled off his and Annie's packs.

They all knew what they had to do. They had to split up. For the first time since Annie and Jamie came to Aurora, the children were going to have to potentially face their demons without one another.

15

Setting the Star

*T*his *is a bad idea*, Annie thought. *A very bad idea.*

She had Purcee in her pocket, but a kitten for company didn't make her feel any safer.

And this is just like a horror movie, she thought as she moved along the mountainside alone. *It's dark, there are monsters. Yep, just like those horror movies that Walden used to watch.*

She used to think her foster brother was the worst monster she'd ever have to deal with. She'd been so wrong.

Annie pressed herself along the trail, which pushed against the rock wall of the mountain like a tiny crack against a skyscraper's side. Annie was no more than an ant, inching along its great vastness.

There was no wind, just the sound of her little ant feet as she walked along the path. She sniffed. The cold made her nose run. She slowly shuffled sideways. In the distance, something scuffled. She stopped for a moment, listening. Not a sound from her left, the way she'd come, scrambling along the rocks and boulders, nose tingling from the stench of burning metal and decay. Ahead of her, to her right, she couldn't hear anything either. Below her was the machine, shining in the moonlight, humming incessantly. The moon loomed big over the mountain, an intense ivory circle. It cast silvery light onto everything. Without it, she wouldn't have been able to see.

The vampires were out, and the trolls. Anger welled up inside of her.

Stop being such a wimp. You've faced worse before, she told herself, checking her position. Some pebbles scattered beneath her feet. She brushed the hair out of her face with a shivering hand.

She sniffed the air trying to smell the odorous scent of trolls, which is similar to skunk spray covered up with twenty bottles of cheap perfume. She couldn't smell anything. She listened again for the scuffling noise. Nothing.

Okay, let's go.

Taking three more steps, she bumped into a boulder, skinning her knuckles. She smashed them into her mouth and sucked on them.

Suppose the vampires smell my blood? They'll swoop down and rip me apart, suck me dry, demon blood or Stopper blood, or whatever.

She closed her eyes and took a deep breath, trying to rid herself of the horrible images flashing in her mind. The grandmother elf didn't die for nothing. She wasn't going to let her down. Opening her eyes, Annie scrambled up another thirty feet and pulled out the diamond as big as a fist. It glinted in the moonlight, its many cuts catching the light and turning it into rainbows of colors. Something so beautiful didn't belong in a place so drear and grim, but Annie placed it in a safe position on the trail, tucked between boulders, one point of a star.

The machine in the valley didn't hiss or hum or explode or anything at all fantastic like that. Annie surveyed the landscape below her as best she could in the moon's light. Everything seemed the same.

Maybe the others haven't finished yet, she worried. Purcee poked his head out of her coat; she kissed the top of his kitten nose and he softly mewed and rubbed against her chin. She barely noticed. Maybe they'd caught Jamie or Eva or Sal-Goud. Maybe Bloom and the grogans were lost.

There was nothing she could do. She checked the diamond one more time, making sure it was hidden well enough, but in the right place.

"Good luck," she whispered to it.

She sighed and turned away, crossing her fingers for luck and hurrying to meet up with the others.

SalGoud could barely move his legs as he walked across the dark gray terrain to his point of the star. His logical brain couldn't understand what was going on. Normally he strode through mountains with long, galloping strides. When he walked with his friends, it was always more like crawling. Now, he had the opportunity to go fast and with ease, but he couldn't. Every step made his bones want to crack. Every step stretched his muscles as tightly as they could go.

I have to get there, he thought, looking up at the fat moon, which seemed to laugh at him as it traveled the sky.

He walked on. In the valley below him, trolls were rounding up elves and shoving some into a cave and others into a building that seemed to be made of compressed dirt. Some elves were still tied to the constantly humming machine.

"'Show thy dangerous brow by night, when evils are most free.' Shakespeare," he quoted. His voice sounded ragged as if full of pebbles and dirt. He swallowed and that, too, was hard to do.

I am turning to stone, he realized. *All stone. Soon I won't be able to move.*

And for a moment his lip quivered and he thought of Ned the Doctor and how sad Ned would be if he didn't return for their long walks and philosophy talks through the blueberry barrens. Who would Ned teach his healing ways and which herb to pick in which phase of the moon? No one would bring Ned the Doctor stories of the school day, all about Odham's bullying and the silly things Megan said to him at the lunch table. A tiny tear squeezed its way out of SalGoud's eye and it was not made of water, but actually was a small quartz crystal. It landed hard on his cheek, but he didn't stop to examine it because he was afraid if he stopped, he wouldn't be able to move again.

Something was wrong with his hands. He didn't really want to look, but he couldn't help himself. Instead of his soft skin, granite formations, ripples of malachite and quartz shone up at him. He wondered in his head, *Why is this happening to me?*

And the answer came back.

"It's the machine and what it has done to the strings," he said, voice choking. "They're changing me to stone. The closer I get, the stronger it becomes."

In SalGoud's pocket was a dwarf's scabbard, ornate and covered with dwarfish writing, runes, and golden pictures of battle triumphs. He had to get it to the spot, he had to get it there. He would be brave. He would die a hero. A great gulp caught in his throat. He'd never finish his book of quotations. Maybe Ned could finish it for him, he thought, as a crow fluttered up into the night sky.

"'To him who is in fear, everything rustles.' Sophocles," he quoted and realized that it made him feel braver to quote.

He took a few more steps, creaking and swaying, and looked around, checking his position with that of the moon and the machine. He was there, in the drop-off place. He let the scabbard fall from his granite hand. It bounced and rested in the middle of the trail. He could not trust himself to bend down and move it. Who knew if he could straighten back up afterward? Who knew?

Turning around and moving like a very elderly man, he began to make small steps back the way he came. A crow landed on his shoulder. It fluttered a wing against his stony cheek, like a kiss.

"Hello, bird," he whispered. A whisper was all his voice could manage now.

The bird cawed, adjusted itself, and motioned toward the valley below, and the last elf disappearing into the cave, his walk slow and defeated.

"'He who helps . . . helps in the saving of others, saves himself as well.' Hartmann von Aue," SalGoud quoted, his voice breaking midsentence.

The crow cawed in agreement.

SalGoud managed another step, rolling his bulk forward. He seemed to weigh as much as a mountain.

Below him on the trail, he spotted through his clouding vision a group of trolls heading his way. They pointed at him.

They were wearing cowgirl and cowboy outfits, which looked ridiculous against their slimy skin. They started running toward him, tassels bouncing, but curiously, he did not feel afraid. He took another step toward them.

"'These wretched ones who never were alive.' Dante," he told the crow.

The bird nudged his ear. The trolls were almost to him. He closed his eyes and thought of Eva, hoped she was safe and not rushing off and attacking a gaggle of orcs. He hoped she forgave him about the dwarf jokes. He worried one more time about Ned the Doctor being alone without him. And the elves . . . He had failed the elves . . .

His breath was like a whisper and he managed to say one last quote to his new crow friend, "'The weight of this sad time we must obey.' Shakes-peare. Shakes . . . Shakes . . . peare again."

The crow nodded and sighed as the boy stopped moving, cast in stone, midstride on the trail. It was the last quote Sal-Goud said. The trolls heaved up his lifeless form and carried him away—and the crow flew off to bring the other birds the sad news.

Eva didn't care one dwarf ax strike about stealth. She cared about success, and rushed up the trail to her drop-off place headfirst, pumping her squat legs for all they were worth, bumping into boulders, jumping over rocks, stubbing her toe, smashing her hip.

One rock knocked her totally off-balance, sending her flying like Supergirl, arms outstretched in front of her, before she hit the hard earth with a crunching noise. She scrambled back up to her feet.

"That'll be a good bruise," she grumbled and started running off again. She was going to do this, to get her treasure in the appropriate place, to break this machine. And when she did? Not only would the elves be free but she would clear her family name, making up for her mom's mistake. She had to be successful. There was no other choice.

"They will sing songs of my family's glory," she announced, running harder. "Our names will be back in the *Rolls of Awesome Dwarfness*."

She made it to her spot in no time and heaved out the dwarfish sword that she carried. Holding it with two hands in front of her, she marveled at the craftsmanship for a moment.

"A beautiful weapon." She sighed and put it down on the ground, kicking some dirt on it so no one would see. She looked at the machine. Nothing happened.

"That little elf punk better have not lied," she said and bit her lip. She had expected fireworks or a great devastating explosion, to show her that her mission had been accomplished. Maybe Annie or Jamie or SalGoud hadn't made it. She knew Bloom would never be caught. "Freakin' freak."

Maybe the grogans got lost.

Worried, she bit her lip again and adjusted the strap of her overalls.

"I'll go help them." She turned around the way she came and smacked right into the arms of a vampire, the bad, bloodsucking kind.

———

Bloom strode gracefully along the trail, counting each easy footfall as he moved up and toward the farthest point of the star. He kept his pack on and in it was the dwarfs' golden shield, which he would set out. The pack seemed heavier now somehow.

It's because it's heavy with importance, he thought.

The Golden Arrow was safely in the quiver.

He steadfastly refused to look down in the pit-like valley below him, not because he was afraid of heights. He feared his own rage. If he looked he might rush headlong into a trap, vision clouded with bloodred fury.

My people are down there, he thought as a cloud passed over the gaping eye of the moon, the color of ice. *Maybe my parents.*

He gulped and located a handhold and started pulling himself up the steep face of the mountain. There were no more trails to where he was going. He would have to make his own way.

"Bravery is the ability to face one more second, one more moment of fear," Bloom mumbled to himself and then smiled. He sounded like SalGoud. He hauled himself up another foot and came to a level edge that he could inch along.

Standing up, he made his way toward the drop-off point and then whipped out his bow. He could smell something not far off. The scent of perfume and body odor wafted over him. Trolls. They were close. Pebbles fell on his head. They were above him!

"I swears I smells elf," a squeaky-voiced troll said and then belched.

"Smells good?"

"Smells like dinner."

Bloom froze. There were no good shots he could take. He could see nothing but the distant stars, just mere dots in the sky, and not some place safe to escape to.

"We can't eats 'em. We have to bring 'em back for the Raiff."

The first troll began to hiccup. "That's stupid. *Hic.* They always says that and we never gets to eat 'em. How often do we get elf? *Hic.* It's always bunny or kitty or human children from that city. Never elf. I hates it."

He stomped his foot for emphasis, and an avalanche of rocks toppled on top of and around Bloom, hitting his head and shoulders. He swayed but did not lose his balance and tumble into the valley below. Instead, he inched forward.

The second troll sighed. "He'll cut up our fingernails if we eat 'em. The Raiff will know, I tell ya. Dratty demons."

Bloom cautioned another step. He had to move.

"And he knows things. He gets more powerful every day."

Bloom sneaked another step and then another baby step. Then he heard what he didn't want to hear.

"I smell it, too! A boy elf! *Hic. Hic!*"

"Where? Where?"

There were scurrying footsteps above him, the frantic footfalls of hungry trolls. It sounded as if they were wearing heels. Bloom hoped that would slow them down.

"Do you see him?"

"I smell him!"

"Where is he?"

"Below—*hic*—us!"

A large troll hand swept down, just missing Bloom's head. He sank an arrow into it and was rewarded with a scream.

"He gots me! Bad elf! Ow. Ow. Ow. Pull it out!"

Bloom ran. He raced along the knife edge of a trail.

"Get him!"

The trolls thundered after him, but they were up higher than he was and couldn't reach. Still, they kept just a step or two behind him, and he knew that where he had to put the shield was where they were, up above him, and a hundred feet ahead. He had to get there. He had to save the elves. He *would not be* the last elf. He would not stand alone. He had been the only for too long.

The trolls' running steps displaced more rocks and pebbles. They rained down on his trail. The weight of their feet shook the earth.

Bloom ran as fast as he could, keeping one foot in front of the other in order to not fall off the mountainside, and then the trail sloped up.

"I see him!" a troll screamed.

The troll's sour breath hit the back of Bloom's neck. He tried not to gag. He threw the dwarf shield in front of him, perfectly hitting a spot on a barren tree. It dangled there above the trolls' reach, he was sure.

He allowed himself a split second of relief when he saw it dangling there. He'd done his part. No matter what happened, he'd know he helped save his people.

A huge hand smashed his back. He fell down. His skin-armor flared green, coiling itself around his skin, protecting his flesh. He'd forgotten about it. Bloom whirled around to face his attackers. The troll who hit him screamed in pain and held up his hand. Bloom gasped. Burns covered its skin.

Bouncing up to his feet, Bloom grabbed his bow. He'd dropped it when he fell. The arrow . . . The Golden Arrow . . . He still had it. He wasn't going to use it yet, just a regular one.

The troll was crying, big green tears that caused its black mascara to run in waves down its slimy face.

"Eats him! Eats him! He hurted me!" the troll demanded.

The other troll smacked its lips. It took a step toward Bloom. Another. Bloom pulled the arrow back on his bow and released the shaft. The arrow pierced the skin near the troll's heart. The troll ripped it out and kept coming.

Bloom did the best thing he could think of. He ran.

The grogans all went with Jamie since everyone decided he wasn't much of a fighter and needed all of them. He regretted this pretty soon after they tromped off away from the others, circling down into a ditch before heading up a hill. And then turning around. And then turning around again. Jamie and the grogans were lost. Of course, they were lost because the grogans decided not to listen to Jamie, who told them to head west. They all thought they should go east, because they could smell a fight east.

"Argh! I want ta get me hands on a trollsie," Pagan of Joe growled, sticking a spoon up in the air and waving it mightily.

"Aye. We'll rip 'em ta pieces," said Levesque of Jon. "What day ya say, lads?"

He stuck up his fork and looked brave and rather stupid.

"Ta adventurin' and fightin' and adventurin' some more!!!" the army yelled, and then they all clapped one another on the backs and smacked one another in the arms and ran off the wrong way.

Jamie argued and stood his ground, but the men paid no attention. He had no choice but to follow. The little fighting grogans had the ruby-studded dragon that they needed to set out on the western ridge.

"Why do you like fighting so much?" Jamie asked. "Why? Aren't you scared of getting hurt or dying?"

Nye of Alisa bounced up onto his shoulder. "We're always scared. We're little and we have ta be loud or people forget we exist. Fightin' makes it easier, ya know. And it's how it is for us wee ones—we're fightin' just ta live. When nobody pays attention to ya, ya've got to *grab* their attention. Anything is better than being invisible when you're visible, ya know?"

Jamie thought he did.

16

Crows Can Be Good

Eva bellowed curses on vampires' coffins and their undead mothers' fangs as she dangled upside down off a vampire's bony shoulder, pounding her fists into his caped back.

"A dwarf can't be caught!" Eva yelled. "I myself have escaped the dungeons of Ireland, broken the bonds holding unicorns, fought my way out of the lairs of evil queens. Mere vampires cannot bind a dwarf!"

She slammed her whole upper body into the vampire's back. It did nothing.

"Oh, we dwarfs have escaped . . . we have escaped . . ." She sighed and gave up. "Jeez Louise."

Annie heard Eva's bellows, tucked Purcee into her pocket, and ducked behind a rock, searching around her. There had to be a way to ambush whatever had hold of Eva, to grab her back. She desperately wished for someone to show up and help her.

The nasty smell of old shoe and granny perfume permeated the air. The earth moved with the heavy footsteps of approaching trolls.

At first, Annie didn't recognize the heavy statue they carried. It was large and long and covered with different-colored rocks, and she was distracted by the ridiculous outfits the trolls were wearing. Why, she wondered, did they have to look like that? Then she noticed that the statue had glasses on it and was wearing clothes that looked remarkably like SalGoud's.

"Oh, no!" she gasped and leaned forward, squinting to get a better look. Just as she did, a shadow crossed the moon behind her.

"SalGoud?" she whispered.

The female vampire, dressed in a nurse's white uniform beneath her cape, turned to the trolls, lips curling with distaste. Annie recognized her as Vampire Sue from the Raiff's fortress. Beside her trotted a hideous vampire dog, a springer spaniel. There was a male vampire, too, wearing a hard hat like construction workers wore.

"We've got the dwarf. You have the giant?" Vampire Sue asked the trolls.

"Yep." The troll's voice came out huffy. It was hunched over, carrying SalGoud's feet. The other troll had his arms. "He's a heavy fellow."

"Why is he stone?" Sue asked, running a finger along his leg and then knocking her knuckles on it. It gave a rattling sound.

"Don't know. Raiff says the good change, the closer they get to the machine. Some turn stone, I guess."

Sue turned away and said to her vampire companion, "So we have just the Stopper, the boy, and the elf left."

Eva twisted her body at the waist, still dangling upside down. "You'll never get Bloom. Never. He's the best elf around. He's quick and smart and stubborn and . . ."

Eva saw SalGoud and roared.

She bit at the vampire's cape and spat it out, pummeling him again with her fists.

He rolled his eyes as she demanded, "What have you done to SalGoud? I'll kill you! I'll take your fangs and turn 'em into my earrings. I'll take your tongue and turn it into a necklace. I'll . . . I'll . . ."

"Shut her up!" Sue ordered. The vampire holding Eva dropped her on her head. She passed out. He picked her up again, smiling. "It always works on dwarfs. Hardest heads around, but quickest way to get them unconscious without actually killing the annoying things."

Annie couldn't take it anymore. She tried the only thing

she knew how to do, closing her eyes and feeling for the strings. They were everywhere and nowhere, twisted beyond recognition by the Raiff's horrible machine. Still, she tried.

"Stop," she whispered.

A troll grunted nearby.

"Stop," she said again, balling her hands into tight little fists. Purcee mewed, and a vampire looked in their direction and took a step toward them.

"Stop."

She was so desperate; she wanted to start crying from the sheer distress, but instead she whispered it again, fear welling up in her throat like a volcano ready to burst, "Stop."

"You can't do it," announced a pompous voice that came over her shoulder. "You aren't a Stopper anymore, little one. Now, you're just a Nobody."

Annie slowly turned her head, her hand on the short sword beneath her cloak. The woman behind her smiled, revealing a mouth full of perfect teeth in an oversize head. She had the look of a former beauty queen gone horribly wrong with perfectly stretched skin that was too tight across her face. A massive crown perched on top of her blond hair.

Annie gaped.

The Queen. It had to be.

The Queen's smile faded. "I'd say nice to see you, but is it ever nice to meet the hideous girl who ruined your happy plans? And stole your grogans? No. I think not."

The Queen's ears flattened against the side of her head like a dog's. Her teeth extended into fangs. She was some sort of shapeshifter, turning herself into a vampire.

"You're—you're not in Scot's Land," Annie sputtered.

"Not anymore." She preened. "The Raiff brought me here to the machine. It's not up to full power yet, but it is so close and when it is—we shall get out of here. I shall go back to the real Scotland and not this jumbled mess. Children will be easily found and eaten. Power will be unlimited. I shall be rightfully worshipped."

"You can't eat children!" Annie whipped out her phurba and lunged, but the Queen merely reached out her hand and knocked the dagger away.

A vampire scurried after it and tossed it back to the wicked woman before pinning Annie's arms to her back. Purcee slid out of Annie's coat and skittered off. The Queen didn't notice.

"You have less than two hours before it's full strength. You goody-goodies, thinking you could save the day? Too little too late as always." The Queen sauntered up to Annie, touched her chin lightly with the end of the dagger. "I could kill you now for vengeance."

"Vengeance for what? I haven't done anything to you." Annie stared into her eyes. She would not be weak, wouldn't even think of it.

The Queen nicked Annie's chin, making a tiny cut. The blood dripped down and Vampire Sue licked her lips.

"But killing you now wouldn't be any fun. Would it?" the Queen asked, making another nick. This time on Annie's neck. "You wouldn't get to see us win."

Annie glared at her, unflinching.

The Queen paced away. "Of course, I could just let Sue here have you, slowly rip out your throat, drain your blood."

Sue sniffed at Annie's neck.

The Queen pivoted on the balls of her feet, rushing back up to Annie so quickly that Annie didn't really see her move. "But that wouldn't be any fun. Maybe she can do that later. First, why don't I use you? See what power the Raiff can get from you for his machine."

Sue lifted Annie up, trapping her arms to her sides. They flew through the air to the wall where the elves were connected to the machine.

"No!" Annie yelled, thrashing. "No!"

But it was no good. Sue closed her fingers around both of Annie's wrists. She shoved Annie against the wall and began the connections.

Annie focused all her energy on just one thought: *Bloom.*

A good distance away on the other side of the valley, the young elf was rushing along the mountain, twisting his tracks, feigning and feinting like a soccer player trying to out-maneuver his opponents.

The trolls kept coming.

It was just as he was leaping over the remains of a burned-out tree trunk that Bloom heard her call him.

Bloom!

It shook his brain to the core.

He didn't think about how she could do that. He didn't think about what it meant. He just knew he had to get to Annie.

It was a split-second decision. He crossed his fingers that his armor would protect him and he stuck his tongue out at the trolls before he did it. Then, turning toward the edge of the mountain's sheer face he leaped and fell, plummeting a good two hundred feet.

I will not survive, he thought as he began falling the great distance down.

And he hoped he was wrong.

Above him, over three hundred crows and ravens swept across the face of the moon, and even with his elf eyes all Bloom could see was the dark.

17

Caught

The boy who thought he was the last elf fell.

And then with a rush so sudden that Bloom had no time to react, the crows and ravens surrounded him, fluttering their wings with all their might. He bounced among them, his armor glowing green and covering every inch of his skin. The feathers of the birds brushed against it, and slowly, slowly his fall continued. He moved mere inches at a time, buffeted by the birds' wings, by their maneuvering of the air.

Finally, with a thud he landed on his feet.

The birds covered the air above him, hovering. He lifted his hands up to them, and leaping and yelling sang out, "Thank you. Thank you."

He knew they'd saved him. His armor may have protected

him some, but not enough, he didn't think. He probably wouldn't have survived. Most of his bones probably would have been broken. It was kind of a dumb move to jump off the cliff, but, hey, it worked out.

He grabbed the closest crow from the air and planted a kiss on its beak. He didn't know why they saved him, but he was so grateful.

"Angels!" he said as it indignantly squawked. He let it go and yelled again, "Thank you!"

Then he turned and ran across the valley floor toward Annie.

It wasn't long before the grogans realized that they hadn't found the fight they were looking for and that they might as well listen to Jamie.

They were halfway up a canyon wall and strewn out along the edge of a barren crust of a once-live tree. Grogans stood on one another's shoulders to create a multilevel pyramid. It was precarious because grogans are not good at standing still. There were lots of near falls off the shoulder and off the tree and onto the bumpy hillside below them.

The biggest one, Farrar of Shaun, balanced at the top, cursed at the others to be still so that he could have a "wee good looksie about."

Jamie stood below it all, completely unamused.

Farrar of Shaun cleared his throat and made circles of his fingers and brought them up to his eyes, like binoculars.

"I think we go that way!" he announced, pointing backward over his head, toward the Pass of Sighs, which of course was entirely the wrong way to go.

Jamie cleared his throat.

"Or, perhaps 'tis this way," Boucher of Steve said, climbing up the pyramid and stepping on Levesque of Jon's head for a better look. Levesque of Jon grunted.

Jamie scratched at his ear, worried, and then tried something different. He pointed. "Guys . . . You said you'd listen to me."

If the grogans were paying any attention at all, they would have known exactly which way to go. They were not paying attention.

Light of Nathan rolled his eyes. "Argh, only one way to settle this one, laddies!"

Every single grogan's eyes lit up and they yelled, "Fight."

As one, they tumbled off the pyramid and began to settle their arguments with a series of hair-pulling maneuvers and arm-biting moves. Crows crossed the moon's face and a cold wind stirred up the dirt on the mountain floor. Since they obviously weren't going to listen, Jamie gave up. He could steal the dwarf's item from the grogans and set it out there himself.

His ears perked up and he uncovered his eyes.

What an idea!

Eva woke up in an ugly room, the wan faces of several elves peering down at her.

"She wakes," said one closest, touching her gently on the head.

"So . . . many . . . elves . . ." Eva moaned, slightly shocked, and tried to sit up, but kind hands pushed her back to the ground. To her dismay and humiliation, she realized that her head was resting on the lap of a lady elf. She groaned. How embarrassing. First to be knocked out. Then, to be resting on an elf lap like a baby.

"Your head hurts?" asked the lady whose potato sack–covered lap was her pillow.

Her head throbbed like there was an orc ax stuck in it but Eva said, "Not much."

She touched the egg-size lump poking out of her scalp and looked around at the dreary room they were in. Cement walls, pale and plain, enclosed them. Wires were wrapped around the elves' arms and legs, black and coiling cords like snakes. Patches of blood stained the wall.

"Where are we?" she asked.

"Inside the mountain," said the closest elf. The one with whip lashes covering her naked arms. "He keeps us here at night. If he kept us chained to the machine at night, too, we all would die, and then we'd be of no use to him. I am Aster, and you and your friend are?"

Eva shot up too quickly for the elves to stop her. "SalGoud!"

How had she forgotten? It must have been the lump on her head. She stumbled to where SalGoud's still form lay on the floor. An ant crawled along his stony leg. She touched him with a shaking hand and whirled around, voice strong and demanding, "Is he dead?"

She wasn't sure if she wanted to know the answer.

Aster shook her head. "We don't think so. Just rocked."

Eva turned back to him and shuddered, crouching low to sit next to him. Her lip trembled a bit and she crossed her arms in front of her and found herself wishing, ridiculously enough, for her teddy. "Can you fix him?

A male elf dressed in scraps of plastic bags like the kind you find in grocery stores shook his head. "No. Not here. Our power doesn't work well here."

He waved his hands around to indicate the wires and cords. "The electricity drains us."

"And the machine," Aster said walking toward Eva. "Did you come to save us? You had others with you? An elf boy?"

Eva glared at her. "How do you know that?"

Aster smiled weakly and sat next to Eva and SalGoud. She barely had strength to talk let alone stand. The man helped ease her down to the floor.

"The birds told us," she said, reaching out to fix Eva's pig-tails, slowly putting the hairs back in their proper places. "The birds have been working with us since the beginning. This place crushes their light souls as much as it does ours. Not everything in the Badlands is meant to be here. Some of us were brought here by the Raiff when he was exiled. Some of us were trapped here, like the birds, the children I hear of in Scot's Land, other creatures . . . But you were indeed sent here from Aurora to save us? Lichen arrived?"

Eva huffed and heaved SalGoud's heavy hand so that it would rest in hers. "Yeah, fat lot of good it's done, too. Hard to save anybody when you're trapped like a hermit crab in a fourth-grade science class."

Aster brushed a piece of hair that had strayed again from Eva's left pigtail. "For years we had no hope, and then you came. Do not give up yet."

"Dwarfs never give up," Eva growled and she proceeded to tell them her name and how they journeyed there. She exaggerated some of the battles, of course, as dwarfs tend to do. But the elves appropriately oohed and ahhed as she explained how she triumphantly beheaded seventy-two orcs single-handedly.

Aster stopped her gently in midstory, grabbing Eva's stout hand in her own long-fingered grasp, and she whispered to Eva, "What is the boy elf's name?"

"Bloom," Eva said matter-of-factly.

Aster's hand slid away and she repeated in wonder, hand over her heart, "Bloom."

As the moon continued to rise, Eva became more and more frustrated with her confinement. The walls seemed to close in on her, and the elves seemed too pale to be much use, although she knew that some of their old power still surged within their spirits. Looking at SalGoud made her feel as if her heart, too, had been turned to stone. It lodged in her throat's bottom like a boulder that would not move.

She paced the corners of the room like a wild tiger stuck in a zoo's cage, and occasionally she would growl like a tiger, too, and hit at the wired wall with her fist, until eventually cuts from the wire ripped her skin and Aster begged her to stop, so that her blood wouldn't attract the vampires.

"They taunt us already, banging on the door, sniffing for our blood," said an elf named Greenland, as he motioned with his eyes for Eva to sit on the floor.

Eva plopped down beside SalGoud and pouted. "You should kill them."

"They are already dead, little dwarf." Aster took a piece of potato sack and ripped it and began to wrap it around Eva's hand.

"They could be deader," Eva boasted, sticking her chin up in the air. "One of those pale blood drinkers wouldn't dare come in when I'm here, cause I'd show 'em what . . ."

Her words were cut off by the swinging open of the door. Eva panicked and pressed back into SalGoud, but then remembered her dwarfish valor and stood up, ready to face whoever was coming.

"What do you want," she bellowed, putting a good deal of contempt into the word "you."

The Queen didn't even glance her way. She nodded behind her and vampires pushed into the room, each taking an elf, pushing the elves' hands behind their backs and marching them toward the doors.

Eva kicked the one holding Aster, and he rewarded her with a flash of his fangs behind his snarling lips.

Eva marched up to the Queen, putting her hands on her hips. "Let them go!"

The Queen held up a hand and sniffed at the air. "Do I smell fresh blood?"

Eva glared at her; she wouldn't back down. Her little lips pressed into a tight line and she swallowed. She'd stare that Queen into submission.

The woman laughed. "I know who you are, dwarf."

She made Eva's race sound like an insult.

Eva didn't respond. She was trying to figure out how she could stop the vampires from marching the elves out. If only she had her ax.

"I said, I know who you are. I know who your mother was. I know your family is no threat. A line of dwarfs with no courage and therefore no use. Am I right? And who do you think I am?" She lifted her eyebrows and sauntered around in a happy circle, arms stretched wide and dramatically as if she was about to begin dancing the cha-cha and was just waiting for her partner.

"An idiot?" Eva crossed her arms in front of her. "Yep. That's it. I think you are an idiot with a weird crown that's super tacky even for a troll and you seem to have an unhealthy fixation on your looks 'cause you keep licking your lips and making faces like you're posing in a magazine or something."

One of the elves laughed and the vampire pushed him harder, bonking his head on the door.

"She is her royal highness, her great majesty, Queen of Scot's Land," the vampire hissed. "When the Raiff isn't here, her rule is law."

"Well, since the Raiff is trapped here in the Badlands thanks to Miss Cornelia, I'd say he is always here, so her rule is never law. Duh." Eva rolled her eyes, but she was really a bit afraid and terribly angry. Nobody could insult her family. Nobody.

The Queen checked her reflection in a small mirror that was in the pocket of her robes. "You are just like your mother, dwarf, aren't you? All talk. No valor."

With a great roar Eva pushed her head down and ran at the Queen full force, attempting to knock her over. The Queen sidestepped Eva's rush, and she smashed into the wall with her head. The Queen laughed as Eva slumped to the floor.

"We are taking the elves back out, dwarf. So you and your stone giant will be alone here." She gestured at the motionless SalGoud with a cock of her head. "Looks like you won't have much in the way of conversation."

Aster stopped walking. She was the last in line and her voice was a dry whisper when she spoke, "Not at night. You never do it at night. We are too weak. We need rest. We will not survive."

The Queen shrugged. "So what?"

"You will not be able to use us anymore."

"Then the trolls will have a good meal. And here's the thing—we don't actually need you much longer. There's no need at all for you after tonight. Tonight everything changes."

The vampire pushed Aster along. She disappeared into the blackness of night.

The Queen bent down close to Eva's ear. Her breath smelled of broccoli and it hit Eva's flesh with an unpleasant hiss. She blinked her eyes to make sure they stayed open.

"We have your little friend, dwarf. We have the Stopper," the Queen said. "We've tied her up, too, and are taking her power as I speak. I don't think she'll last long, not being an elf. Should die in, who knows, maybe an hour? The trolls are taking bets. You want in?"

Eva growled, trying to stand back up, but she was too hurt. She keeled over onto SalGoud's feet, unconscious.

"I hear that you saved her once, dwarf, with that snowmobile. It won't happen again. I'll see to it." The Queen laughed and walked away, not even bothering to close the door.

18

Using the Darkness

The moon continued its rising despite the terror that occurred below it. Vampires shrieked across the sky. Weakly protesting elves were chained once again to the machine's walls. They gasped from the constant pain. A giant lay still as stone, a dwarf snoring, unconscious next to him. A young Time Stopper's life ebbed slowly out of her. Another boy stole a dwarf treasure from arguing grogans and raced against time.

Jamie pulled himself forward, scooting his belly along the dirt. One inch forward, another.

He had to be careful. The grogans would never let him take over the task by himself. He had to slink. He had to steal. He wasn't a stealing type of boy. He scooted another inch. The ruby-studded dragon was just a few feet away.

"Left, I tell ya!" shouted Taylor of Davis into Levesque of Jon's ear. Levesque of Jon did a back tuck and landed with a bump on Pagan of Joe's face.

Two more feet. Jamie scooted. One and a half feet.

With a downward swoosh of air, several grogans stood in front of him, utensils ready and pointed at his nose.

"Now, Jamie, ya weren't gettin' any ideas, were ya?" Staggs asked, hands on his hips, while the grogans flanking him waved their utensils menacingly through the air at Jamie's nose.

"Yeah, laddie, 'cause the grogans don't take kindly to thievery," said Levesque of Jon, shaking his head.

There was a flickering of movement behind the grogans to the right.

A furry cat streaked behind the grogans and snatched up the splendid toy dragon, zipping by before the grogans even noticed.

"Unless we're the ones doing it!" Staggs yelled and they charged Jamie, who, seeing the dragon gone anyhow, did the most intelligent thing, which any kid would do. He ran.

***

Annie's arms were shackled to the machine. Wires wound around her legs and arms. Pain and cold coursed through her.

A tiny whimpering noise left her mouth as she stood against the hard mountain wall, hands wrapped in electrical cords and wires. She followed the wires to the machine that sat, large and forbidding, in the center of the valley. It hummed with renewed energy.

My energy, thought Annie. *The elves' energy.*

It was hard to even think. The horrid buzz of the machine, like a gigantic bumblebee on super steroids, resounded in her ears, vibrating her teeth, making her shake. And with that buzz, it seemed all of her energy, all of her life, all of her soul, was being sucked away.

She closed her eyes and tried to feel the strings. If she could stop time maybe the machine would stop, and that nasty noise would stop, too, and she could be free and life would be good and . . .

It didn't work.

Maybe the cold . . .

She tried to make ice, to freeze the air around her, to . . .

That didn't work either.

She batted the back of her head against the mountain wall, good enough so that there would be a dull ache.

Ah, that was better. The new pain made the humming quieter for a moment. Something touched her cheek and she opened her eyes to see the Queen's wicked face before her.

"I brought you company." She caressed Annie's cheek with her perfectly shaped finger. "Poor little orphan, shouldn't be left alone, chained here, dying, ready to be the key to the Raiff's successful return. Oh, yes . . . He will return to Aurora even without you to open the portal. The machine will give him the power to do it himself. And then . . . Then we take the town, the island, the state, the world. There will be no end to our power. It serves you right, stealing my grogans."

The Queen laughed and moved her head so Annie could witness the vampires bringing the rest of the elves along the little trail. Annie gasped. They looked so thin and pale and so terribly sad in their potato sacks and grocery-bag clothing. She'd always imagined the elves looking like Bloom, sort of golden and glorious, with clothes made of earth and sun.

As the elves shuffled by, their sad eyes seemed to still somehow reflect tiny sparkles of hope. Bruises marred the skin of some, giant dark patches of remembered pain. Red welts disfigured the skin of others. Some had bite marks on their necks.

The Queen watched Annie's expression change from sorrowful and shift into fierce. She laughed, delighted, and clapped her hands.

"You thought you would save them, didn't you?" she said, getting in Annie's face again. Her nose was just centimeters from Annie's. "Well, you failed. Failed. Failed. Failed! And tonight, tonight, you all will die. The Raiff's machine will suck your souls completely away and you will be empty, empty shells. He'll be able to make the portal all by himself, no Stopper or dragon needed, and we'll march through together, triumphant."

Annie glared at the Queen. She smashed her forehead against the Queen's as hard as she possibly could. It made a cracking sound and the Queen whirled around howling. A nearby elf gasped.

Annie saw stars, but the pain made the machine's noise a little less once again. She grinned. Eva would be proud of her.

The Queen turned back to her, scowling, as horns grew out of her head, joined with a gigantic bump.

"Do you have any idea how hard it's going to be to cover this up with makeup, Annie? Any idea?" she asked, coming closer but far enough away to be safe from any more head butts. "Do you have any idea of what this queen can do?"

Annie shrugged.

"What are you afraid of, Annie?" she asked. "I can become your fears."

With a whirl of movement, the Queen transformed into a vampire that looked more like Dracula than real vampires. Blood ran from the vampire's mouth.

Annie rolled her eyes and said in a voice braver than she thought possible, "Whatever."

Steam came from the Queen's nostrils. "How about this, then?"

Another blur and she became a troll, dressed in a tutu

and high pink heels. A muscle twitched in her large jaw and she huffed out, "You smell good enough to eat."

Annie shrugged again as if it wasn't intimidating at all, and the Queen grunted. Annie was so cold. Frost started to form in her hair.

Another blur and the Queen transformed into Walden Wiegle, a whip in his hand, processed-cheese food remnants streaked around his lips. Annie refused to react. She was satisfied to know that her lack of fear was making the Queen furious; the anger was rolling off her in icy waves so thick that they turned to steam in the air they touched.

"Or this?"

With a fleshy fist, the Queen slammed Annie in the stomach. It made a horrible noise, but Annie didn't make a sound, despite the explosion ripping through her body.

Her mind flitted back to all those times Walden had hurt her, sat on her, shoved underwear (tighty-whities) in her mouth, called her names, hit her, put Cheetos in her ears. She gritted her teeth.

The Queen as Walden grinned. Her voice came out with a triumphant laugh, "So this—this is what you are afraid of. Then this is how you will die!"

She raised the whip above her head and a nearby elf screamed, but Annie did not flinch. She did not move.

"But not now," the Queen teased, putting the whip down and returning to her normal form. "I'll wait till you're almost drained and then I'll kill you. I'm sure the Raiff will let me."

She blew her a little kiss and turned to walk the elf line. "After all, it shouldn't be too easy."

"The Raiff needs me!" Annie yelled after her. "I'm not afraid of you or him."

The Queen whirled around. "Not anymore. He can feel the strings now. A little more energy—energy that you and the remnants of these elves provide and—poof! He'll be a Stopper again. Stopper and demon perfectly blended. The strongest of all evil. And you? Hold on. Let me laugh for a sec. Wait for it . . . Wait for it . . ." She held up her hand and guffawed. "You'll be dead." The Queen eyed her as if she was looking into her soul. "Oh . . . Now I know what you're afraid of. Your biggest fear is this."

The Queen transformed into Jamie, dear, sweet Jamie, but then she began to morph, mimicking the process by which Jamie would turn troll. Her body grew large, green, hideous. She smelled rancid.

"Jamie won't turn troll," Annie snarled.

"Oh, he will. And then he'll eat you . . . Whatever good is in him will be taken away by the machine and then he'll reveal his true nature. We all do, don't we?"

"You lie."

"Everyone lies, Annie. But in those lies are also truth." In troll form, the Queen paraded down the line of elves. When the Queen finally disappeared, Annie turned her attention to the two vampire guards standing about thirty feet away. They were playing thumb wars, their bodies silhouetted against the moon. She shook her head.

Thumb wars?

Maybe she was delirious.

The elf tied up next to her made a small noise like she was hurt. The woman was lovely, even if close to death. Her skin flashed pale in the moonlight but held hints of the glory it might have once been. Her hair, too, was pale, but seemed to promise that it once shone gold. The wicked wind picked it up and lashed it about, as it did with Annie's own.

Annie swallowed. She'd never seen a female elf up close before. When the wind blew the elf's hair Annie could see the pointy ears. They weren't so pointy that they looked like cartoons, but there was a definite point about them. Annie wished she could move her hands and touch her own ears.

The elf turned her head to look at Annie. They both smiled at the same time, despite the pain they were in.

"I feel like I know you," Annie said, looking at the elf's familiar green eyes, the set of her hair upon her forehead, the distance between her nose and brow. She was embarrassed for staring. "I'm sorry. I'm rude. My name is Annie."

The elf nodded, "Aster. You were brave with the Queen. You acted like an elf. No boasting. No show of fear."

Annie looked at her kind twinkling eyes and wished what she said was true. She sighed and her heart ached as she thought about the elves being here for so long and the end being near. "You remind me of my friend. His name's Bloom. He's the last elf in Aurora and we came here to save you, but it doesn't seem as if we're doing it all that well, which stinks, because Bloom really, really wants to save you. He's so lonely. His father died when the Raiff attacked Aurora. And he's hoping that his mother might be alive. Do you know her?"

Even as she asked the questions, Annie stared out into the night, at the machine below them, at the moon, and thought of Miss Cornelia. She never should have snuck away. She hoped Purcee the kitten was all right and not eaten by trolls or werewolves.

Aster's voice distracted Annie from a bit of her worry.

"He is my son," the elf said, voice breaking. "Bloom is mine."

"Yours?" It made so much sense. Aster looked familiar because she looked like Bloom. Bloom's mother, his actual mother, was alive!

"Oh, I'm so glad. Oh, you have no idea. He was so worried you'd died. I mean, all those years he thought you were dead and then to hear that you're alive is like a miracle," Annie gushed. The emotional outburst seemed to warm her the tiniest of bits. "I just can't believe it. Bloom has been looking for you. He wants so badly to find you. He's a really great elf, you know."

Tears leaked from Aster's eyes.

"Oh." Annie's voice dropped a notch. "He's okay. He's still alive, I'm sure of it, and he'll save us. Bloom always saves people. It's what he does."

"Really?" Aster's voice had a bit of a twinkle in it.

"Oh, he's helped me a million times. When I fell off a cliff . . . when I fought the Raiff . . . a million times. We found the Golden Arrow in Ireland. That was all Bloom there."

Aster smiled and murmured, "The Golden Arrow."

"We need it to break the machine. Anyways, he'll be so happy to see you." The words poured out of Annie and she looked at Aster, who was glowing it seemed, glowing with happiness. "We'll find a way. It's okay." She tried to make her voice sound positive, to give Aster hope.

"Annie, you are a Stopper, right?" Aster whispered so the vampires wouldn't hear.

"Uh-huh, but it's not working," Annie said, voice sinking.

Aster pointed with her finger toward where the Queen was perched on the machine doing a happy victory dance that involved a lot of butt wiggling. "But you have the demon blood in you, too."

Annie recoiled and looked down at the ground. She was so cold. "How do you know?"

"I can smell it, just the faintest bits of it there, underneath your goodness. You have Raiff blood in you and magic

Tullgren blood, too. Maybe even a little elf," Aster murmured. "You're really a mix, aren't you?"

Annie tried not to cry. She hated Bloom's mother knowing, hated it. It was bad enough she was too little and a foster kid that no one had ever wanted, now she had to have demon blood. Tears crept down her cheeks, embarrassing her even more, and of course her hands were tied so she couldn't brush them away.

"Annie." Aster's voice was warm and soothing. Annie could imagine her singing Bloom lullabies.

"Annie," Aster said again, forcing Annie to look at her. "Having demon blood in you doesn't make you a demon. Just because you are a Stopper doesn't mean you'll turn bad like him. Cornelia didn't. She is of the same bloodline, the Raiff's bloodline, and she epitomizes good. She cares for others above herself, forgives, is kind."

Annie stared at her. Her eyelashes were thick like Bloom's and long. In the distance, crows began to caw.

"Damn birds," a vampire shouted.

"Demon blood will help you here," Aster said. "If you feel it in your body you can use it to feel the strings. But your Stopper blood fights it, which is why you are so cold."

"Will I be able to stop time if I use the demon side?" Annie asked.

"The Raiff couldn't, but powers manifest differently in different people." Aster shook her head and kept her voice to a whisper, "I don't know. Demons do have great powers, like trained Stoppers, like Miss Cornelia. You can use that to break us free."

"Really?" Annie asked.

"Really."

"It's so . . . It's awful when I feel the demon blood inside of me, when I use the powers of it," Annie said after a moment, shuddering. "You don't know what it's like . . . It's cold and heartless. It's like all the love in the universe has been turned to hate."

Her feet ached from standing. She thought about the ice balls she'd thrown at the orcs. Had that been her demon blood? Maybe she had been using that all along. All this time, being so cold.

She bit her lip and steeled her shoulders square against the cold mountainside.

Aster's voice came gentle as a breeze: "No, I don't know what it is like. But all of us have both good and bad within. It's our choices that make the difference. It's what we do with our power that makes us good or bad, not what's in our blood, or who our parents or grandparents were, but what is in our hearts."

Annie gazed up at the moon, so far away, just like Aurora, and said in a voice much too loud, "I have to try."

Aster nodded. "Yes, yes, you do."

19

Here, Kitty, Kitty . . .

Bloom's feet ran swiftly and silently along the earth as he headed toward Annie. The way smelled of trolls and danger. He was no fool. He knew what he was getting himself into.

With every footfall, he chanted her name in his mind. "Annie. Annie. Annie."

If she died, if SalGoud or Jamie or Eva died, it would be his fault.

"I brought them here," he whispered. "Me."

He gulped and sucked in the horrid air that smelled of burning metal. He was in the shadow of the Raiff's machine, racing past it toward the side of the pit where the elves were stuck to cords and wires.

The evil of it all was almost too much for Bloom to

handle. There was no green anywhere. Even in daylight the world here was brown, ruined by the machine's electricity, burned beyond recognition, dried out, all the life sucked away. And that was what the Raiff was doing to the elves.

Bloom's feet wouldn't move quickly enough to satisfy him. He wished he could just get there. As it was, his body trembled, terribly weak, as if he had a horrible flu and all his muscles were too tired to move.

"It's the machine," he said aloud.

The machine drained them all. The twisting of the strings brought additional weakness to the humans, stone giants, and elves in the area and beyond, touching the people in Aurora as well. It was hurting good magic, possibly all over the world.

Bloom *had* to stop the machine, but right now his priority was Annie. He could feel her weakening. He wasn't sure how he could, but he could. He raced past the machine and headed toward her. Something cracked—nearby off to his right, and he stopped, sniffing the air and listening.

Trolls.

And something else.

A kitten.

A kitten? Bloom wondered and then he remembered, smacking his forehead with his hand. Purcee.

Creeping forward, he inched closer, hiding behind boulders and tree stumps, until he could see and hear what was going on. Three trolls, all dressed in hideous purple taffeta prom dresses with flouncy hoop skirts beneath them, had surrounded a small cat that clutched a golden-plated, ruby-studded dragon in its mouth.

"Here, kitty, kitty . . . ," the trolls kept saying in squeaky voices, scrambling around trying to catch the feline.

Bloom smiled as Purcee feinted and ducked out of the smelly trolls' long-nailed fingers, but the little cat could not get beyond their panty-hosed legs and escape. And the dragon in Purcee's mouth had to be placed at a certain point of the star.

That's why the machine still runs, Bloom realized. *Not because Lichen was wrong, but because the grogans failed. And Jamie. Where is Jamie?*

As if answering Bloom's thoughts, Jamie appeared on an outcropping above the trolls and Purcee. He nodded at Bloom, indicating that he saw the elf there.

"Hey! Trolls! Up here!" Jamie hollered.

The trolls startled and looked up. The moment they did, Jamie leaped off the outcropping, squarely landing on a troll's head, dislodging its wig of long dreadlocks, and sending it squealing. It was enough of a distraction for Purcee, who darted over to where Bloom hid. The cat shimmered and changed back into his adult form, dropping the rubied dragon into the hands of an astonished Bloom.

"Place it," the cat said with his overblown French accent.

"Hurry. Annie has been captured. We distract ze trolls and you do ze rescue."

He looked over his shoulder at the sound of Jamie yelling.

"Do a good job, Bloom. On you, we all depend, not just little Annie, but ze entire world, yes?"

He clapped the boy on his shoulder with his little furry paw, and Bloom watched, wide eyed, as Purcee turned into a half lion–half man creature twenty times the size of his normal cat body.

Purcee winked. "Be safe. Go. I think it's okay that I am in adult form. They obviously already know we are here, no?"

And Purcee, a golden-haired, gigantic, ferocious Purcee, bounded over to the trolls to help Jamie, who was glad of it, since a troll was stepping on his foot.

Purcee's giant lion claws slashed across the leg of the offending troll.

"My hose!" it cried, stepping off Jamie, clearly more concerned about losing a pair of precious stockings than the gaping wound on its leg. Purcee roared and it echoed throughout the canyon. The rage of the lion pulsed in Bloom's blood as he tucked the ruby-spotted dragon toy into his shirt and ran toward the point in the star, worried about Annie and Jamie, but knowing he had no choice. No choice at all.

Forgive me, Annie, he thought. *But I have to save us all first, before I save you.*

But, trapped on the machine, bound and stuck, Annie was focused on saving herself and didn't need Bloom right then. She just needed to believe she could do it.

"You can do this, Annie," Aster whispered. "You *must* do this."

Annie closed her eyes. She smelled the bitter stench of the trolls, like skunk and old sock, the metallic heat of the machine, the mustiness of the vampires, and beneath it all, way, way beneath it, the crisp pine smell of the elves.

She sighed.

The machine buzzed incessantly in her head. She searched for the strings, the old way, the Stopper way, by opening her mind and accepting her power, but there was no power there.

She snapped open her eyes, pleading. Her voice shook. "And what do we do? What do we do if I can get us free?"

"We run. We fight. We break the machine."

"You're too weak to fight, though."

Aster eyes fluttered a bit, as if she could barely keep them open. "If we are freed we will have hope. If we die fighting, but with hope in our hearts, then it is a far better death than what awaits us here, tied to the machine."

Annie bit her lip.

The elf smiled faintly. "Use the power of the machine itself. Use the demon's cold within you."

Annie closed her eyes again. To her left, an elf moaned and the Queen laughed, hideously. Annie remembered the grandmother's head on the Pass of Sighs, remembered the power that surged through her and Bloom then, circling around Jamie. Some good still did exist in the strings, she knew it, but she couldn't find it.

"The machine," Aster whispered next to her.

Annie listened to the humming in her head, that horrible machine noise. She let herself loose into it; the cold of the machine matched part of her blood.

I am part of it, she thought. *Part of the machine.*

"Harness its power, Annie," Aster whispered. "Hurry. That queen is walking back toward us. Use the cold, Annie. The cold."

Annie barely heard her. The sound of the machine filled her head, and then, and then . . . There was a horrible crashing of cold that raced through her body, wave after wave of it, and she let it come. Aster watched her turn blue and then white, even her hair becoming the color of snow. She glowed in the dark.

Others saw it, too. The vampires jumped to attention.

"What the . . ."

"Man . . ."

"My lady! Queen! Come quickly!"

Aster prayed to the grandmother and whispered, "Hurry, Annie."

Annie opened her eyes and looked down at her skin. She looked like a ghost, a solid ghost. Through foggy eyes, she saw the Queen racing toward her, her arm outstretched, conjuring up something to hurt her. She turned her head away and with one easy step moved forward and broke all the wires and shackles connecting her to the machine. She raised her hands and the vampires racing toward her were knocked over by blocks of ice that flew from her fingers. Everything inside her that hurt, hurt no more.

She whirled on her heel to face Bloom's mother, a question in her voice. "Aster?"

The elf was beaming with a wide joyous smile just like her son's. "The cords, Annie. Break our cords."

Annie nodded slowly, still in shock, and she snapped her fingers, once, twice, thirty-six times. The cords connecting the elves snapped in half, hissing, sending little electrical bursts of light everywhere, like tiny explosions or fireworks. It set the tail of a nearby werewolf on fire.

The elves cheered and pulled themselves free.

"Mutiny! Mutiny!" the Queen screamed to her scattered troops, calling for backup and help. "All return. All return."

Annie lost sight of the Queen in the chaos. Aster clutched Annie's cold hand and then hugged her frozen body against her own weak one. "Good job, Annie. Good job."

Annie pulled away a bit, against her will. It felt so much like having a mother, and how she'd always wanted to be hugged by a mother. "Can I break the machine?"

Aster shook her head, ducking as a vampire flew past

them. "No. Only dwarfs' things and the Golden Arrow can do that. But you can call to the power with your coldness, and then use the power for goodness."

Annie clutched her hand. "So what now? What do we do?"

Aster looked at the pandemonium, as the horribly weakened elves tried to keep the vampires and trolls at bay.

"We fight," she said straightening her back, the potato sacks rippling. "Do you feel strong enough to fight, Annie?"

Annie thought of the ice blocks she'd smashed the vampires with. She smiled and wiggled her frozen fingers and for a moment felt even more like Eva. "I feel very strong."

20

The Wires Break

Eva woke up in a fog. Her vision blurred as she tried to blink herself into battle-readiness. SalGoud's stony self didn't move. Groaning, she struggled to her feet, making her way to the open door. Out in the dark, the sounds of battle raged. Her blood quickened and her palms itched for fighting. She glanced back at SalGoud's unmoving form. He would be alone here, all alone and unprotected, if she left him.

"No," she said, shuffling back toward her friend. "I'll stay with you."

Bloom, too, ignored the sounds of the battle and silently ran toward the point of the star where he had to place the dragon.

Vampires spotted him, a blond head bobbing across the dark land. Swooping down at him as he ran, the vampires tried to lash Bloom with their whips, or catch him up to their cloaked forms, so they could fly away with him.

Dodging the whips and hands, Bloom didn't slow down. He pulled his arrows out, one after the other, sending them shooting over his shoulder as he ran. The arrows pierced the vampires' skin, again and again, but didn't stop them. Bloom was only slowing them down, and only slightly. He could smell the animal sweat of the werewolves bounding down the mountainside toward him. They'd be there soon. He'd be completely trapped and outnumbered.

It didn't matter. Saving the elves mattered. Saving his friends mattered.

Bloom ran. His thighs screaming from the hot ache of exertion, he finally found the spot he was looking for. He pulled the dragon from his shirt. It caught the moonlight and glowed. A vampire swooped down toward him, fangs bared. He sidestepped the attack at the last minute and she turned around for another strike. Ducking, Bloom put the dragon down, scurried back on his hands and feet, and set another arrow in his bow. He let it fly. It hit the vampire in the chest, sending her reeling away.

Bloom wiped dirt off his cheek and looked at the dragon. Was it in the right place? Wolves' paws thundered closer. He could smell trolls clambering toward him.

"Work!" he yelled at the dragon, kicking it. "Work."

The dragon fell over on its side and tumbled a foot or two on the sloped ground and then it happened. A great ear-splitting squeal filled the air like feedback on a sound system, high, brain-piercing. Bloom stumbled backward, his hands over his ears. Across the valley werewolves, vampires, elves, and humans did the same.

The noise came from the toy dragon. It split in half and a much larger dragon burst from the shell. It split in half again, and once more emerged a larger dragon, and so on. Each of the rubies expanded to the size of dinner plates. The process happened over and over until the dragon was twice the size of Grady O'Grady, towering over them.

She opened her mouth and roared at the vampires before bowing to Bloom, who climbed on her back without hesitating. A troll who finally made it to the area screamed and tried to lunge for Bloom, but the dragon merely stepped on him with her giant foot, and the troll moved no more.

The five points of the star glowed golden in the dark, shooting up great globs of light into the sky. The dragon stopped her shrieking noise and Bloom could hear small sounds in the distance. It sounded . . . It sounded like the cheering of elves . . . Could it be?

With a great slow rustle, the dragon unfurled her wings and they headed up toward the center of the valley, their flight smooth and graceful. A scurry of vampires charged toward them, but the dragon lazily moved her head and breathed fire at them. The dragon swooped high above the valley and now Bloom could really see it, the golden outline of a star, glowing like a fire along the dark land, shafts of light connecting the points. Something vibrated in his backpack and he twisted it to the front of him, and pulled out his Golden Arrow. It burned hot, but he could touch it, the green armor that suddenly appeared again on his hand protecting him as the sun began to rise.

Use it, came the dragon's voice in his head.

Bloom looked around him in the sky. Nothing moved.

Use it on what? he asked.

The machine.

The machine waited below them, still vibrating, looking like a monstrous, boxy octopus with too many tentacles leaching out its poison.

Shoot it where? Bloom asked.

The center.

Bloom nodded, notched the arrow, and released it. The arrow whizzed downward and downward, leaving a line of golden light in its wake. The beauty of the light took Bloom's breath away. It struck the center of the machine and disappeared.

Bloom stared, mouth opened. *Nothing's happened!*

Wait, grandson. Wait!

Bloom tilted his head, confused. *Grandmother?*

Yes.

You're a dragon toy?

I am everything.

As the dragon spoke, the machine hissed and began to spit steam out of its sides, a great rending noise, and it cleaved in half as the sides sizzled and melted. Rain began, great sheets of water, so thick and fast that Bloom couldn't see anything. It stopped suddenly and the night was gone and so was the death. The valley had transformed back into a vast, green meadow. Trees sprouted leaves, their trunks whole and no longer broken. Crows soared through the sky, singing melodies of happiness and triumph. Where the machine was, was now a field of flowers, purple, yellow, blue, and white. Everywhere, everywhere in the valley there was now life. The lands beyond were still ravaged, but tiny bits of grass were sprouting here and there in the landscape.

The dragon swooped low to where the elves stood cheering. Their vampire enemies had disappeared, cast down by the sun. The trolls had turned to stone. As Bloom and the grandmother dragon flew past them, they shouted and waved, throwing flowers, smiling, singing. Some had tears in their eyes. Some had tears running down their cheeks. Some, like Annie, just stood there and cried, clapping, and waving at Bloom and screaming with joy inside, because the machine was gone. She could feel the strings. And they all lived. They lived!

Jamie and Purcee crested the hill just as the explosion happened. The blast staggered them backward, dropping them to the ground. Something itched on Jamie's back, itched horribly, but that didn't matter. What mattered was the gold light, the cheering, the crows singing, the strings vibrating in the air.

Purcee, who had changed back to his normal cat size, hopped up first, standing and staring. "They have done it! We have done it!"

The cat grabbed Jamie around his waist, dancing and hugging him triumphantly. "Celebrate, my young friend! We have saved each other and the elves!"

Jamie cheered. He slapped the cat on the back, smiling. But then, the itching came again and he couldn't resist scratching it. His hand touched something . . . funny . . . something just coming out of his skin. He pulled up his shirt and turned to Purcee. "Purcee! What . . . Is something on me? A giant bug?"

The cat gasped and stepped back. "No . . . No . . . Something is growing out of your back."

The cat stepped forward again and yanked Jamie's shirt down.

"Am I turning troll?" Jamie gasped.

"Heaven forbid!" Purcee said, taking Jamie's hand in his paw. "Come, let us see our friends. Cornelia will set right whatever it is when we are back in Aurora. You wait and see."

In the prison room, Eva ran toward the door. In front of her, a dragon flew past, her wings beating fresh, flower-smelling air in her face. On her back was a golden boy who smiled and waved. He cupped his hands around his mouth and yelled to her, "Eva! How is SalGoud?"

Eva turned around toward her stone giant friend and saw cracks forming in the stone. A quiet rumbling began, and first his fingers moved, then his toes. She raced back to him and began pulling away the cracking rock, revealing skin beneath, warm skin. SalGoud gave a great sneeze and a good part of the rock layer covering his face fell off. The corners of his lips turned up in an attempt at a smile.

Eva whacked him in the stomach and raced back to the doorway, her heart thumping wildly. She jumped up and down on her stout little legs and cupped her hands around her own lips and bellowed.

"He lives, Bloom! He lives!"

21

The Queen Is a Worm, but We Knew That

Although the machine was gone and the elves were free, Annie knew that they were all still in danger. The Raiff, the Queen, and all their minions were not going to be happy about the turn of events.

She knew they would strike.

"Behind me!" Annie screamed, waving the elves into a formation.

The sun brought a moment of quiet to the valley, and it definitely made it a fairer fight. The trolls and the vampires were gone, but there was still the werewolves and some kelpies and satyrs, nasty things with teeth and muscles.

Annie worried the most about the Queen and the Raiff. Where had he been all this time? If only the sun eradicated demons the way it did vampires. No such luck.

Annie stood, alert, her eyes scanning the scene before her. Werewolves crouched behind trees, ready to spring. A kelpie ran along the valley floor, his horse hindquarters springing him forward.

"Do you see the Queen?" she whispered to the tall male elf standing beside her.

He had dark skin and deep curly hair and his name was Bass. He once loved the sea, but hadn't seen it for years. Now he thought he could almost smell it, but knew that to be a distraction. If they could get out of there safely, his long legs would walk him home to Aurora and he would see the ocean again.

Annie sensed him tear away from his thoughts. He stared into the cracks and crevices of the mountain's side and said roughly, "No. She hides."

"The Raiff?"

He pressed his lips together before he spoke. "Not terribly near."

Annie allowed herself to inhale. If the Raiff wasn't close by, that was good. If the Queen was hiding, that meant she was scared. They'd only have to contend with their followers, at least for now. But where was the Raiff? Was he getting ready to go to Aurora?

Eva yelled, "Annie! Annie, you ain't dead! How the heck did that happen?"

From behind her, the dwarf flung herself into Annie's thin frame, almost knocking her over. Annie laughed for a moment, looking at Eva's grin and the dirty face of the tall boy behind her.

"SalGoud." Annie's heart leaped in happiness.

He opened his arms. "In the flesh. Or at least, not in the stone."

Annie hugged him, too, quickly. "We don't have time for reunions. We have to get the elves out of here. We haven't seen the Queen or the Raiff."

"Good," Eva hissed, hammering her hand into her fist.

"But the Queen took my pack. We have no weapons," Annie continued.

"No weapons!" Eva panicked, throwing up her hands and stomping.

"And Jamie and Purcee are missing," Annie continued.

SalGoud shook his head. "And Bloom?"

"Bloom broke the machine," Annie explained. "He's flying on this ruby-studded dragon—maybe he's trying to spot the Queen or the Raiff. I'm sure he'll be right back."

Eva was still shaking her head, stomping in a circle and mumbling, "No weapons. No weapons. How the vampire widow's peaks are we going to battle without weapons?"

There was a great rumbling below the edge of the mountain. Annie, Bass, and SalGoud peeked over, hands to their lips, telling Eva to be quiet. Beneath them, scurrying up the mountain's steep face were the grogans, huffing and puffing and hauling a whole assortment of knives and bows, swords and arrows.

Light of Nathan stopped and the rest of the grogans stopped with him. He put his hands on his broad hips and smiled. "Did I hear the young dwarf warrior say she 'as no weapons? Well, I hope this'll do."

Eva peeked over the edge and jumped up delighted. "Where'd you get 'em?"

Light of Nathan winked. "Ah, ya know us grogans. A fine bit of thievin' is all. I'd say the vampires and trollies that had 'em won't be using 'em anymore." He cleared his throat. "It's the least we can do after gettin' lost and almost ruinin' everythin'."

Annie handed out any extra weapons to the elves, taking a small sword and her phurba. It was good to have it again.

Staggs cleared his throat. "We will accept your thanks in the form of yeasty beverages!"

"And songs of praise," added Spellacy of Sam.

"Most definitely!" Eva bellowed, snatching up her ax and kissing the side of its blade.

"Aren't you going to be kissing us?" Levesque of Jon asked, offering Eva his cheek.

Before she could respond, Jamie and Purcee came over the hill. Annie rushed to them, checking them for injuries while listening to their stories. She hugged them both, and Jamie moved so that she wouldn't touch the two bumps on his back.

"You aren't going to tell her zat something is growing there?" Purcee whispered.

Jamie couldn't answer. He didn't know how. Everyone was so happy. He didn't want to ruin it, not right now. "Still not green?"

"Not a bit," Purcee reassured him.

Bloom was concerned about the lack of any Raiff sightings. It made his stomach uneasy.

"We have to search for him," Bloom said to the dragon, still sitting upon her, "before we go back and celebrate."

I agree.

"You won't leave me?"

Not until you are back in Aurora or the Raiff is gone.

Bloom touched the dragon's back. He had one more question. "My mother?"

Lives. She still lives.

"We will make sure it stays that way," he said quietly.

And they flew off, searching for the Raiff. The hot air of the Badlands did nothing to stop the dragon. They soared above treetops and mountains, circling in an ever widening pattern, looking for the demon. Bloom notched his bow, holding on to the grandmother dragon with just his legs. Below them, orcs and other monsters all seemed to be marching in one direction, toward the sea. They headed that way as well, traveling swiftly over the forest, farther and farther away from Annie, Jamie, and the elves.

Bloom's senses all seemed to be on overload. Every sound, every smell, brought him closer to the Raiff. And then . . . there he was . . . just standing there . . . short blond hair making him easy to pick out among the orcs and werewolves. He didn't even look worried. They had just destroyed his machine and there he was ordering his minions around like it was just a regular day.

Bloom released an arrow. The Raiff caught it with his hand, breaking it, smiling as he looked up at the boy and the dragon.

"You come all by yourself? For me? How sweet?" The Raiff patted his chest. "Don't you love my army?"

"You took all the elves. You killed so many. And for what? For revenge? To get back to Aurora?" Bloom's hands were sweating. He had not had time to wipe them.

"Your heart is full of hate, elf." The Raiff smiled. "I like that."

Bloom shot off several of his longest arrows, quicker than a human ever could manage. The Raiff scurried out of the way.

"Turn them to fire, Grandmother," Bloom said, as he shot off another set. The grandmother breathed on the plummeting arrows, alighting them with flame. They landed in a perfect circle around the Raiff, who bellowed, infuriated. He breathed on them, encasing himself in ice. He roared in rage, trapped by an icy circle of his own making.

The others need us. There is . . . trouble.

"That should hold him," Bloom said, a slight smile on his face. "Let's go back."

The children and elves and grogans began the long walk out of the valley. Annie's skin had faded from its snow-white color and she was now back to being just plain old pale. Annie and Eva led the way with SalGoud and Bass behind. All of them were helping the frailest of the elves, who were gradually gathering strength but still were terribly weak.

"Too weak to be any good in a fight," Eva mumbled.

Annie hushed her but she was thinking the same thing, trying to calculate their odds against the Raiff, the Queen, and wolves, wishing Bloom would come back and help. The ax in her hand made her feel stronger though, safer. It looked a lot like the one the grogans brought Eva, but a little lighter. SalGoud had a sword. Bass had a bow. Aster did as well. All the elves, all the grogans were armed.

But will it be enough? Annie wondered. *Enough to keep us safe?*

A massive noise crumbled from the mountain above them. They stopped. The mountains stretched up forever, farther than their eyes could see, a dark mass of boulders and dust. Something was up there.

"What is it?" Annie whispered, planting her feet, trying to get ready for whatever might be hiding up there.

Jamie stood beside her. He placed his hand on her shoulder. "It feels bad."

Bass and Aster shot arrows up into the mountainside. One arrow hit a werewolf's arm. He yelped, leaving his hiding place as he yanked out the arrow and threw it back down before running away.

As he did the rumbling intensified. Giant boulders and rocks cascaded down the mountain, raining down upon all of them, sending up a stench of smoke and dust.

"Cover your heads," Bass yelled, pushing Annie, Jamie, Eva, and SalGoud forward as the rocks pelted them.

A huge boulder smashed behind them, blocking them and Aster from the rest of the group. Bass cursed. Aster hugged Annie to her, and after a moment the dust settled.

"Everyone all right?" SalGoud yelled.

"Fine. Fine," came an answering voice, the elf named Greenland. "We can't press through."

Bass pushed against the boulder. It did not budge. "Stay there, we'll think of a way."

But there was no time to think.

A wicked laughter echoed all around them. A line of werewolves in human form towered on the mountain ridge twenty feet above their heads and there, ahead of them on the trail, was the Queen, eyes gleaming and horns out.

"I am so sick of bad guys," Annie muttered.

The Queen took a step forward. "Let me assure you, little Stopper, that we are much more sick of you."

Annie's hands clenched into fists around her ax, knuckles whitening. The crows cawed in the distance. There was a rush of movement beside her, and suddenly Eva was in front of her, ax out and ready.

"I wouldn't take one step closer, buddy!" she said, hitting her ax handle into her palm.

"A baby dwarf from a long line of half-adequate dwarfs with fainting tendencies, oh, scary . . ." The Queen rolled her eyes and deliberately stepped closer, morphing into the shape of the Raiff. She reached out her hands and ice shot out of them, directly at Eva.

"No!" Annie yelled. Bass pushed Eva out of the way, and drew his bow, shooting arrows in quick movements like Bloom's. Annie watched in horror as the arrows bounced off the Queen.

The Queen pointed her hand at Bass and the thin elf began to levitate into the air. He had the dignity to not kick his feet in midair, but simply rested, waiting to be dropped or tossed.

"Put him down!" Annie yelled.

The Queen shrugged and, with a movement of her hand, sent Bass soaring up the mountainside to where the werewolves waited.

"They'll eat him!" Annie screamed, and stepped forward. "You monster. They'll *eat* him."

"So sad . . ." The queen mocked and cracked her fingers. "Who should they eat next? You do know that needing to feed isn't evil. It's just part of existence. I personally prefer children, but those werewolves? They will eat *any*thing."

She considered Aster, Eva, Jamie, SalGoud, and Annie, pointing her finger at each one in turn. "Eenie . . . meenie . . . minie . . ."

A French voice called from the top of the mountain where Bass had disappeared, "I am up here with him, Annie. I fight ze werewolves. We will be done as soon as we can."

"Purcee! Be safe!" Annie turned back to the demon.

The Queen pulled out her own hair a bit, but it was the Raiff's hair, still short and light blond. "How does he stand this?" She dropped the hair on the ground casually. It was like she didn't have a care in the world. "So many rescuers, Annie. So many lives you put in danger. For what? So you can have the power?"

"I don't want any power," Annie said, staring into the Queen's mealy eyes, thinking, thinking, thinking.

"Stupid!"

" 'Absolute power corrupts absolutely,' " SalGoud quoted.

The Queen flashed out her hand and a sheath of ice leaped from it, wrapping around SalGoud's mouth. "Silence, giant. How about you quote this? There will be no more Stoppers on my watch. There will be no more rescues on my watch. I declare that it is now the time for demons and giants. The Time of the Demons. It sounds good, doesn't it? Catchy? I think there's a good sound bite in there. The TV newspeople will eat that up. That is . . . if the trolls don't eat them up first." She winked and chuckled, obviously pleased with herself.

Annie shook her head. "Your watch is over, Queen lady. Your machine is gone. You chose the wrong side."

The Queen shuddered, a great angry wave rippling up inside of her, so fierce that Annie could actually see it build beneath her skin.

"*You* are over!" she yelled, lifting her hands, ready to attack. Her face puckered up with anger and concentration.

"Original comeback," Eva muttered, pulling herself to Annie's side.

Annie didn't pay attention. She had lifted her own hands and pulled almost all the remaining cold within her out, whipping it toward the Queen in the shape of a huge ice ball. The balls met midway and they shattered against each other, flinging ice shards everywhere.

They all shielded their heads with their arms.

"Annie!" came a voice beyond the ice. Annie glanced and there was Bloom, on the dragon. "Annie!"

But she couldn't pay attention because the Queen was whipping a boulder right at her. Annie flung back her own ice ball and again they clashed in the middle, the shards cutting her forearms and ice sticking to her hair, to Eva's and Aster's and SalGoud's, little crystals of it, almost looking like snowflakes stuck there.

But Jamie—Jamie had no ice on him. Jamie looked . . . warmed.

Annie wiped the wet from her eyes just in time to see the Queen pitch another boulder toward them. She held up her hands and it burst to pieces. She looked at her hands, surprised. The Queen whipped another ice ball at them. Annie pointed at it. It hovered in the sky and fell apart like a cracked egg.

"Yeah, Annie!" Eva yelled, hitting her in the arm.

Annie actually giggled.

The Queen roared and chucked the next boulder at SalGoud. He punched it out of the sky. The Queen stomped her foot on the ground so hard the mountain trembled, and before anyone knew what she was doing, she lunged forward grabbing Aster by the arm. She pulled her to her tightly so that Aster's back was against the Queen's chest.

"One more move and I kill the elf," she threatened, eyes white with fear and hate.

———

Jamie trembled as Annie gasped, holding back Eva, who was trying to attack the Queen with her ax.

There was a roar from above them and the dragon with Bloom upon her back landed in between the rest of them and the Queen. Everyone scurried around, quickly moving between the dragon's legs.

"Mother," Bloom said from the dragon's back, his voice cracking. Jamie glanced over at his friend. Tears filled Bloom's eyes. The hand on his bow shook. "Mother."

All the need and missing and love of a good ten years was tied up in that word. Jamie's heart sank—to have her so close, to have her taken away. If that were his mother how would he feel? If that were his mother what would he do? He'd never had a mother, never had a real father, just a pretend one, but these people were as close as he'd ever gotten to it.

There was no way, no way, that the stupid Queen, human turned demon-y shape-shifter or not, was going to screw it all up now.

"No more violence!" he yelled.

His eyes squeezed shut, and the Queen's hands dropped from Aster's side.

"Safe." Jamie pointed at Aster, love filling his heart, and the woman floated through the air until she landed on the dragon's back, green markings surging across her skin. Aster drew a deep breath and wrapped her arms around Bloom. Bloom gulped and hugged her back.

"Oh, my beautiful boy," she breathed as the coils grew more leafy and intricate. "How I've missed you."

"I—I missed you—I missed you, too." Bloom's voice was overwhelmed with emotion.

"What a fine, fine elf you have turned out to be," she said, hugging him closer as one by one, the green vines covered all the elves, flashing across their skin. Then they coated the dragon and finally, faintly—much more faintly—they twisted around Annie's skin.

She was the least elf of all of them, Jamie supposed.

"How does it feel, Annie?" he asked. "Does it feel okay?"

She gasped up at him. "It feels—amazing . . . It feels like I'm part of something, something so good. And warm. I feel warm."

"Annie!" Eva's voice was high-pitched and squeaky. "Annie! What are you doing, Annie?"

"It's not me," Annie breathed out, trying not to fall over. "It's Jamie."

Bass and Purcee came inching down the mountainside toward them, trying to sneak past the Queen.

Jamie glowed next to Annie, eyes squeezed shut still. He grabbed for her hand. "Help me, Annie. I don't know what I'm doing, but I know I'll be stronger with you."

Annie clenched her hand around his, squeezing it tightly. "Always."

Jamie cleared his throat. It just felt like . . . like magic was using him. Good magic.

"I call on the power of the water and the wind, the earth and the fire." Jamie's voice came from somewhere else. He didn't even feel like it was him talking. "I call on the helpers of the strings, the beatings of our hearts. I call on the powers to banish you, Queen. I call on the powers to bind you to stone, to bind you with iron, to bind you with salt."

The mist swirled around the Queen, trapping her like a whirlwind.

And then Aster echoed Jamie's words.

"Aro nehar glinno sehume . . ."

Aster's arms wrapped tightly around Bloom, but despite her exhaustion, there was power in her eyes and those were focused on the Queen.

"Aro neloo criminshe tal . . ."

The Queen battled back. Jamie could feel her tugging against the mist. It was taking all of his energy to keep it around her and then he heard another voice, a lovely voice that joined with his own.

"I call on the power of the water and the wind," Annie yelled, "the earth and the fire. I call on the helpers of the strings, the beatings of our hearts."

"No!" The Queen's voice rippled with rage. It blew like a hurricane wind, right at Annie. "No!" She pointed at the little fighting men. "Grogans! I command you to help me!"

For a moment, the grogans panicked, running about in a circle of dismay, but then Farrar of Shaun shouted, "Nah! We da not need to! She's na human anymore, lads! She's all demon now!"

Annie stumbled backward, trying to get out of the grogans' way and landed on SalGoud. SalGoud helped her back up. Through it all, she never let go of Jamie's hands.

Annie gave a slight nod and started again. "I call on the powers to banish you, Queen. I call on the powers to bind you to stone, to bind you with iron, to bind you with salt."

Neho linra yasha . . .

The grandmother's silent voice joined in.

Lintra nesono . . .

"Does anyone have any salt?" Spellacy of Sam yelled. "We need salt. You can't bind without it."

"I have some," Farrar of Shaun grumbled, whisking out three tiny packets like the kind they give you at fast-food restaurants. "I was saving them for my ketchup."

"Toss it to them," Spellacy of Sam said. "They have to make a circle around her."

Eva ripped the packets open with her teeth and trotted terribly close to the screaming, writhing queen, trapped inside the winding mist. Eva snarled at the woman and then spilled the salt in a circle around her. First one packet, then another, then, finally the last, just barely enough to make it a full circle.

The Queen screamed and hunched her shoulders angrily. Mist—a white mist—leached up from the salt circle on the ground.

"No!" she screeched, punching into the air. "No!"

And then, plop, she was gone. The mist dissipated,

revealing a circle of salt with a few stones in the center but no queen.

"What happened?" Annie whispered. "Where is she?"

"There." Jamie pointed at the center of the circle. In the Queen's place was a tiny little worm that seemed to be made of stone.

Everything was absolutely still for a moment and then Aster's voice broke through the quiet. "Thank Heavens."

And that set the cheering in motion. The grandmother dragon pushed away the rock blocking the rest of the elves.

Bloom and Aster kept hugging, and Eva thumped her chest and said, "Hey, what about me?"

Bloom opened his arms up and said, "Come on, Eva."

And Eva bounded into the hug, lifting Bloom and his mom a few inches up in the air with her enthusiasm.

"I love elves!" she yelled and then looked sheepish. "And I'll show any of you my ax if you ever tell anyone I said that. That is not going into the songs of glory. Got it? Got it?" Nobody answered. "Good."

Annie stared at the stone worm and sighed, wondering what to do with it. She glanced at Bloom and his family, wondered about her own family, if she'd ever find them. Or Jamie's.

And what *was* Jamie?

He was shivering now, obviously tired. His eyes met hers

for the briefest of seconds before he turned away as SalGoud clamped his hand on the top of his shoulder. "Good job, Jamie. Lovely teamwork, everyone! Lovely! We should get going."

SalGoud was so tired and dirty. One lens of his glasses was cracked. Annie made her way to him. "How are you feeling, SalGoud? Are you okay?"

His shoulders slumped. "I would like to be done with this."

"And you, Jamie?" Annie asked.

"I have had enough adventuring and violence," Jamie said. "I just want to go home and sleep in my own bed and have some of Gramma Doris's pies."

"Me, too," Annie said nodding. "Me, too."

Jamie cleared his throat. "Something is happening to me, Annie."

She pulled him and SalGoud to the edge of the group. "I know. What do you think it is?"

He shook his head. "I have these knobs on my back. I thought they were troll or something. I didn't want—I didn't want to show you."

"Jamie! We're friends! You're supposed to be able to show me anything." Annie threw her hands up in the air. "You're supposed to trust me."

SalGoud's eyes widened. "May we see?"

After a moment of hesitation, Jamie turned around and

lifted up the back of his shirt. "I—I— Don't tell me if it's gross, okay?"

Annie's breath fluttered out of her mouth.

"What? What is it, Annie?" Jamie pulled his shirt back down.

"It's not ugly at all, Jamie . . . It's . . . It's . . ." She didn't know how to say it. "It's like these feathers are sprouting from your back."

"Is it troll?" He whipped around, face stricken. "Please say it's not troll."

"Not unless trolls grow wings," Annie whispered. "They don't ever, right, SalGoud?"

The giant's eyes widened. "No . . . No, trolls don't have wings. But . . ."

Annie and Jamie both turned on him.

"But what?" Annie demanded.

"Angels do." SalGoud pushed his glasses higher up onto his nose and announced, "We need to get back to Aurora. Now."

22

Open the Portal.
Open the Portal Now.

A crow dropped a note.

SalGoud grabbed and read it. **THEY COME. HURRY**.

They hurried.

Despite their victory over the machine and the Queen, none of them wanted to stay in the Badlands a moment longer than they had to. They had to get to the portal and back to Aurora, and they really had to be quick. They Raiff was probably lurking about somewhere, angrier than ever.

They ran, and behind them the noise of galloping orcs and kelpies grew closer no matter how quickly they tried to move.

"Maybe they aren't coming for us," said Bloom, but he knew that wasn't probable. They'd thrown the Raiff into his own dungeon once before when they'd rescued Cornelia, even if it was only for a moment. They destroyed his machine, rescued the elves . . . sort of . . . Well, they would be rescued if they could get them somewhere safe. They turned the Queen into a worm. They had a golden dragon that the elves rode upon, too weak now to run.

"What should we do?" Annie asked, panting as she ran full throttle ahead. Bloom reached out and yanked her back, causing her to stumble a bit and windmill her arms to catch her balance. She was so distressed she hadn't realized how close they were to the beach, but suddenly sand whipped into the hole in her sneaker and they were standing on the shore behind hundreds and hundreds of trolls and kelpies and satyrs. Goblins and gremlins scurried along the boats, readying them. Ghouls hissed out orders, occasionally cracking whips that reminded Annie of the one the Queen had used.

The dragon landed next to them. *My energy is too low. I must turn or risk true death.* Before any of them could respond, she began transforming back into a toy as the elves climbed to the ground.

Jamie squatted down low and bit the corner of his lip. "Okay. Well, this complicates things a bit."

He surveyed the scene for a moment. "Purcee, I need you to transform into your largest form."

Suddenly behind Annie, Purcee was a lion-man again, in just his underpants. Annie realized she should probably be grateful he had those on.

The unmistakable sound of orcs pounding through the ruined forest pierced through the din on the beach.

"We need a boat!" Jamie whispered. "We can use the dragon to transport one of the elves with us, if she turns back full size . . . which it doesn't look like she's doing . . . but we need boats for everyone else."

Eva threw her hands up in the air. "Maybe one will just magically appear. Oh, yeah . . . Here boat . . . Here boaty, boaty, boaty."

The elves exchanged glances and even the grogans acted embarrassed by Eva's sarcasm.

SalGoud sighed. "She's had a hard couple of days . . ."

Jamie wasn't paying attention. He was too busy planning.

"Purcee will get us boats," he said, slumping down again. "Tie up our hands. We are your prisoners. Quick!"

Purcee did as he was told, loosely binding their hands with long, burned-up strips of black bark. Annie imitated Jamie's slumped posture, and Bloom and the other elves tried to slouch, but it didn't work. Elves don't do well at looking defeated.

"Don't even try," Eva said. "Elves look defiant to the last."

Bloom stared, stricken. He should have known that.

Aster murmured something in his ear and then staggered, weak again, so weak, all of them.

"No one say anything," gasped Jamie as they walked forward, Purcee pushing them along. "Purcee does all the talking."

"Great, I am very good at this conversing, at ze talking," he growled. The grogans growled with him and went invisible.

Purcee had placed his hand over Annie's mouth to make her seem more hostage-like. Without slowing his stride, Purcee pushed them toward one of the smaller boats. Annie and Bloom gagged from the stench of the trolls. A winged female swooped down in front of them. She wore a nurse's uniform beneath her cape. The name tag read: *Tisiphone*. Next to her was a horrid twisted otter. It had little fangs sticking out of its mouth, and ghastly eyes.

Annie gulped.

Tisiphone sniffed the air near Bloom. She moved a hand up to her permed blond hair and stood with her feet planted and hands on her hips.

"What's this?" she asked Purcee.

"I'm to take ze hostages over now," Purcee snarled, curling up his lip and exposing his sharp teeth for effect. "Raiff's orders."

Tisiphone's face darkened when she gazed at the prisoners. Her eyes lingered on Bloom's ears. "I thought the elves were not returning."

Jamie shot Bloom a warning glance.

"Who told you that?" Purcee bit back. He sounded absolutely evil and sure of himself. Annie was impressed. Who would have thought the kitten capable of such deception? "They told you wrong."

Tisiphone looked stunned, as if she had never been wrong

before. Purcee ignored her and lifted Bloom, Annie, Eva, and Jamie into the boat one by one. SalGoud stepped in himself. Bass and the other elves stumbled in after them, swaying from the effort. The grogans, wisely, stayed hidden inside Bloom's cape. Purcee threw in the weapons and then sat down, picking up the oars. The boat was crowded. They loaded into another one as well.

"Well, push us off, infernal goddess of vengeful destruction," he ordered Tisiphone.

She beckoned some orcs and they all pulled the boats toward the water. Purcee picked up the oars and licked his lips lasciviously.

"See you on the other side," he yelled back to the group on the beach.

A big troll in a police uniform hollered after them, "How's the water? It horrid?"

Purcee bent and lapped up some with his tongue.

"Delicious!" he yelled back.

The trolls shrieked and clutched one another, their ugly fat knees wobbling and lower lips trembling. Purcee only lapped up some more.

Eva rolled her eyes and laughed. "Ham."

Purcee said nothing, just kept rowing toward the strings.

Once they were a good enough distance away from the beach so that they could not be overheard or seen, Jamie slipped his hands out of their bonds and told the others to do the same. He looked behind them and then toward the strings ahead. SalGoud checked his watch. The face sparkled like raindrops on a birch leaf and the band was golden flowers interlinked.

"It is still daylight in Aurora, just for another hour," SalGoud said. "If we can cross before they catch us, then we'll have an hour's time. They won't go after us until it's night. The trolls and vampires can't be in the light because they would die instantly, and the Raiff's power is greater at night."

"If they catch us?" Annie asked, craning her head back to examine the figures on the beach. More creatures ran out of the woods to join them. "They just let us go."

Purcee growled, pumping the oars harder. "They will realize their mistake soon enough."

"They already have." Bloom motioned toward the beach, where there was now massive activity. A horrible roar rushed out across the ocean toward them. "Seems like the Raiff is there."

"He escaped the ice," Bloom said.

"He is made of ice, almost. It is his element." Aster squinted. "He's getting into a boat. He's sending the flying creatures ahead."

Dark forms quickly took to the sky, causing Annie's stomach to lurch in horror. Those nocturnal terrors hanging in flight were enough to make many a grown man faint. But Annie did no such thing. Adrenaline surged through her veins, urging her to run. She grabbed her small sword and tried to paddle with it, slicing the water with it, matching Purcee's strokes.

"Good, Annie," said Aster. "Bloom. Do you have any silver-tipped arrows?"

He nodded, pulling some out and notching his bow. "Luckily, I do now."

She had told him a long time ago that silver was one of the few things that could stop a werewolf. She raised her trembling hands, palms out, toward the strings. "Be ready to shoot. Now is not the time for mercy, Bloom. It is the time for skill. Annie, we will help you with what power we have left. Please try to speed us up. Jamie, I'm not sure what you can do, but anything would help."

"Call for friends," SalGoud suggested. "Jamie, call for the merpeople. They love you. And they can come back and forth, unlike everyone else."

Jamie imagined Farkey, the merboy from the fountain. "Let me try."

Farkey . . .

Annie could tell that the Raiff was speeding up, too. He stood at the helm of his long boat; several trolls were rowing it in unison. They didn't look happy about it, but the satyr whipping their backs kept them going. The Raiff's red cloak whipped behind him. Annie grew cold. *He will catch us. He will kill us.*

She kept paddling, trying to feel the magic—any magic—that might help.

"Don't watch, little Annie," Purcee said, his catlike muscles rippling with the exertion of rowing. "Just paddle."

Bloom had no such escape. Nor did he want one. If he was going to die, he would die fighting beside his mother.

He notched his arrow as a creature swooped close, arms outstretched, ready to knock off Purcee. Bloom let the arrow loose. It whizzed through the air, striking the flying half man in the heart. The man recoiled and fell into the sea. Bloom had no time to celebrate or think. He notched another arrow and shot again. This time it was the flying man with a black cowboy hat. He bared his fangs. Bloom shot and hit his mark.

Another arrow downed the next—a griffin. Then came Tisiphone, low and close to the water, her otter by her side. Her fingernails were like claws and they were outstretched, ready to rip Annie off the boat. Annie calmly looked at Bloom. Just as calmly, he shot Tisiphone in the neck moments before she reached the boat. Her little otter, hidden behind her, made it, latching onto Eva's back. Eva yelped and tried to shake it off. SalGoud shrieked and wrenched it off, hurling it through the air. It tumbled into the sea.

"Are they dead?" Eva sputtered out.

Purcee grimaced. "Most likely not. Infernal ones are hard to kill. They're more likely to be decommissioned for a while."

Annie glanced at Bloom. His hard face held watchful eyes.

"Annie, we need some speed," Aster said, eyeing the Raiff's quickly approaching boat.

She nodded, handed her paddle to Jamie, and lifted her hands above her head.

"I can't feel the strings yet," she shouted.

"Nor can we," an elf murmured back, face broken and tired. "They haven't returned to their original resonance, not completely. The Raiff's machine still taints them."

"He's getting closer!" Jamie shouted.

The Raiff was catching up.

The boat rushed forward. Annie held her small sword in midair. Dozens of mermen and mermaids appeared, lifting the boat above the water. One of the mermen, with dark green hair and dimples, winked at her. She smiled, astonished, and pulled her sword back into the boat. She didn't want to accidentally hurt anyone.

Behind them, the Raiff slapped his hands together and between them formed a gigantic ice ball. He flung it forward and it careened after them.

"He'll freeze us," Bloom whispered.

Aster sat calmly, with her hands folded in her lap. "No, he won't."

Annie didn't know if she should believe her. The ice ball rocketed toward them. The Raiff's face took on an expression that could only be called gloating. Bloom's arrows sliced into the ice, slowing it down, but not enough. Annie ducked and grabbed onto Eva, braced for impact. The ball grew bigger and closer, ready to engulf them.

"Oh no," Annie said, remembering the cold of the Raiff. "Please, no. Oh no."

She looked at Bloom in horror. More of his arrows sped into the ice ball. One arrow. Another. He shot them so fast, Annie couldn't count them.

"Duck!" he yelled, pushing her head down between her knees, and jumping down himself into the shelter of the boat as the ice split apart. "Open the portal, Annie."

"They'll follow us."

"Not for an hour. There is time." Bloom kept shooting.

Annie grabbed Aster's hand and focused. Jamie grabbed her other hand. "Let me help."

"But how?" she gasped.

"No idea, honestly," Jamie said. "It just always feels better when we're holding hands."

Annie swallowed hard and stared into Jamie's brown eyes. They were full of goodness and kindness despite everything he'd gone through. She could almost see the strings in them. That was it, wasn't it? The strings were in all of them, resonating, the absolute molecules that made up everything and could be twisted for good magic or evil, if you just let yourself feel them. She wanted the good. She wanted the Jamie kind of magic.

"You're so beautiful. Everyone is so, so very beautiful," she whispered, and she reached out and sensed the strings, manipulating them. Power surged within her, warmth spread from her hands to Jamie's and Aster's and then back again.

Then—in front of them—the strings. Marvelous and singing, beautiful and perfect, they shimmered as the portal back to Aurora, away from the Badlands, formed.

"Yes!" the grogans bellowed.

Jamie's hand tightened in hers. "It's so perfect."

The toy dragon trembled and then lifted up to the sky, transforming into a dragon again. *I will hold him off. Stay down.*

"But, Grandmother!" Bloom's voice was a plea. "You're too weak."

I must save you. Go quickly.

She flapped her wings and soared away, back toward the land, away from the portal. As she did, the Raiff's ball of ice exploded, sending chunks spraying in all directions, even back toward the Raiff's boat. The infernals and orcs screamed in terror as some of them were hit.

"My nose!" one yelled.

Bloom reached up his hand and caught several of his arrows, which had flown back toward them with the ice. He placed them into his quiver and smiled as Annie released Aster's and Jamie's hands.

"Such an elf," Aster said, slowly lifting up her arm and tousling his hair.

Bloom smiled and turned to look at his mother. Annie turned with him, just in time to see them all pierce the strings.

The Raiff's howl died to their ears the moment they entered the portal. All they saw was the beauty of the strings.

23

Home Again, Home Again, Jiggety-Jig

The joy that Annie had once experienced going through the strings with Grady O'Grady doubled as they passed through them again. She grabbed Jamie's hand as the boats pushed through the portal that she and the strings had created. "It's so beautiful."

"Does it still feel off?" he asked, quietly, leaning toward her.

She thought for a second. "Yes, but . . . It feels like they are trying to become right again, you know?"

Jamie swallowed hard. For the first time in days and days, Annie was smiling and he didn't want to ruin it. The joy of the strings had changed her face back into something lovely and calmer, far less tense, even if it was just for the moment that she was relaxed.

Bloom and SalGoud were hunkered down with Aster and the rest of the elves, feeling foreheads, checking pulses. The mermen and mermaids were still beneath the boats, and Eva was staring at the strings with her mouth wide open, awed. Purcee was rowing even though they were too far above the water for his paddle to reach it.

They floated out of the strings and into the regular world of Maine. The cold air blasted against their skin and they huddled together as the merpeople towed them back toward the rocky beach and home. The ocean was dark, frozen, but it felt so good to be back. The rest of the occupants of the boats cheered. Elves hugged one another. Eva screamed in victory. The merpeople laughed, joining in. Aster pulled Bloom into an enormous hug. Jamie and SalGoud gave each other high fives and tears leaked out of Annie's eyes because she was so happy, so incredibly happy, that they had escaped the Badlands.

"Crikeys, it's cold here," Boucher of Steve said, hiding in Bloom's cloak pocket and vaguely ruining the mood.

"Never thought I, Levesque of Jon, would live ta see the regular world, or Aurora," Levesque of Jon bragged and then ducked into Annie's hair for warmth.

Eva wiped her nose. For a second, Annie thought she'd been crying, but she couldn't have, could she?

"The Raiff will wait for at least an hour," SalGoud

announced. "Like the mayor, he hates to be alone. He wants his reinforcements."

"He'll be angry," Bloom said.

"Furious," Aster agreed, closing her eyes because she was so tired.

"Let us hurry, then," Purcee declared just as the grandmother dragon broke through the portal. Ice encased her wings and she tumbled out of the sky, turning into a toy again as she fell.

"Catch her!" Bloom yelled, cupping his own hands and reaching up. She landed in his hands, tiny and silent. He gasped, looking at Aster, horrified. "Is she . . . Is she . . ."

"I don't know," Aster said. "Put her in your cloak pocket and keep her safe. She has done so much for us, always. I believe she's just drained of her energy. She may take years to recharge."

The toy wiggled a bit in Bloom's hands. "She still . . ." He wasn't sure the word for it. "Lives? She's a toy again but she lives."

The mermen began singing as they crossed, an ocean shanty that Annie had never heard before.

His beard is black.

His soul is, too.

Best not go home.

He waits for you.

"Bloody freakin' mermen, now they're singing about him," Eva grumbled, pulling the oars into the boat and commenting that they'd be good troll head-bashing weapons.

Nobody needed to row anymore. The mermen did all the work, having carried them through the portal to the other side. And in this way they crossed the calm ocean to Aurora. Bloom kept a lookout for the Raiff. Annie watched with anxious eyes as the sun edged toward the horizon. Eva grumbled constantly as the mermen sang.

He likes to swear.

He likes to dance.

He likes to sniff his underpants.

Bloom began to laugh. The elves joined in. Eva just growled and mumbled to herself about how sea men are entirely too frivolous, especially considering the dire state of things, and laughing would just encourage them. No one paid attention. The mermen, encouraged by the laughter, continued to sing for the rest of their voyage across the sea.

His arms are hairy.

His nose is, too.

He feeds his trolls goblin poo.

After glancing over his mother, Eva, and the elves, Bloom met Annie's eyes and mouthed the words "Thank you."

She pressed her lips together to keep from crying. They'd brought the elves home but in doing so they'd opened the portal, and that meant the thing they feared most was going to happen. The Raiff was going to return.

And then what? she wondered.

And then there would be war.

24

Worms Become Wicked

When the group of children, elves, and grogans landed on the shore, the sun was terribly close to the end of its day's journey. They had merely a half hour or so before the Raiff's forces began to arrive. Leaping out of the boat, the stronger survivors helped the weakened elves to shore. Bloom gave his cloak to Aster, and Purcee helped her wrap it around her shoulders.

"But what about you?" she asked.

Bloom didn't meet her eyes. "I'll be fine."

Nobody wanted to speak because they were afraid.

"They will make the crossing difficult for the Raiff," Eva said, turning back to the group waiting for her on the beach. She clapped her hands together. "No time to waste. Let's go."

It had been decided on the trip that they would split up and warn the town of the Raiff's crossing. Everyone was sure he'd still cross and try to grab Miss Cornelia or Annie and force them to stop time so that his beasts could kill freely.

"He is a determined demon," Aster had said. "Losing us will only iron his will."

Bloom, SalGoud, grogans, and Purcee would bring the elves to Aquarius House and head to the forest to begin the warnings. Annie, Jamie, and Eva would head to the town. They would gather up all the creatures they could and meet at Miss Cornelia's house. Nothing could enter there without her permission.

"I will not invite the mayor over for tea and carrots again," she had said back in the Badlands when confronted with his betrayal.

Annie shivered in the cold, both from worrying and from remembering, and Aster smiled at her. When she'd first come to Aurora, the mayor had hugged her and put her up on his shoulders, praising her return. It hurt that all that kindness had been fake. She shivered again.

"We will be warm soon, Annie," Aster said, placing her hand on the side of the girl's face, "all snuggled up in our cozy houses. We have you to thank."

Annie nodded. She wanted to believe her, but, well, Annie was noticing that no one had moved the plan to the logical conclusion. Everyone would hunker down and be safe at Miss Cornelia's house, but then what? Would she and Miss Cornelia never be able to leave, because if they did the Raiff would capture them? They would be stuck all their lives. No matter how much Annie loved Miss Cornelia and her wonderful house, she didn't like the thought of never being able to leave. And what about the rest of the world, outside Aurora . . . the regular people? What would happen to them?

There was only one thing to do. She had to find a way to stop him, to fight him, no matter what the cost to herself. She had to.

Annie gritted her teeth and steeled her mind, and Aster slowly dropped her hand. "Things will be okay, Annie."

"I know." Annie tried to make her voice sound braver than she felt. Bloom lifted his hand goodbye and turned. She wondered if she'd ever see him again.

———

Annie, Jamie, and Eva made it to the town as quickly as they could, following the beach and then scrambling up a hill. They went from house to cottage to burrow to den, knocking on doors. Joyous that they had returned, people hugged the children, screaming delight even as the threesome explained in quick voices was what wrong.

The happy mood quickly changed. Young children grabbed their mothers' legs. Men hushed their dogs to listen. Fairies flew in circles, horrified, and held hands with the pixies. The good vampires slept. They all lived in a group at the bottom of the florist's. Since the sun was out it was too early to wake them up, so Annie scrawled out a note explaining and telling them to be careful, while Jamie went next door to inform the family of goblins that lived in the library.

They found Helena and Mr. Nate at the bakery. The duo started dancing a jig, they were so excited to see the children, but Eva said, "We got bad news."

Mr. Nate's expression changed as he stared at Jamie who explained what was happening. Mr. Nate pulled him into a rough hug. "I thought I was saving you by bringing you here and now . . . now this."

"You did," Jamie said, his words slightly muffled by the fabric of Mr. Nate's red flannel shirt. "You *did* save me."

"Let the boy go! I can't feed him when you're hugging him!" Helena exclaimed and then shot several sugar-dusted doughnuts into Jamie's mouth the moment he was free. The sparkly sugar reminded Annie of Jamie's wings, hidden beneath his shirt and coat now. They were black and white feathers, small, easily concealed. She couldn't imagine how it felt to him. And she didn't have time to imagine. Not right now. She would if they survived. *When* they survived, she corrected herself. They had to survive. They had to.

"We knew he was coming," Mr. Nate said stoically as Helena kept flying mini doughnuts into everyone's mouths. "We've been preparing."

"You need strength for battle!" she insisted as she pushed a chocolate cream mini doughnut into Eva's mouth. "We all do!"

"We will help tell the others it's begun," Mr. Nate said, shrugging on a coat covered in cinnamon. "Cornelia warned us it would be soon, but we didn't think it would be so soon."

"And the elves?" Helena asked, sending a pink shimmery stream of sugar directly into everyone's mouths. "For strength."

"They're at Cornelia's. Ain't no use. The ones that survived are weak. The demons had them strapped to a machine. Stupid demons," Eva muttered through a mouth full of baked goods and pink sugar. She lifted up her ax. "Let's go."

It was taking forever. A kindly giant gave Annie a long coat to keep her warm as she continued the telling. She tried to imagine Bloom racing through the forest, warning the creatures of Aurora who preferred trees to houses as shelters. As she did, she watched the families of Aurora stream up the hill to Cornelia's. They loped and ambled and scurried down Main Street and up her long driveway. There were a lot heading for the shelter of the home, but it wasn't nearly half.

"We have to split up," she told Jamie.

He looked at the sun. Half of it had already disappeared below the horizon. "Annie . . ."

"It will be okay." She hugged him.

"I'll get fireworks!" said Eva, running off.

Jamie's eyes seemed a little misty. "I think we should stay together. We're supposed to always stay together, remember? Forever friends."

"Forever." Annie didn't know if he was saying that they should stay together because he was scared or if he thought it made more sense, but she trusted him enough to agree.

Still, his worry overwhelmed him and he blurted, "I think something is happening to me, Annie. Something big and unstoppable."

Annie spoke quietly, grabbing Jamie's hand in hers. "I think something already has. There are feathers on your back. You have magic in you."

"I know that SalGoud thinks that I'm an angel or something, but . . . but I'm afraid I'm becoming what I don't want to become."

He couldn't make himself say the word—troll. He didn't want to become a troll.

Annie didn't want to say the word either.

Jamie had spent so much time worrying about becoming troll, trying to fit in, to take care of everyone in Aurora even when they were afraid he was a monster and were threatening to kick him out of town. He was the least monsterish person she'd ever met, would ever meet. A surge of love leaped inside her chest, warming her heart, and they hurried through the dark, cold almost-night. "I think you— You should just embrace it, Jamie. Whatever it is that you are is awesome, because you, Jamie, are awesome."

"You are, too," Jamie said, squeezing her hand a bit.

"Eva would say, 'I know,' here."

Jamie laughed. "Yes, yes, she would."

They hurried from house to house. One group of werecats didn't believe them. Annie gave up after wasting precious minutes and moved on, leaving them to purr over their whiskers and contemplate the mouse soup they were planning on having for dinner.

"It's taking too long," she said. "We'll never get them all."

Jamie pointed up at the town hall, a white sideboard building, square and rough from the sea's battering. At the top stood a tower and cupola, the only adornments on the stark building.

"What?" Annie asked. "Does someone live there? Vampires or something?"

"No. The Belles. The warning system, remember?" Jamie knocked on the door. No one answered. He pushed it open. "Hello?"

No one answered still. It was dark inside.

Jamie flicked on a light switch. A piece of yellowed paper stuck to the plaster wall with a red thumbtack read:

• ATTENTION •

Ring Bell Only in Cases of DIRE Emergency.

Do Not Activate for Mere Tarasque Sightings or Vampire Conventions.

In Those Instances Contact the Mayor at 211 Main Street.

For Other Ultimate Horrors, Including End-of-the-World Oblivion Problems, Please Ring Bell for Town Evacuation.

"Brilliant!" Annie gave Jamie a hearty pat and bounded toward the stairs at the side of the building. They must lead to the tower and the bell. "Why didn't Eva do this?"

"She probably forgot?" Jamie offered. "Plus, I think Eva will use fireworks whenever it's even remotely possible, don't you?"

They flew up the old wooden stairs, which ended in a door. Annie opened it without hesitating and burst into the bell room. She smiled. The bell was right where it was supposed to be, suspended in the air with its ringing rope dangling down, but as Annie lunged for it she spotted a bulky figure in the shadows. Just as she grabbed the rope to ring the bell, he stepped out of the darkness and into the light.

"I wouldn't do that, Annie," came the figure's voice, cold and bitter. A hulking presence clapped his hands together, stretching up to his full height. His beard glistened with ocean water and snow.

"Mayor?"

The mayor smiled, a wicked smile. In his hands he clutched his whip and his other arm was locked around Jamie's neck, trapping him and strangling him all at once as Jamie's feet dangled helplessly above the wooden floor.

25

The Belles

Jamie collapsed onto the ground at the mayor's feet, unconscious.

The mayor pointed at Annie. He cracked his whip. It lashed right by Annie's cheek, but didn't touch it. "You're next."

Annie froze. Jamie was crumpled on the wooden floor. Jamie . . . She hadn't kept him safe. She broke her promise.

"I'm here to make Aurora great again, Annie," the mayor said. "You can't think that I'd wait in the Badlands with everyone else. I'm too important for that. I'm here, getting ready for the Raiff's raid of Aurora. I followed you right through that portal and none of you noticed. I'm sneaky, and I get my way. That's what I do. That's what the Raiff does. We win."

Annie gritted her teeth. Aurora would never be great without Jamie or Miss Cornelia. It would never be awesome if the mayor or the Raiff were in charge. Biting her tongue, she pulled on the bell's rope with all her might, grabbing the dry prickliness of it with two hands and bringing it backward as quickly as she could.

Its loud chime resonated deeply, shaking the entire room. For a moment, triumph mixed with Annie's worry for Jamie. She'd done it. Another ring and everyone would be warned. They could run to Miss Cornelia's. They would be safe.

Just as she turned toward Jamie, the mayor's whip lashed out and twirled itself around her ankles. Annie's legs slammed together, tied up tight. She lost her footing as the mayor yanked her toward him. Still, she didn't let go of the rope.

The bell clanged again. Shuffling her legs backward to get away from the mayor, she tried to get one more ring in.

He would not let go.

She thrashed, trying to get free. "Get off, you maggot."

"Oh, so terribly threatening. Where are your little elf friends now, Annie? Have they abandoned you for what they presume to be the safety of Aquarius House? After you spent all that time rescuing them? How typical of elves." The mayor pulled his whip tighter so that Annie was completely stretched out, caught between the bell's rope and the whip.

"You used to be nice!" Annie shouted. "I trusted you. We all trusted you—except maybe Canin. Remember when you hugged me? Remember the fairies and pixies at the tavern and how much they loved you? Why would you do that to us? You were our leader."

"Cornelia never let me truly lead."

"That doesn't mean you have to hurt her, hurt all of us. Think about the fairies if you don't care about me or Corny or . . . or . . . or anyone."

He started laughing. "You are so weak, Annie, just like your parents. You worry too much about others instead of caring about your own power and destiny. Let me tell you a secret—people like that boy over there? They aren't worth your time. They are nothings and only get in the way of you grabbing your own power."

"Jamie isn't a nothing. He's full of good! Full of it. Jamie is strong and kind no matter what. He cares about other people. He wants the world to be happy and safe."

"You're so naive. Goodness means nothing, Annie. It's all about power. Haven't you learned anything yet?" The mayor yanked his whip a bit harder and pain seared through her legs. She wouldn't be able to hold on much longer.

She thought of the pixies and fairies and mermaids, the young dwarfs and werewolves, the hags, even Megan. All of them were in danger because of him. And now he had the gall to call Jamie, the best boy she'd ever met, a nothing? Anger filled her.

Annie pulled up her knees and tried to kick at him. It didn't work.

"Do you really think you can fight me?" asked the mayor. "Defeat the Raiff? Your parents thought that, too. Your mother screamed as she died and your father disap—"

"Don't talk about my mother!" Annie kicked again. It didn't work. Again.

It didn't have to.

A snarling, leaping form flew over her. White fur and dewclaws smashed squarely into the mayor's chest knocking him so hard that he fell backward.

"Tala?" Annie gasped.

The dog's sweet brown eyes met hers. They were full of love and . . . and . . . determination?

The mayor scrambled to his feet. "You can't take me down that easily, dog."

Tala winked at Annie, and turned to face the Mayor, hackles raised and growling. The mayor lunged for him and their bodies met in midair, but the momentum of Tala's leap pushed the mayor backward again. They landed against the side of the bell tower and broke through the rotten boards that encased the bell so many feet above the ground. The two of them disappeared through the hole.

Annie hurdled up, ripping the whip off from around her ankles, gasping.

Tala!

He'd fallen out of the tower with the mayor, and the tower was so high—too high to fall from.

"Tala!" Annie screamed, scrambling to the hole in the wall. The last moments of the setting sun had cast pink and purple shadows across the sky. In the distance, the dark shapes of vampires approached from across the sea. The moon was out, and with it Raiff's creatures. She couldn't see Tala or the mayor anywhere.

A great sob ripped through her.

Tala.

And Jamie.

Annie's heart shattered in two.

She had to get Jamie somewhere safe. She grabbed him by the ankles and dragged him behind some boxes. Hopefully, nothing evil would find him there.

A roaring noise made her turn to the hole in the wall. Then in the sky, fireworks burst into words:

Every 1 get to Corny's. Raiff coming.

Eva had done her part. From behind Annie came a flutter of activity and then dozens of small flouncy forms whizzed by her, out into the night air. Each glowed in the dark and was female, she thought, dressed in elaborate ball gowns such as the kind women wore in the South during the time of the Civil War. They scattered out toward the town, each of them singing out in a lilting southern accent, "Ev-acu-ate.

Ev-ac-u-ate. E-mer-gen-cy. Please, y'all must head to the big house. Evacuate. Emergency."

Annie slumped to the wall, head in her hands. She'd lost Tala, the only dog she'd ever owned, a dog so great he saved her from her foster home when wolf dogs were attacking. Jamie was unconscious and maybe really terribly hurt. The Raiff was coming, and she couldn't stop him. She couldn't stop anything. Suddenly nothing seemed worth it at all. She slammed her fist against her head and then slapped it on the floor.

"No!" Annie screamed. She didn't care who heard her. Let all of the Raiff's evil cronies hear her. Let all of Aurora. Did it matter anymore? "I can't give up. No!"

The last of the Belles flitted by her, fluttering her yellow fan as she passed. "E-mer-gen-cy. E-mer-gen-cy."

Annie raced down the steps, skipping two or three at a time as she ran, and finally slowed down only when she stepped beyond the threshold of the building. She was afraid she'd see Tala's beautiful body, broken and still, crumpled. She took a big swallow and looked around. It was twilight now, and the remaining light was little.

Squinting, she began to look for white fur on the snow—maybe—a trickle of blood, somewhere. The monsters would be coming. Her feet crunched on the snow. She willed herself to be quiet. In the distance she could hear the sound of Aurora residents continuing their ascent to Miss Cornelia's house.

"Hurry," she whispered as she searched the ground for Tala. "Hurry."

From above her came a whimper. She jerked her head up to look in the direction of the noise. Hope surged.

"Tala?" she called into the darkening sky.

Above her, a vampire Annie didn't recognize flew away from her, heading directly toward Miss Cornelia's, Tala's body in its arms.

"Don't hurt him!"

"I live here!" the vampire shouted down. "I'm one of the good guys. I will bring him to Corny's! He's only a bit hurt."

Tala was alive! Annie wanted to do an impromptu backflip to celebrate but she was so tired.

"Thank you!" Annie yelled back, hand over her heart. "Tell them Jamie needs help, too! Tell them—"

The vampire was already gone. Annie ran off toward Miss Cornelia's to get help for Jamie. She was sure someone— the hags, Cornelia, Ned the Doctor—could make him better as long as she hurried and got help in time.

She'd only run a block or so when strong fingers grabbed her arm. She whirled around, phurba drawn, ready to strike. Relaxing the moment she saw that it was Canin who stopped her, she let out a big sigh. She hadn't realized how tense, how nervous she was.

"The others?" he asked her in a hushed whisper.

In an equally quiet tone she explained what had happened. He nodded and pointed at Miss Cornelia's.

"Everyone else is there, almost. We have to hurry," he whispered. "You are the most valuable right now, and here you are the least safe."

"One of us needs to stay and guard Jamie," Annie insisted.

"I can go get him and carry him back," Canin said just as there was a sharp noise in the direction of the playground.

Annie grabbed at Canin's warm, hairy arm. He motioned for her to crouch down. She ignored him, standing beside him, instead. Terrified, she was not about to cower. Her chin firmed up. Her grasp on the hilt of her dagger tightened.

A gusting wind that echoed out loneliness swept by them. The swings at the playground all swung back and forth. The merry-go-round squeaked on its unoiled gears and began to slowly circle. The tetherball loped toward its pole and back out again.

Annie held her phurba out in front of her as Canin shifted behind her so they stood back-to-back.

Another snapping noise came from the opposite direction. Were they surrounded? Fear welled up in Annie's throat. She hoped it wasn't the Raiff's vampires. She hated the Raiff's vampires. Aurora ones? Totally different story.

The nasty smell that hit her nostrils informed her that it was definitely trolls, not vampires. There was a sudden movement above them and a net made of silver fell over them, snagging them tight.

"Not a net!" Canin growled, thrashing about. Normally he would be able to tear right through a net, but not one of silver. Silver was toxic to werewolves and terribly strong. He began to curse. "Stupid shoe-loving idiot maggots. Darn makeup-wearing whelps."

Annie tried to calm him down. All his thrashing made it worse. "Shh."

Two trolls bundled them up and one slung them over its shoulder. Annie and Canin hung upside down, and Canin's elbow filled part of her mouth. She spat out the fur and twisted her head enough so that she could see out into the night.

She wished she hadn't.

Down below her, at ground level, the mayor clapped his hands gleefully.

The mayor!

"You—you slimeball," she hissed at him and instantly wished she could have thought of something nastier to call him. Slimeball just wasn't strong enough. If she survived this, she'd need to get insult lessons from Eva.

Annie struggled tremendously against the net binding her, but nothing gave. She tried to rip at it with her teeth, gnawing against it, but it did nothing other than make her teeth hurt, the way teeth do when you've bitten into aluminum foil. She had to get free. She had to trick the mayor somehow into letting her go.

The mayor trotted behind the trolls. The net bounced against the troll's shoulder as he carried Annie and Canin away. The mayor lifted up his hand to show her a tiny wound.

"I got a splinter when I fell. But that's it. Do you know why? Because I'm a giant, and giants are outstanding specimens of the magical variety. Not only are our brains strong, but our bodies, too. You do know, I almost pity you because you're weak, just like your parents. You can't protect yourself at all, too goody-goody for your own good."

He picked up some snow and made it into a ball. He taunted her for a second, bouncing it up and down in his hand before he threw it smack into her face.

Annie thought frantically as the snow melted against her skin. She thought about how the mayor needed so much love and glory. He'd been so nice to her when she first arrived. A plan came to her.

Forcing herself to look contrite, she said, "I might as well tell you this now, since I'll probably never see you again once the Raiff gets through with me."

She paused dramatically.

"What?" he picked his teeth with his fingernails, dislodging great chunks of pizza sauce. Annie forced her stomach to calm down.

"You can't laugh. It's embarrassing."

She made her voice softer than it was normally. Canin snorted. She elbowed him in what she thought was his stomach although it turned out to be his butt.

"Ouch," he grumbled.

"Sorry."

The mayor lifted up his hand and bellowed at the trolls, "Stop."

The trolls halted their march. Annie shuddered as the mayor came closer. Up on the hill she could see the lights at Miss Cornelia's house. There were all sorts of activities going on in there, shapes moving behind the windows. If they could get there, they would be safer. Even if she could stop time now, though, it wouldn't help because of the net. They had to get out of the net.

The mayor moved close to the net so they were face-to-face. His breath assaulted Annie's nose. It seemed like he'd eaten a pepperoni pizza with extra garlic and anchovies at his last meal and had not brushed his teeth afterward. He had a funny little smile on his face. "Tell me what it is, Stopper."

Annie gulped. This was harder than she'd imagined. The words stuttered out—"Because . . . because . . . I . . . I . . . like you. In my head, I imagined that you were my dad and that you just didn't know. And that I would be . . . that when you found out . . . you'd make me a winner like you."

The mayor's eyes widened with shock.

Annie rushed out the words. "I've always liked you ever since I came here and you hoisted me up on your shoulders. I knew there was no hope that anyone so fantastic would ever have a daughter like me. I'm such a reject and so skinny and stupid. I knew that there was no way I could possibly be good enough for you, someone who has millions of fairy and pixie admirers, someone who could run a town? Do you remember when you hugged me, mayor? You were the first hug I've ever had."

He nodded.

It was all true. He *was* her first hug. She *had* imagined he would be a perfect dad. Things had changed a lot since she first came to Aurora. *She* had changed a lot.

"That was so great," Annie gushed on, while Canin made vomiting noises. "I liked you so much, mayor, but I knew that I wasn't worthy. This is sheer torture. To have to look at you upside down, knowing that I'll probably never see your face again and now I have to see it upside down rather than right side up. Oh, it's so unfair."

She gave out a melodramatic moan and then used Megan's famous puppy dog pout. The puppy dog pout required a trembling bottom lip and saucerlike eyes. It worked really well on the mayor. He started fumbling all around, looking over his shoulder and up at the sky.

"Enough," he mumbled, obviously at odds with himself. "Okay. Let her out."

"HUH?" the big troll squeaked.

"Let her out, I said. I want to hug her, poor thing. How can I resist? She should have had me as a father instead of that stupid, weak, cowardly man."

Annie screwed up her courage.

The troll opened the bag and a great hand reached in, grabbing her and pulling her out, upside down. Canin mouthed the word "careful" as she was deposited unceremoniously on the ground at the mayor's feet. Scuffs marked his winter boots, which smelled as if he'd stepped in some troll poop somewhere.

"Kiss my feet," he said.

"No, Annie!" Canin yelled.

Annie groaned and brought her lips to within a centimeter of the smelly boots that encased the stinky, callus-covered, hairy feet of the mayor. She couldn't bear to touch them with her lips. She made a smacking noise and pretended to kiss them. It fooled the mayor, of course. The mayor was an idiot.

"Stand up," the mayor ordered.

Annie clambered to her feet, grabbing two handfuls of snow and gravel. She looked the mayor straight in his beady pig eyes and then realized she should look down as if she was completely overwhelmed by being so close to him in all his magnificence. If only the trolls hadn't taken her dagger. She looked back at Canin. The troll hadn't actually remembered to close the net bag again and the wolf-man was slowly inching his way up, using his feet to climb on the silver rope. Each step he took looked like torture. Stepping on silver for wolves is like stepping on broken beer bottles for humans. Still, Canin didn't make a sound.

The mayor, however, was a different story. The giant puckered up his lips and made several deafening smacking noises and pointed to his cheek. "Kiss my cheek, then."

"Me—kiss—you?" Annie spluttered and closed her eyes. Things could not possibly be worse. "I thought we were going to hug?"

"I know you want to, and if you don't want to then you're lying and back in the net you go."

The mayor's dry, cracked lips twitched. Annie tried not to vomit.

Okay, Annie thought. *Okay, here goes.*

She tentatively took one step closer. The mayor reached out his arms as if he was readying himself for a big monster hug. Annie swallowed hard and took another step. The trolls giggled. One elbowed the other in its massive gut and said, "Kissy, kissy."

Annie glanced back at Canin. He was almost out of the net.

Okay, now . . .

With one motion, she threw each handful of snow and grit at the trolls' faces and spat into the mayor's screwed-up face. He screamed and began wiping at it frantically.

"Run!" Annie hollered and began booking it out of there herself, straight up the hill toward Miss Cornelia's house. She crossed her fingers that Canin escaped in time, but she couldn't stop and go back because the mayor was fast on her trail. He huffed and puffed up the hill behind her.

"I'll kill you," he screamed after her. "Rip you apart. You could never be a winner! Never!"

She didn't doubt he wanted to kill her, not at all.

Behind her the trolls screamed, "My mascara! She ruined my mascara!"

Annie's sneakers slipped on the snow and she slithered backward. She rushed to her feet again and slid, struggling, and now down on all fours she kept moving up the hill, although not as quickly as she liked. The sneakers had terrible traction. The trolls followed after the mayor and they were so much quicker and the snow didn't bother them at all. She looked up at Miss Cornelia's. If only she could get there . . .

"Eat her, is what we should do, ruining our makeup like that." The trolls had passed the mayor and were almost on her. She stared up at the welcoming lights of Miss Cornelia's. She had to get there. She could feel the foul breath of a troll on her back. She had run out of ideas.

Where was Canin?

She didn't wonder long. A huge snarling wolf lunged at the troll closest to her, ripping off its silky nightgown in one rough tear. The naked troll wailed, "My dress! My dress!"

The wolf spat the fabric out of its mouth. Annie crawled up the hill backward, inching away. The mayor pulled out Annie's phurba and held it in front of him, terrified of the snapping wolf whose eyes and teeth seemed to glow in the moonlight.

He was right to be scared. Canin wasn't as merciful as Annie and he wouldn't hesitate to kill the giant.

The troll in the terry cloth running suit tried to stomp on Canin, but the wolf was too fast and kept darting away just in time, which caused the terry cloth troll to stumble about after him, going every which way and eventually falling on a seesaw. The naked troll got over the shock of being naked and lunged after Canin, walloping down flat on his troll belly, causing the ground to shake as if there was a major earthquake. He barely missed Canin. The other troll reached out and swiped at the wolf, knocking him sideways. Canin's head hit against a boulder. Canin stopped moving. The troll laughed triumphantly and reached out to grab Canin. He would eat him, Annie was sure.

Annie had to distract them and did the first thing that came to mind, echoing the mayor's words of so long ago. "Yoo-hoo. Trollies! Stoppers are much, much yummier than wolves. No nasty fur to floss out of your teeth!"

That got their attention. The tracksuit troll dropped Canin on the ground without a glance. He landed against the boulder again with a sickening crunch. It was all Annie could do not to rush to her fallen friend. There was no chance for that. The troll lunged for her, and Annie was so busy thinking about how to dodge him that she didn't see the mayor himself leap after her, his face glistening with hate, the dagger outstretched and pointed at her heart.

As he lunged he screamed her name, twisting the syllables of it with his stark and fierce hatred: "Annie . . ."

And then he was on her. She dodged the phurba—*my own*

phurba, she thought, shocked—just barely, whirling around to face him. Frantic, she grabbed at his right arm, the one that held the dagger. He beat at her with his large fist, hammering at her shoulder and face, while she twisted his arm, trying to make him let go of the weapon. The trolls simply watched the fight, placing bets.

"I give her two minutes."

"Thirty seconds and he sits on her." The troll fixed his running suit. It had given him a wedgie.

The naked one whispered, "Isn't she the Stopper?"

The other shrugged.

"Well, can't kill her, then. The Raiff wants her."

Finally relieved of his wedgie pants problem the troll squeaked back, "We don't kill her. Mayor does. Then we eats."

Impressed by the logic of his fellow imbecile, the naked troll nodded.

Meanwhile, Annie staggered around, slipping on the snow, trying to keep the dagger from slicing into her. The mayor's face turned bright red. He switched the phurba into his free hand and in a quick movement plunged it into Annie's belly on the right side.

Her hands dropped from his arms and she looked down to see what had happened. He pulled the phurba out. She stared up into his eyes. There was nothing there, nothing in his eyes. He pulled back the dagger to strike again. Then a great force yanked him backward, flinging him out of the air and completely out of Annie's sight.

But Annie had stopped looking.

Her body fell to the snow. She lay on her back, her hands slapped tight against the wound on her stomach. Above her the stars in the night sky twinkled, little pinpricks of light. They seemed to be spinning. She closed her eyes. She was so cold everywhere, except for her hands on her wound. The blood flowing onto them was warm.

Bugaboo-Boo

Back at Miss Cornelia's, there was a moment of absolute silence as Bloom, SalGoud, and the elves burst through the front doors and into the parlor where Miss Cornelia, the entire town council, Gramma Doris, and so many others were bustling about, trying to understand what the merpeople were trying to tell them.

Farkey pointed an algae-draped finger at the new arrivals and shouted into the silence, "See! The children and the elves! They have returned."

There was one more moment of shock and two more moments of silence before the room erupted in applause and cheer and joy and hugs. Gramma Doris bundled the elves into hugs, commanding Dr. Ned to take care of them upstairs with Lichen.

Miss Cornelia opened her arms, smiling. "Welcome home! Welcome home! Aster! Bass! Everyone! Oh." Her hand fluttered to her heart. "It is so lovely and right to have you home again. We will have you well soon. So soon." She paused for a moment and her eyes lost their smile. "Bloom! SalGoud! You have done it! But where are Annie and Jamie and Eva?" She gasped. "Don't tell me they have—"

"Thar warning the others," shouted Nye of Alisa, materializing with some of the other grogans and winking at a pixie. "And ye best get ready because the Badlands are a'comin' to ya." She coughed, bowed, blushed at the pixie, and cleared her throat. "We're going to go guard outside. Come on, men!"

"We heard about the pies," West of Stuart said as he scurried back out the front door. "We're really looking forward to ya pies here!"

Bloom and SalGoud quickly explained to Cornelia what was happening, and the happy reunion was soon over. Flustered pixies flew in circles smashing into the walls or the trees that surrounded the mermaids' pool. Worked-up giants wrung their hands nervously and bit their bottom lips. Red Nose the giant bit his lip so hard he drew blood, which compelled several of the good vampires to faint dead away on the floor. Good vampires have a hard time dealing with blood. This fainting frenzy forced the mermaids to pound their tails in the pool in an attempt to splash water out onto the unconscious vampires' faces to revive them.

"Oh my word." Gramma Doris threw up her hands. Five

banana cream pies materialized out of thin air and flew into the faces of several vampires and one merman.

"Doris," Cornelia scolded.

"I couldn't help myself. I can't stand it when they go on like this. It's disgraceful."

Cornelia didn't disagree. She put her fingers between her lips and whistled. The shrill sound moved throughout the foyer, and quiet magically reigned.

Cornelia stood partway up the spiral stairs in the foyer and for a moment looked simultaneously frustrated and amused. Clapping her hands together to get the focus of the bunny who was lapping up some of the water on the carpet, she began to explain exactly what was going on. She was barraged by questions, of course, mostly from the vampires who were revived and dripping. Vampires as a group tended to like to hear themselves talk, more so even than the giants.

"It is all fine and good that we are here," shouted Purcee. His French accent was a little overwhelming and caused Red Nose to snigger. "But what of ze Stopper and ze boy and ze dwarf and ze wolf? It is dark. Still, they are not here."

"Too true. Too true," the pixies began murmuring, fluttering their wings and zigzagging about.

Miss Cornelia closed her eyes and nodded. She held up her hand for silence. Instantly the crowd quieted.

"You all know now what the Raiff is up to, and it seems to me we have two choices. We can stay here in my house and wait. Due to the charms once again protecting it, we will be safe here, but we will not be able to influence the events that play out."

"If the girl stops time, we will all be here forever, stuck . . . ," a goblin muttered, pulling at his fingers anxiously. A worried-looking kobold nibbled on the end of his pipe, nodding and rubbing his hands on his brown knee pants.

"True, we will be stuck, with no movement, no thought," Miss Cornelia said, looking at him and then directing her gaze at others in the crowd. "But we will be unharmed. And perhaps Annie would find a way to start time again to free us."

"Ha. That girl's a pipsqueak. I doubt she's old enough to think of anything other than when she'll eat her next lolli-pop, much less find a way to unstop us," grumbled a Buga-boo, who was standing near Tala, looking more or less like a piece of dust with hollow eyes. Tala growled at him, baring his teeth. The dog's side was covered with bandages, but he looked none the worse for his fall. The Bugaboo stuck out his tongue, knowing he was safe. Miss Cornelia had a strict no-fighting policy in her home.

Miss Cornelia ignored his comment completely and con-tinued to speak. "If we leave the house, we may be able to find our friends. We may be able to bring Annie back here with us. Or we may be caught."

"And eaten by trolls!" Gran Pie's son yelled from his

position on the floor, where he was doing a one-handed handstand.

"Or sucked dry by vampires!" a little dwarf grumbled, biting his own lip so hard in his nervousness that he drew blood and yelped.

The Bugaboo said, "It's all for naught."

"True, terrible things could happen," Miss Cornelia said, gazing down at the townspeople gathered below her, making eye contact with each and every one, or at least all that had eyes.

Helena and Mr. Nate barged into the room. "They're here! The Raiff is here with his minions."

Gramma Doris fluttered over, wrapping her arm around Helena. "We know."

"Have Jamie and Annie returned?" Mr. Nate asked. "And Eva?"

"Not yet, no," Doris murmured and explained quickly what was happening and how the hags were ministering to the elves, whom they had brought upstairs, and how the mermen were off fetching medicine as they spoke, and that they were discussing strategy.

"We must determine our course," Cornelia told them all.

Bloom's heart beat frantically in his chest. He had never been so angry or so afraid, but mostly it was the anger that took over. How could they even think of doing nothing?

"We stay and we die," he said. "Maybe not a real death,

but we will be frozen here forever if the Raiff makes Annie stop time. And he will. She has struggled these few days and made it through, but only barely. She is brave, but she has never seen a world like this before. And now, we cower here and surrender her to him. Why? Because we want one girl to bear the whole responsibility of a town she has only just moved to. She and Jamie and Eva and SalGoud have already done more than any of the rest of you to keep us safe. What kind of creatures are we?"

Nobody said anything.

Bloom pulled on a borrowed cloak, loaded his quiver. "If we stay here, we are no better than the trolls. We are wannabes, talking of courage and friendship and conviction, community and goodness, but in reality being nothing at all."

Gran Pie placed her hand on his shoulder. "I am not all talk."

He nodded. "Neither am I."

"Nor I!" shouted Purcee. He pranced over and climbed up the boy's cloak in order to sit on Bloom's shoulder. The bunny hopped up next to him, trying to look stern, but really just looking like a bunny.

"Nor I," chimed a pixie, who then looked surprised that she said it.

Leodora Lenci Leksi came to stand by Bloom. "Nor I."

Arrius Herman, Aelfric Darling, and Nicodemus Metal Smith moved forward. "Nor I."

"Nor I." SalGoud cleared his throat as if he was going to quote someone, but Ned the Doctor clamped his hand over SalGoud's mouth.

"Nor I."

"Nor I."

The Bugaboo rolled his eyes and slunk away just as Eva and the rest of the grogans bashed into the front foyer.

"Ach, what have we missed?" Eva bellowed. "Has there been any fighting?"

"Or warrin'?" Taylor of Davis asked, popping out on top of Eva's head. "That we missed while we were outside?"

Staggs clung to her pigtail and waved a table knife about. "Or adventurin'? Have we missed more adventurin'?"

"And cake making?" asked West of Stuart, the grogan who liked to bake. "Because I'd totally love some Louisiana Crunch Cake right now."

Helena eyed the grogan. "If we defeat the Raiff, if we survive all this, I will make enough Louisiana Crunch Cake to feed the entire State of Maine and give it all to you grogans."

West of Stuart's eyes glinted and he twirled his fork in his hand. "Deal!"

Eva's father and Cornelia passed out torches and weapons. The elves, Miss Cornelia, and the youngest children stayed in the house where she would read them stories and let them swim in the merpeople's fountain. They couldn't risk having Miss Cornelia captured, just as they couldn't risk having Annie captured. Her staying behind was logical, but SalGoud could tell by how she kept pacing and wringing her hands, that she didn't want to do it. As the citizens of Aurora and its forest marched out the doors, Miss Cornelia and the children gave them each a flower and a kiss.

"I am still weak," she said, "but with the machine's demise, my powers are slowly returning. Be careful."

Bloom was the first to leave.

"I will find her and Jamie," he said, teeth gritted and eyes concerned, as he gazed at Miss Cornelia.

He looked so young, so alone. He spent so much time trying to do what was right and be brave, just as she'd taught him. She prayed that she taught him well enough and nodded at his determined words and kissed his forehead, planting a flower in his cloak pocket for luck.

"To remember the light," she told him as she placed it gently into his pocket. He nodded.

The bunny began to munch on the yellow petals.

"Come back, Bloom," Miss Cornelia whispered as he stepped into the night. From an upstairs bedroom window, Aster stared out at her son's departing form, whispering blessings as she placed her hand against the windowpane.

Bloom glanced back and raised his bow in salute.

And he was gone.

Raiff Blood

Finally, the worst had happened. Annie was dying; she knew it. Flat on the ground, with her back sunk into the cold snow, she wanted to open her eyes and stare at the stars one last time, maybe see Grady O'Grady fly across the moon, something, anything, but she was too weak. Annie realized she wasn't tough enough to fight the Raiff, not even the mayor, by herself. She never was.

"Drink this, Annie."

A hand lifted up her head and placed something cold against her lips. She knew whoever it was wanted her to drink, but the actual process of drinking seemed completely beyond her. *What was it again?* she wondered. *Did you have to part your lips? Was your tongue involved somehow? Or maybe it was your toenails?*

Her thoughts didn't even make sense anymore and her heart beat weakly in her chest.

"Annie, drink!"

Strong fingers moved her lips, parting them enough to squeak some water into her mouth. Freezing liquid made its way through the tiny opening to slosh around behind her teeth. It tasted salty.

Fear filled her as she struggled to open her eyes.

"Swallow," the voice commanded.

Slowly, she did. The glacial liquid moved into her esophagus and down toward her stomach. The cold inside her grew. She shuddered, her whole body quaking uncontrollably as she remembered the mayor thrusting her own phurba into her. Groaning, she remembered Aurora, the wicked Raiff. She had to stop him! And Jamie . . . Jamie was hurt. He seemed so far away. All her friends did, but even though it was colder, her heart seemed a tiny bit stronger now. She struggled to sit up.

"Easy," came the voice. A hand stroked her brow and she eased herself back down, thinking how comfortable it would be to just stay there, letting the hand smooth her forehead, to just keep her eyes closed. She could stay there forever, if only it weren't so cold. But no. She couldn't. She had to fight the Raiff. She had to save Aurora. Images of the grandmother in the Pass of Sighs and the little girl in Scot's Land, how she imagined her own parents' death—all pushed their way into her brain. She couldn't let that happen to anyone else. She was supposed to save them. That's what Time Stoppers did. She had to get up.

"Drink more."

Again, the cold liquid came. She swallowed it more easily this time. A little strength returned as the nutrients flooded her system. *Who's taking care of me?* she wondered and opened her eyes.

She wished she hadn't.

A man—no, a demon—sat in the snow next to her. One arm cradled her head. A hollowed-out rock filled with clear liquid rested in his hand. Beyond him lay the mayor's gigantic, motionless form. Annie saw the night sky above them, streaked with shrieking vampires. Two hideous naked trolls were hiding behind a boulder. And beyond them was Canin, fully human again and moaning in pain.

The Raiff smiled down on her with a look of pure caring and kindness, a look that had to be pretend considering who it was who had rescued her.

"Welcome back, Annie."

She shut her eyes and tried to pull the fur that someone had given her more tightly around her. Someone had given her? It must have been the Raiff.

A wolf howled in the distance.

"Drink some more, Annie. It will help you heal." The Raiff's voice was even and flat, but still commanding.

She peeked open an eye. "It's not poisoned?"

The Raiff threw back his head and began to laugh, "Poisoned? Hardly. It's the reason you aren't dead already."

"The mayor stabbed me," Annie said, voice flat.

"The mayor is an idiot."

Well, she and the Raiff both agreed about that.

"I have taken care of him," the Raiff said.

Her hand went down to her wound, finding it beneath her clothing. Her shirt and jeans would be ruined from the blood.

Why had he saved her? She had to think quickly.

He wanted to use her to stop time. If she died there would only be Miss Cornelia, who had already toughed out Raiff torture once. Annie doubted that she herself could be so strong. The Raiff probably knew that, too, she figured.

Annie looked at the Raiff's perfectly constructed face. He had a cleft chin, dimples in his cheeks, and crinkles around his eyes when he smiled. He smiled for her now, trying to be charming, Annie supposed.

She struggled to push herself up into a sitting position. She had never felt so weak.

"What did you give me to drink?" she asked. Each word was difficult to form. Her voiced sounded ragged and colder than it normally did.

He reached a hand behind her back to steady her. "My blood."

If she had been strong enough she would have lifted her

hand to her lips and covered her mouth, or thrown up, or punched the Raiff right in the nose.

She wasn't anywhere near strong enough.

She was too weak to even keep her head steady on her neck. It kept drooping forward as if she were some sort of cloth doll propped against a headboard. She could tell she was becoming stronger though, little by little. The wound in her side throbbed.

His blood, she thought, shuddering. *I have his blood*. The coldness of it reached her stomach, spread through her like a virus. It was almost exactly like the mist had shown her—only there she had been drinking from his wrist. But, the despair, the shame were the same—only it hadn't been real yet. Now, it was real.

The Raiff watched her struggle and petted her hair like she was some sort of puppy dog. A tiny corner of her brain thought it seemed nice, almost like having a mother or a father taking care of you when you're home with the flu while everyone else is having field day at school, running through the obstacle course, throwing water balloons at one another.

"What does it mean?" she asked. "What does it mean that I have your blood?"

He used his free hand to fix his hair. An unruly lock had strayed. The Raiff obviously hated anything to be out of place. Behind him one of the trolls did jumping jacks. Each leap shook the earth and made Annie cringe. The Raiff finished with his hair and then held up his hand, pointing a long, thick finger at the troll. It instantly vanished. In its place was a cockroach. The bug scuttled between the now-vacant pair of red pumps and ran off toward Canin, still lying in the snow, taking deep ragged breaths but otherwise unmoving. Annie's heart clenched to see him like that.

Why hadn't the Raiff taken care of him, too? she wondered for a brief second. She knew why. He wasn't the Stopper. He was expendable. Like Jamie. Everyone was in such danger. She had to help them somehow.

Proudly, the Raiff watched the cockroach leave. He blew on his finger the way people blow on the tip of a gun in bad movies. A flame shot out. Annie gasped and the Raiff chuckled, "Good parlor trick."

"Why did you do this?" Annie asked.

"Which *this* do you mean? Kidnap the elves? Try to manipulate the strings? Have the Queen tie you to a machine?"

"No. Yes . . . But I was asking about giving me your blood."

He scrutinized her face. "My blood saved you. Demon blood is a powerful thing. Great healing properties. Vampires and demons, even werewolves, heal much faster than humans or Stoppers. We can survive a great many things because of it. Even those vampires your friend Bloom so expertly shot today have survived. A little worse for the wear, just as you are. But they didn't die. I didn't want someone so sweet and young and determined as yourself to die yet either, at least not tonight.

So, I drained a little of it from me to save you." He showed her his wrist. He must have drained it from there into the cup. There was a small cut there, already healing. "Without it you would have died, and we couldn't have that, could we?"

He smiled a sickly sweet smile that matched his cotton-candy tone of voice. Annie met his eyes. They reflected the snow.

"Why not?" she asked, although she knew she shouldn't. She said it loudly as if she was feeling strong and brave. Her heart skipped a beat. The world seemed to freeze around them. It was her alone against a demon. Maybe it always had been. This was the destiny she had always been stuck with, the one she had been hidden away from for years. It had caught up to her. What had Megan said again? *That she would fall with evil.*

He kept on stroking her hair. "Because you are going to help me. Aren't you? You and I are going to be great friends. There's no other choice since you destroyed my machine. No other choice for either of us."

The Raiff stood, picking her up in his arms as if she were a sack of apples. He nodded into the darkness. A horse whinnied in response. Its hooves crunched through the snow. A moment later, a black stallion appeared before them. Green smoke curled out of its nostrils. Red flared in its eyes. The Raiff leaped up onto its back, seeming to float into the air. He never let go of Annie, merely sailed back down, perfectly astride the horse.

"Very impressive, aren't I?" He preened.

Leaning Annie back against him, he held her there by wrapping his arm around her. He kicked at the horse with his feet to make it move forward.

"Where are we going?" she asked him, weak and now even dizzier from the horse's movement.

His arm clenched her more tightly as they galloped into the night. "To my troops. And to your destiny."

That was exactly what Annie was afraid he was going to say.

Alone in the top of the bell tower, Jamie suddenly opened his eyes. He took a gasping breath. One inhalation. Another. Warmth filled his body— It was so warm as he stared into the darkness.

And then he remembered— *Annie. The mayor.* He rushed to the stairs and called down. "Annie?"

There was no answer.

He crept to the open window and peered into the night. It was darker than he expected, dark and evil. Vampires crossed the moon. Griffins soared by the beach. They must be gathering there.

His back itched and his shirt and coat seemed stretched to the breaking point. Something was there. He knew it. Every molecule in his body seemed to buzz, alive and waiting. He counted silently in his mind. He had to be brave. He had to see what was happening to him. Didn't he?

Yanking off his coat and shirt, he peered over his shoulder. Wings unfurled behind him. They started just by his shoulder blades and extended to the right and left. They were gold and white and black and they were . . . they were magnificent and huge and powerful. He reached his hand back over his shoulder to touch them. They were real. Feathery light beneath his fingertips, but strong, too.

His breath whooshed out of him.

They were beautiful.

They were part of him.

He couldn't believe it.

Wings.

"Am I really an angel?" he asked into the night.

He didn't even know what angels could do. What had he noticed? He could protect people. He could sort of feel things without seeing them sometimes, hear thoughts. . . . Was that it? He helped make the Queen a worm.

But angels were most often good. He knew that. In stories, angels were almost always good.

He dropped his shirt and coat on the wooden floor. He didn't need them anymore. Warmth filled him, protected him. Black lines spiraled across his arms, down to his hands, covering his skin with designs, much the way the green lines had covered Bloom's skin.

He didn't know what being an angel meant, but he liked it. He liked it a lot. It certainly seemed a million times better than being a troll.

That reminded him that Annie was out there, and so were the rest of his friends. And he knew that he couldn't really think about who or what he was anymore. He had to go help them somehow. Trolls were probably coming. The Raiff was probably coming.

Slowly, so slowly, he focused on moving one wing and then the other. They twitched and then flapped. His feet lifted up off the floor and as they did he felt so much better than he had ever felt in his entire life. How could this possibly be who he was? This beautiful being. He smiled and felt the miracle of life, and acceptance. He was James Hephaistion Alexander, angel. He had wings. He was not a troll and never would be. And he had friends, real friends that he had to take care of. He stepped out of the window into the air.

It was time to fly.

The Raiff's horse galloped straight to the cliffs that overlooked the ocean. Storming through the night, silently and quickly, the ride made Annie nauseated. Or maybe it wasn't the ride. The Raiff's actual blood was inside her. She thought about Jamie. Canin. Tala. Bloom. Eva. The elves. How could she know if they were okay?

Everything seemed absolutely hopeless.

The demon's arm circled around her, gripping her tightly, ensnaring her. Her wound throbbed hopelessly and she had to fight against falling asleep, which was normal when a body was fighting to survive. SalGoud told her that before. He was so smart and gentle. She couldn't let anything happen to him either, not to any of them.

But how could she even help?

She had demon blood inside her, really inside of her. It wasn't just that she was related to one. She had it in her, making her better, keeping her alive.

She didn't even know what she was anymore. Stopper? Demon? Both.

"No," she muttered. "I refuse. I refuse to be bad. I won't. I won't."

This, she realized, must have been how Jamie felt all those weeks he thought he might turn troll. Poor Jamie. But Aster, Bloom, they all insisted that it wasn't what was inside of you that mattered, not your species, not even your DNA, but what you did, the choices you made.

She had to make the right choices.

The Raiff whispered to the horse, which blended perfectly with the night shadows. At his words, the horse came out of his run to stand still at the top center of the cliffs. The sea pounded below them. Above them, the moon lit up the scene on the beach hundreds of feet below.

The Raiff's arm swept the horizon. "My children."

Annie looked down, expecting to see the familiar beach, the gray stones and pebbles, the dried pieces of algae that never made it back to the water. Instead, the beach teemed with dark life. Boats scattered about the shore. Orcs and trolls, werewolves, gremlins, kelpies, satyrs, and vampires stood in perfect rows, motionless. They were connected to one another. Each had a hand or a hoof or a claw on the other's shoulder. Annie had never seen anything so sinister looking, so ugly.

"What are they doing?" Annie whispered, forgetting for a moment who she was with.

The Raiff smiled. "Waiting."

"For what?"

"Us."

Annie gulped. They were waiting for her to come down there and stop time. If she touched them when she stopped . . . Then they could destroy the world. Nothing beautiful would be left, not one flower, not one tree, not one bunny. It would all be burned up, torn apart, sucked dry.

Below them, a troll suddenly shot out his foot and kicked a kelpie in the ribs. The man-horse flew through the air, knocking over several goblins in the next two lines. They in turn knocked down a group of trolls.

"This is all part of the plan, Annie," the Raiff said, voice full of hope. "First, I took Cornelia, used her as bait to get you, the young one, the strong one, the one I could give my blood to and change. I didn't think you all would escape, and I didn't think you could destroy the machine, but . . . in the end? What does it matter? You had to open the portal to get them back home. That allowed us through. My backup plan was spot-on. I might not be able to control the strings anymore, but you can, and you will, for me."

"I won't do it," Annie blurted and instantly regretted saying anything. In her veins, the Raiff's blood grew even colder as if it was punishing her for her choice.

He looked to the sky and moaned theatrically. His voice came out smooth and convincing: "Annie, these are your people. Not the goody-goodies of Aurora who are ready to scapegoat you and blame you, sacrifice you to me. Here, you will always belong. Here, you will always fit in. Wouldn't that be nice, Annie? Wouldn't that be a welcome change? I know about your life before, never feeling wanted, shuttled from one dismal hovel to another, no one loving you, no one taking the time to know you. Don't you deserve more than that, Annie? I can give you that. The whole world—it can be yours."

Annie's breath left her body in one long sigh. She didn't know what to say. Nobody had ever offered her the world before.

While the hags stayed at Cornelia's and helped nurse the elves back to strength, Bloom, Eva, and most of the town's still-healthy inhabitants set out immediately for the beach.

They knew the Raiff would cross on the ocean and gather his troops in one place to ensure that a time stop would work for all of them. A few Big Feet went with Helena to scout out the town and the forest to look for Annie, Jamie, and Canin. But they didn't hold out much hope. They tried to convince Purcee to come with them, but he refused, brandishing his saber.

"No, no. I will fight at ze beach. I will fight for my love, no matter where she is," he purred.

"Ew." Eva brandished her sword and rolled her eyes.

Bloom and Gran Pie led the citizens of Aurora, much to the chagrin of several werewolves and giants who didn't take kindly to the thought of a boy and a Big Foot being in charge.

"He's still a baby," Red Nose grumbled. "No job for a boy."

Bloom cringed from the insult, turning away and continuing to run toward the sea. Gran Pie, however, would have none of it. With a horrid growl, she lifted the giant with one hand and hissed at him. The giant gasped from the smell of her breath.

Eva had no time for insults either and bellowed, "It is a job for a friend. This elf has more courage in his piggy toe than you have in your whole immense body, giant."

Gran Pie dropped the giant into the snow with a thud. Without a second glance, she loped on, quickly catching up to the elf. Some pixies giggled as Red Nose wiped the snow out of his beard and clambered back to his feet.

"Shut up," he grumbled, running on to catch up.

They reached the sea and stopped so that the Raiff's follow-ers wouldn't hear them coming. They were at a site about a quarter mile away from the cliffs. Here, the beach met the forest. They hid behind the trees. Aelfric left them, cruising along the treetops so he wouldn't be detected, and came back with a report.

"They are there, all of them," he hissed as he landed silently between Bloom and Gran Pie. "There are hundreds lined up on the beaches, all touching. Some griffins and vampires are still joining them."

"Annie?" Bloom asked anxiously.

"She is not on the beach."

This put them in a quandary. How did they rescue the girl when they didn't know where she was?

"The Raiff?" Eva asked as the vampire gulped some milk straight out of a carton. It ran down his chin. Flying was thirsty work.

"He is not there either."

"So what do we do?" Red Nose asked, looking contrite and still a little snowy. A red carnation was stuck to his parka, tied to the zipper the way people tie on ski lift tickets. Gran Pie nodded with approval at the new deference in his tone.

Touching the toy dragon in his pocket for strength, Bloom scanned the nervous faces of the town's citizens clustered behind them. Some were hairy. Some were bare. Some were covered with fur. Some were only a couple of inches tall. All the visible ones looked angry and worried. All of them looked determined. That same determination made its home in Bloom's bones. Fear was there, to be sure, but Bloom had already lost so much to the Raiff and his supporters. He would either lose everything or nothing more. That was his choice. He took it.

"We break the lines," he said, pulling out an arrow. "We attack."

The grogans cheered and raised their silverware and said as one, "Now, yar talkin'. Ta battle!"

Up on the cliff, Annie bit her lip and shuddered. "I don't want the whole world."

The Raiff laughed at her like she was a toddler having a tantrum. "Of course you do. Everyone does."

"I only—only—want friends," she stammered. "And family."

The Raiff flicked away the thought as if he were flicking away a fly. "Humans always want friends."

"You were human once," Annie said softly.

"Once," he said, staring out at the sea. "Once I was a Captain. I was married to a woman who only wore white. I fathered the line of Stoppers that would sire you."

Her?

The night suddenly seemed much darker. His twisted interest in her made even more sense. But that meant when he killed her mom, when he tortured Miss Cornelia, that he was doing that to his own family. There was no good left in him at all. She couldn't ever be like that. She wouldn't.

Annie's voice broke, but she managed to gasp out, "Then you know. You know what it's like to need friends, people who stick by you, people who are brave for you."

"A Captain has no friends. He has his men. He commands them with fear and respect. They are much better than friends." The Raiff motioned toward the beach. "Look at them."

"That's not what I want."

He wasn't listening. "I'll give you them. I'll command them to be your friends."

Annie could hardly imagine herself exchanging girl gossip with a gremlin, or talking about books with a vampire sniffing at her neck the whole time, or working on tumbling runs with a troll.

"No one will dare touch you, dare tease you, or they will have to face me," the Raiff said coldly, and though Annie couldn't see it, she could almost imagine that the Raiff had once been hurt, too, maybe betrayed. "Such as the mayor. He hurt you and now he is nothing."

"*You* set the mayor after me. He was working for *you* and you just killed him! That's not how you treat friends." Stubborn conviction filtered into Annie's words. "And I *have* friends, real friends. I have Jamie and Eva and Bloom and SalGoud and Tala."

"A pitiful boy, a pathetic dwarf, an elf who has no idea how to be an elf, and a stone giant who quotes thoughts that are not his own. And a dog that is not a dog."

"At least they don't try to kill me."

"My blood *saved* you," the Raiff said, his voice just as fierce. "None of your new little friends saved you. They left you alone, with just that pathetic boy to protect you. Where was the beloved Miss Cornelia? Where was the little boy elf? The joke of a dwarf? The pompous giant? Hiding and safe? Or did they abandon you to the night to warn others? As if this entire town is your sole responsibility? That's what they tell you, isn't it? *The Stopper keeps the town safe. The town relies on you.* You are nothing but a tool for them. They were just using you, Annie. They don't care about you at all, just about their precious town."

"Liar!" Annie screamed, wrenching herself away from him. She caught him by surprise and broke free, slipping off the horse's back to land with a thud on the ground. The impact knocked the wind out of her.

The Raiff hurtled off the horse. His smile was wide but Annie could see the anger glittering in his eyes as he strode toward her.

"You'll hurt yourself, Annie," he said, reaching out a hand.

She refused to take it, although she knew she couldn't quite manage to stand up by herself yet.

He grabbed her arm, hoisting her up.

"Where are your friends now, Annie?" he hissed. "Safe in their little house while you have to face the dark night, wounded and alone?"

Annie closed her eyes. Her friends *would* be safe at the house, she hoped. She wanted them out of harm's way, but a little bit of her really wished that they were here to help, that she wasn't so alone.

The Raiff heard her thoughts. "I am with you. You aren't alone."

She opened her eyes. His face was horribly close. The lines of it were so straight, so strong, and it should have been beautiful, but the evil inside of him made it horrible, hard to look at, twisting the beauty into something disgusting.

"Stop time for me, Annie. Let me take you down to the beach. Join us."

"Never."

She tried to punch him, but she was too weak and too slow. He easily avoided the impact.

"You won't hit me again." He laughed. "You're brave. I admire that. Bravery is a good thing. Often inherited. Don't you want to know about your parents? Maybe meet them?"

"They're dead."

"Maybe. Maybe one isn't. Cornelia doesn't know all the things I know."

Annie gasped. "What sort of things?"

"Woof." The Raiff's eyes twinkled in the moonlight. She opened her mouth to speak, but her attention was caught by someone screaming on the beach below. Dozens of rushing figures darted across the beach toward the Raiff's creatures. An arrow shot through the air and into a kelpie's side. It screeched.

An arrow!

Annie squinted. At the point of all the runners, dashing straight down the beach, ran the lithe form of a boy. She recognized his blond hair and his graceful stride. It was Bloom! And he headed right for a gaggle of trolls and vampires and werewolves, Gran Pie racing beside him. Eva trotted at the rear of the group, grogans riding in her hair. And others . . . So many others . . . Annie's heart crashed as she counted the Raiff's forces and compared the numbers to the citizens of Aurora. Her friends would be crushed.

The Raiff's grip on her arm tightened so much that she gasped in pain. She didn't want to miss what was happening on the beach, but she glanced quickly back at him. Horns had sprouted out of his head and his eyes glowed in the horrible pale mask of his face.

"Fools. I will kill them all," he said. "Come."

He whipped her up to her feet, never letting go of her arm. Below them, the trolls and werewolves broke line and began charging toward Bloom and the good citizens of Aurora. They *would* kill them all, Annie knew. They were outnumbered. And more were coming. Trolls were thundering into Aurora, the Gnome of Protection obviously gone again somehow. Satyrs came through the portal on boats.

The people of Aurora had no chance. It would be a massacre.

From below came the unmistakable voice of the sweet, crazy werecat calling a charge, "For Annie! For ze little Time Stopper beauty! We fight! We fight!"

She swallowed and collapsed to her feet. Horrible pain shot through her stomach. Blood coursed out of her wound. The Raiff didn't let go of her arm when she fell as she'd hoped he would.

"Get up!" he hollered, but she paid no attention. Instead, she crossed her fingers and quietly whispered the word, "Stop."

It didn't work. She was too weak. Ah, she couldn't believe it.

The Raiff grabbed her hand, knowledge shining behind his now-red eyes. "Stop time."

"Never."

Did he hear her try? Did he know she couldn't? He'd kill her in an instant if he knew how useless she was.

"Don't be a fool, Annie," snarled the Raiff thing. He began to do his horrible trick of making her freeze. The icy cold feeling spread from her arm and up toward her head. She staggered backward toward the edge of the cliff. "Your mother was a fool, protecting you, fighting me. One good blast of ice took her out. She wasn't strong . . . especially when that dwarf distracted her . . . She was too busy worrying about the dwarf and looked away from me . . . and then . . . poof . . . dead . . . but your father . . . peripheral damage."

"What did you do to my father?"

"His own magic did it to him. Those Tullgrens have such silly magic. Never easy to control. Emotional fools, all of you, fools."

"What did you do to him?" she repeated, anger icing over her words.

"He did it to himself, sobbing, sobbing over your mother's loss, over you. He thought you were dead. We all thought you were dead, but no . . . Just hidden away. Fools."

"I am not a fool," she said.

"Oh. Really. Well, let me tell you . . . *you* are such a fool that you haven't even recognized your own father. None of you have. Right here all the time in front of everyone's noses. I saw him though, watched as his sorrow turned him into a dog. He turned into a white, furry, foolish, emotional dog."

Her father? Was Tala?

Her heart surged with love. He'd found her. Her father had found her at the Wiegles' after all that time. He had never given up hope.

The Raiff laughed as a screech shook the air and a milk-drinking vampire from Aurora appeared in the sky just feet above them. The vampire dived toward the Raiff, who let go of Annie for a moment to ward off the attack. A black streak of ice shot out of his finger and struck the vampire in the chest, causing it to wheel backward, head over heels.

Coming from behind one of the trolls, Megan was running toward them, hair flying out behind her like a beautiful supermodel filming some sort of romantic movie scene, but nothing was romantic here.

"Annie! Get away from him!" she screamed. "Annie! The prophecy! Be careful!"

Annie sprang away from the Raiff as best she could, stumbling a bit more toward the cliff edge, but the Raiff lunged after her, screaming. He knocked her down, her head and shoulders and a good part of her chest hung over the ledge. She could see straight down into the battle. Her eyes found Bloom. He swung his sword at some orcs circled around him. His mouth shouted her name.

The prophecy.

Megan reminded her. What had it been? *That she would fall with evil.* Her own grandfather thought the same. He had drawn this very thing, hadn't he? Drawn her death.

We must not lose, she thought. *We must not.*

But she had no real hope, at least not for herself.

Twisting around she clawed at the Raiff's hideous face.

He laughed. "You can't hurt me, Annie."

Megan screamed Annie's name. "Don't do it! Annie! No!"

Annie thought of Jamie, Bloom, and of Aurora. With the

Raiff around no one would be safe even if they had a Time Stopper who could actually stop time when they needed to. There was nothing else for her to do. Twisting toward him, she grabbed the Raiff around the shoulders and pushed off a rock with her legs as hard as she could, shoving them both over the cliff on which they'd been so precariously hanging. Then they began to fall, and Megan screamed after them.

But it was too late.

Annie grabbed onto evil and fell.

The Battle

Chaos engulfed everyone on the Aurora beach. Screams filled the air. The stomping feet of giants and trolls thundered across the stones, sea glass, and driftwood. Pixies, fairies, and grogans hacked and stabbed their tiny weapons into anything and everything bad, before buzzing away, or in the case of the grogans, vanishing. It looked hopeless.

Bloom shot an arrow directly at a vampire swooping down to bite Gran Pie. The Big Foot roared her thanks and immediately hoisted a goblin above her head, tossing him into the ocean with a resounding splash.

"Everyone watch out!" Mr. Nate screamed as Helena lobbed several Sugary Sticky Spells at the nearest orcs. Caramelized sugar and molasses stuck to the monsters' skin and armor. Within moments, they were desperately trying to lick their way out of their predicament.

"That will give them a nice bellyache," Helena said, sounding slightly satisfied as she sent another pulse of Sugary Sticky Spells at some trolls lumbering toward them.

The air rippled again. White powder swirled around them, coating everyone.

"Oops . . . ," Helena said. "That was not what I planned."

Eva stuck out her tongue and licked her cheek. "Flour!? Ugh."

The air exploded. The creatures on the beach flew backward, slamming into one another and other bodies. Above them, someone screamed, falling to their death. That someone was Annie.

Attention caught, everyone gaped up toward the cliff as Annie and the Raiff plummeted toward the beach, bright light filling the air. The light disappeared completely. For a moment, everything went quiet and dark and then the world zipped back into focus again.

———

Bloom clutched his bow as he sailed rearward, not letting go, mind racing, trying to figure out what had happened. He landed with a thud in a jumble of troll limbs and orc body parts. Someone was whimpering. Half-buried, Bloom started to climb out from the wreckage. Something huge and terrible had happened. That wasn't one of Helena's magic spells. He knew it. It was something much more powerful.

The scream.

Annie.

He craned his neck up to see his best friend falling through the sky, clutching a demon. And then the demon let go of her.

Annie, who was afraid of heights . . .

Annie, who was one of his best friends . . .

Annie was tumbling to the ground faster than he could save her.

The last elf finally extricated himself from the debris and gasped. There was nothing, absolutely nothing he could do.

Annie had heard that when you fall, your life flashes before your eyes. That wasn't how it was for her. She didn't see images from her sad and lonely past. She didn't see the smiles of the people she now loved, feel their arms wrapped around her in a final hug. She saw nothing except the Raiff's wicked face, his glowing eyes, and waxen features. She saw the way his snakelike tongue in the middle of his mouth curled up while he screamed.

He threw her off him as they fell down and down.

Warmth instantly returned to Annie's body. She almost

smiled as she streaked through the air. It was so good to be warm.

She wasn't afraid of heights anymore. She wasn't even afraid of death. She was just afraid of the Raiff winning, of her friends getting hurt, of all of this being for nothing.

"Fight him!" she screamed. "Fight!"

Below them, the two sides shrieked and shouted in deadly combat. Annie couldn't imagine the fairies or pixies fighting the creatures of the dark and hated to think of it—Bloom facing the beasts that had taken away his parents, Jamie and Canin hurt and alone, failing Miss Cornelia. She would be no help to any of them now.

She knew she had to die. That way the Raiff couldn't use her. She pulled in her breath and a quiet ache filled her chest. But perhaps the Raiff would die as well, and Bloom, Eva, and SalGoud would survive. They could gallivant throughout the forest without worrying about evil demon things taking their joy away, the way the trolls took away the elves. Tala could nuzzle Miss Cornelia by the fire, a basket of dog treats by his side. A great sob left her and she thought of Grady O'Grady, of his kindness. She would miss them all.

And Jamie.

She was leaving Jamie when she'd promised to always be there for him, to always be his friend. That was what hurt the most. She was abandoning him, breaking her promise. She hoped he would understand, poor Jamie.

And then like a miracle he was there, right there, swooping beneath her, huge wings unfurled and magnificent. Massive feathery appendages extended from his naked back, black and gold and white feathers that moved with purpose. His dark skin glowed golden, laced with coils, and warmth radiated out from him even as he smiled at her. He seemed more solid and less solid all at once. He wasn't too skinny anymore, but just right. His face when he looked at her was full of concern and joy. She'd never seen anyone so beautiful in her entire life and he was alive, and not a troll, and not hurt.

"Jamie!" His name was half scream and half sob as it burst from her.

He caught her in his arms. The impact threw him a bit off course but he righted them.

"Annie . . . Annie . . . I've got you . . . I think . . . This flying is a bit . . . I'm not quite sure how to steer. Hold on . . ." He stopped flying and simply levitated there, above the battle, holding her. His face twisted. "You're freezing. You're almost blue . . . What . . . What have they done to you?"

"Demon blood. Phurba wound. Bad things." She clutched him and then said, "We need to help them. We need . . . You're beautiful, Jamie. I mean, you've always been beautiful but now it's like the good inside of you is making you glow. And you're warm. I mean, it's crazy how warm you are."

"I think I'm an angel. Officially," he admitted, soaring

toward the beach, zigzagging a bit and going off course before righting them. "It's pretty cool."

"We have to help everyone," Annie said, motioning toward their friends. Jamie landed them both near Bloom, who was crying out orders. Hundreds of the Raiff's troops were filling the beach and the people of Aurora didn't seem like any match for their numbers. Fights were going on everywhere. On the beach. In the sky. Even in the water.

"No trolls in my woods, not on my mountain, not on my beach!" Gran Pie hurtled boulders, one after another, at a group of trolls heading toward some dwarfs.

Eva screamed and thundered after trolls with her ax. "Nobody's hurting my people!"

Bloom shot arrows, frantically yelling for Annie and commanding the others. "The Raiff?"

"He fell with me," Annie said, looking to Jamie, whose wings were folding into his back. His glow faded. "He might be dead. I don't know. I only survived because Jamie caught me."

A nearby orc laughed, obviously exhilarated by the fight. A werewolf vaulted into a mass of trolls. Using a long spatula as if it were a baseball bat, Helena hit biscuits into the air and told Mr. Nate to watch her back.

"Always, my dear," he said. He yanked her down to avoid a vampire hurtling toward them.

Bloom took a moment to turn to Annie and Jamie. "Is the Raiff gone? Gone gone?"

He is not gone . . .

The voice in their heads came from behind them and Jamie pivoted to face the dragon Grady O'Grady.

"Grady! You're back!" Annie sighed with delight and relief. "Please . . . Please help us."

Of course. Sorry for the delay. I'd been held up by a Tarasque. Nasty buggers. Grady lifted to the air and blitzed the Raiff's forces with small well-aimed fireballs. They popped out of his mouth one after another.

"About time, dragon!" an exhausted Gran Pie yelled. A cheer swelled among the residents of Aurora even as Gran Pie muttered, "Dragons, always so late, always such show-offs."

The appearance of the dragon caused instant pandemonium among the Raiff's followers. The vampires soared away and the rest scattered toward the woods. The trolls shrieked the entire time, pulling at their wigs and tripping over one another to get away. The satyrs shook their fists and made a show of it for a moment, but then they, too, fled. The citizens of Aurora streamed after them with their swords and forks and sticks upraised. Now that she was so much closer, Annie could see that the fairies and pixies held swords the size of toothpicks. But they also seemed to be able to shoot little balls of light at the evildoers. When they hit a target the light balls transformed into dozens of angry stinging hornets. Grady O'Grady roared in triumph at the destruction they'd caused, and below them Bloom pumped his fist into the air.

"We won, Annie!" he screamed. "We won!"

Eva was stomping around in a circle-dance shouting, "Who wants my ax? Who wants to sing my glory?"

Her father was roaring in happiness. Jamie smiled down at her.

Annie grinned back and lifted her hand to wave to Bloom, but she was still so shaky and frail that it was hard to move, and she was worried still about so many things.

The Raiff? Annie asked Grady O'Grady with her mind. She was having a hard time forming her thoughts now. Her clothes were wet with new blood.

I can't find him.

Dead?

How do you kill the already dead, Annie?

Annie clutched Jamie, but it was hard for her to even hold on.

"You're so weak, Annie," he said. He swallowed hard. One of his wings folded out and in. "I don't think it's over."

"No. It's like a lull before a storm, I think. Can you protect them, Jamie?" she whispered. "Could you do that for me?"

"I think so . . . Maybe . . ." Jamie focused on his love, on the way Helena fed him and Cornelia took him in, on how Mr. Nate helped him escape his grandparents, and his friends put their lives on the line for him again and again. The love poured out of him in a golden light dabbled with specks of blackness, swirling through the air and toward the still-fighting residents of Aurora.

"Protect them," he whispered, "Protect."

Jamie scanned the landscape for any signs of the Raiff. There were none.

On the beach, all of Miss Cornelia's carefully handed-out flowers that had fallen during the battle shot up out of the stones and sand, attaching green stems and leaves to the earth. Then they began to multiply, becoming a fragrant field of yellow and red, blue and orange, purple and pink. Life returned even in the midst of a battle, even in the midst of night.

"How long will it last? The protection?" Annie asked as the green markings on her skin flared and then vanished.

"I don't know. I've . . . I don't know what I can actually do, Annie, or how long it will last."

Annie's head lolled a bit to the side. She was so exhausted. It was hard to keep her knees from buckling. Pain rippled through her stomach. "I wish it could last forever."

Grady O'Grady had flown off toward the ocean and the portal. They weren't sure what he was chasing after. Up the beach, from the town's side, Miss Cornelia and Doris ran forward to join them. Megan clambered down the cliff trail. Jamie's heart surged to see them. It must be safe now. They must really have won if Cornelia left the house. He started to lead Annie toward them, high stepping past hundreds of jellyfish and lobsters.

Suddenly, a ripple of darkness blasted forward from the

ocean and consumed all of them. The air exploded. Annie and Jamie flew off their feet. Jamie lost Annie's hand. He scrambled up as soon as his body hit the hard sand and sea stones, crumpling so many flowers. Where was she? What had happened? He had to find her.

The world seemed to end. Silence ruled, a horrible, ghastly lack of noise. Then sound rushed back to his ears. People and creatures staggered back to their feet, paws, and claws. Monsters crawled forward, scuttling to attack.

Annie . . . Jamie found her, crumpled up in some flowers and algae, on top of something large and unmoving. She was glowing green from his protection, much like the rest of the townspeople. And there . . . Standing on the beach was the Raiff, demon eyes cold.

Jamie's brain couldn't figure it out. Bloom and Eva were on the beach far behind him. SalGoud was nowhere in sight. Cornelia . . . Cornelia and Doris helped each other to stand. They appeared unharmed. Nobody had died. Not one. Relief flooded through him. He'd protected them somehow, with his last spell.

As he started toward Annie, a body blew past him. A banshee.

The Raiff's voice echoed through the darkness. "You must know that you can't get rid of me that easily."

The demon laughed, wicked and cruel.

Jamie clambered over to Annie, who was lying on top of a dead troll. An arm fell out of the sky and thudded onto some driftwood next to them. Jamie looked away, focusing on the Raiff. "*You* are evil."

"And?" He laughed again, obviously thrilled with the death and destruction around him and then cursed, stretching out his arms. "Are you ready to die, angel?"

Pandemonium occurred on the beach. The Raiff pointed at the chaos. "Hold on. I need a moment to gloat. All my plans have been so perfect. Plus, now I get to kill an angel. I've never done that before."

"Fall in!" Bloom yelled, his voice rising over all other voices. "Your flanks. Guard your flanks."

Crabs and lobsters suddenly spewed out of the ocean, turning over in the tide and then scuttling up onto the beach. Rats poured out of the woods. Bats clambered out of the holes in the cliffs.

"My beautiful friends," the Raiff said, eyes bulging. He coughed.

Was that a sign of weakness? Jamie dared not hope so.

"Hold on. I'll be right back. I have something to attend to." The Raiff disappeared in a swirl of red smoke.

Jamie lifted Annie up off the ground and tried to find where the Raiff's voice was coming from. It seemed like everywhere.

"Annie," he whispered into her ear. "I need you. We need you. The Raiff has brought even more backup."

Annie blinked hard, trying to focus, and finally truly opened her eyes. Two huge human-looking warriors stood behind Jamie. One was golden-haired and smelled somehow of olive oil. The other was handsome with short cropped hair. They wore white cloth garments that wrapped their muscular frames.

"Who are you?" she whispered.

"Hephaistion," said the tall one. "And this is Alexander."

"What?" Jamie asked, looking completely confused.

"Behind you, Jamie. There are two warriors behind you." She paused. "They are sort of transparent. Are you here to help us?"

"Warriors?" Jamie turned quickly. "Where?"

"They are wearing togas. Oh, maybe they're ghosts . . ." Annie's head lolled back on her neck. "They say they are Alexander and Hephaistion. They will help make you strong. Oh. Yep. They are definitely dead."

"Annie . . . You aren't talking sense. That's my last name and my middle name."

Annie's head righted itself. She opened her eyes again, insisting, "They are *right there*, Jamie. I'm sorry you can't see them."

The golden-haired one said, "We are his bodyguards, now that he has turned angel. We are . . . tell him we love him. Tell him we are only here at the most dire of need. Tell him we are proud of him."

"They are like your angel bodyguards or something." She gasped. "They love you very much."

Alexander, the golden-haired one, stabbed a vampire swooping out of the sky, vaulting up and hitting it directly in the heart.

Annie gasped again. "Whoa. Can you seriously not see that? One of them just stabbed that vampire."

"What vampire?" Jamie looked around, seeing nothing.

Annie pointed to the ground. There was a vampire with an ancient Macedonian dagger sticking out of his chest. The dagger vanished even as Annie pointed. "It doesn't matter."

"We have his back, Stopper," said Hephaistion, kicking at a banshee who was slithering along the beach. "Take care of him when we are gone again. And fight the demon. The power is in being together."

Annie nodded, trying to understand exactly what the ghost warrior was saying. He was so unlike any ghosts she'd met before—so much stronger and solid and capable. She searched Jamie's confused face and said, "Look, bring me closer. I need to talk to Cornelia. I don't . . . I don't know how to fight him, but your angel ghost bodyguard friends say we have to do it together. Okay?"

Against his better wishes, Jamie brought Annie toward the demon, who had returned and now stood there, smiling at the death and slaughter going on all around him. Miss

Cornelia bid them closer and then grabbed Annie in her arms for a quick hug. "What has he done to you?"

"He saved me from the mayor, made me drink his blood." Annie made a retching sound. "I'm a demon now."

"You will never be a demon! Don't be silly, especially not now. You wouldn't be so cold and dying if you were a demon. You're a girl, Annie. A Stopper. That is all. To become a demon, your heart has to fill with hate, smolder with it until it twists you into something evil. You have far too much love inside of you for that to ever happen." Cornelia hugged Annie to her and then passed her back to Jamie. "We're going to have to fight now, Annie. Are you up for it?"

Gramma Doris threw her hands up in disgust. "She's half-dead, Cornelia! How can you even ask her?"

"Because without her, we are all dead." Cornelia steeled her face.

Annie felt as though the entire world had slowed down, as if everything and everyone had to be focused on, to be remembered in case they died. No. They must not die.

"I'm ready." Annie leaned back on Jamie, but she felt a bit more solid as the Raiff began to launch ice balls toward them. Jamie's angel bodyguards burst that ice into pieces.

"Well . . ." Cornelia smiled at Jamie. "It appears we have an angel with us with some ghostly angel bodyguards."

Before anyone could respond, a massive scream came from the top of the cliffs. Despite his injuries, a very much alive Canin was throwing a vampire over the side and yelling at it. The distraction was enough for more trolls to come thundering across the beach.

"Aurora is threatened. All fight! All! We have a duty to protect our town and one another!" Bloom yelled, motioning for the others to join him. "Do not retreat!"

The sky filled with black feathers, one after another after another, completely obscuring the moon, the stars, the light of the world outside Aurora.

Miss Cornelia gasped. "Stand ready, Annie . . ."

"For what?"

"We cannot defeat the demon he has become," Cornelia said, ripping off one of her rainbow skirt layers and tying it around a wound on Doris's arm. "Our only hope is to turn him back into the man he used to be." Something howled in the distance and Cornelia flinched. "By Apollo's light, was that a Bugaboo?"

"Miss Cornelia . . . ? What do I do?" Annie asked, wobbling unsteadily as lobsters attacked her toes. Helena growled, clicked her fingers, and dozens of large silver pots fell upside down on the crustaceans, trapping them.

"Well done, Helena. Annie . . . you must reach toward the strings. They are beyond that . . . the darkness he uses to cover it . . . Reach for them, embrace the good and the love inside of them. Cast out the coldness that threatens your heart, Annie. Give into the warmth," Miss Cornelia said. She stiffened.

The Raiff walked out of the cliffs. He had chained Grady O'Grady's wings together and muzzled the dragon's mouth so he couldn't spit out fireballs.

There was a roar of excitement from the Raiff's minions. Annie gasped.

"Stay strong, Annie," Jamie said as the lobsters clattered in the pots and the evil werewolves began a cheering howl that whisked into the wind.

"He's got the dragon!" People murmured and feinted. Some ran away again, but quickly scuttled back, shrieking that trolls were coming. Eva and SalGoud rushed over, smashing past the flowers and lobster pot traps. Gramma Doris yanked off her apron and surged forward, running as fast as her little legs could take her.

There was no other way but to fight. She had to do something. Annie lifted her hands and long lines of gold light, ribbons of them, reached up into the blackness of the sky, and as she lifted her hands, so, too, did Miss Cornelia. Gold billowed into the starlight. It was so beautiful and warm, the opposite of how Annie felt inside.

Jamie held Annie up, supporting her arms with his own.

"She can't do this much longer," he said. "Miss Cornelia . . ."

"Hold steady," said the older woman. "Here come the trolls, not the ones from the Badlands, but locals. The Gnome of Protection has completely failed or it was stolen again—"

Eva groaned. "Not more trolls! No! Not . . ."

"You can do this, Eva," SalGoud murmured. "You have faced them before."

"I'll distract . . . I'll . . ." Eva's knees shook and her face paled. "I can't . . . I won't . . ."

A small man roared onto the field, next to Eva. "I believe in you, lass. You will not fail."

Her father hip checked her and Eva lifted her ax as the giant trolls marched onto the beach, thundering closer and closer to them.

"Hold steady, lass."

Heavy feet cracked the driftwood.

The trolls marched closer and closer.

"You've got this," Eva's dad bellowed. "Got this . . ."

Above them, swooping through the portal were the Saltas, ready to strike. Satyrs and kelpies had also returned, galloping toward the fighters of Aurora.

"Ya have faced trolls, and Bugaboos, crow monsters, and the heavy burden of emotion spells. Ya have tarried with vampires and Saltas and wee devils, ya have, my lass." Eva's father raised his own ax to the sky and began to run toward the trolls. "We will protect the Stoppers at all costs. Run! Fight! Fight!"

Her father's words hit home.

"I have, haven't I?" Eva said more quietly than she had ever spoken before.

The grogans materialized all around her, sitting in flowers, her hair, standing on her shoulders.

"You're a mighty warrior, lass," announced Bench of John. "And we're proud to both fight and barbeque with ya! To many barbeques to celebrate our battle!"

"Ta barbeques and Eva!" the rest of the grogans yelled.

Eva raised her ax even higher and roared, slamming her fists into her chest before thundering after her father, heading directly for the line of trolls. "All charge! I am Eva Beryl-Axe. Join me and they will sing of our victory for centuries."

Ghosts materialized on the beach, one after another after another. They shrieked and rushed forward, attacking a new group of the undead that had also materialized. They looked like pirates and murderers, soldiers and demons. The vagabond ghosts of Aurora shouted a rallying cry and lunged forward, weapons of all sorts in their semi-transparent hands. Tears stained the cheeks of Chloe, one of the youngest ghosts.

"They shouldn't have to fight." The wrongness of it all overtook Annie. Here were innocents, ghosts, sweet pixies, mermen even. And they all had to fight to stay alive. They shouldn't have to do that. The wrongness of it overwhelmed her. None of the citizens of Aurora were perfect, but they were good . . . so good . . . How could they have to face this?

"Think of love, Annie, of goodness," Miss Cornelia called. She slumped a little from the exertion. "We can do this together."

Annie kissed Jamie's cheek. She thought of Miss Cornelia and her friends. She wondered if the Raiff really did know anything about her mother and father and if part of why the Raiff was so evil was because he missed this place so much.

And then out from the darkness came the mayor. He was wounded, and covered in dog bites. In his arms was Tala.

"I found your puppy, Annie." He smiled.

"No! You were dead! The Raiff said he killed you!" Annie shuddered.

"He lied." The mayor shrugged. "But honestly, everyone underestimates the strength of giants. We look dead. We seem dead. We aren't dead." He winked. "Did you want that hug now, Annie? Or wait until later? As you can see"—he lifted Tala up a bit—"my arms are full."

"Don't hurt him!" Annie yelled and with a horrifying shudder, a massive ice ball emerged from her hands, spiraling out toward the giant that held Tala's limp form in his talons. The ball hit the mayor's left leg at the knee, just as he was thrown sideways by an angry SalGoud who had launched himself at a full running tackle. The impact threw Tala into the cliff's side and the dog struggled back up. Then, with a roar of quotes about fighting being wrong, SalGoud thrust the mayor backward again, rolling with him down the beach.

"Not my stone giant, you pompous windbag!" Eva bellowed, running after them. She waved her ax through the air and banged past one troll and another, one vampire and then a kelpie, until she got to the two of them. She grabbed the mayor by his arm and heaved him off SalGoud. At the exact same time, hundreds of seagulls surged out of the holes in the cliff, joined by crows sweeping in over the horizon, and they all soared after the mayor, ripping him from Eva's grip and tormenting him as he screamed.

"He's still alive!" Eva yelled.

Ice formed on Annie's fingertips and vaulted toward the mayor, wrapping him in a giant block of ice. The birds pecked at it, harder and harder, until it broke into a million pieces. There was nothing left of the mayor—just fragments of ice and stone.

The screaming stopped.

"The mayor is dead!" Eva yelled. "For real this time!"

Fighters lost their lines. All was chaos.

The trolls, the remaining ones, surged forward, closer and closer to the Stoppers. Lights burst and dimmed. Screams rattled the beach. Monsters reared and charged and broke fairies in two. A bad vampire hunkered over the lifeless form of Tasha from the tavern, and Purcee left his post behind Annie to try to get him off.

"We're losing," Annie whispered. Attacking the mayor made her feel weaker than ever.

Jamie held on to her tightly, trying to keep her standing. "We can do this, Annie. You can."

"Jamie." Cornelia's voice was hoarse and desperate. "I

know you've only just become an angel, but what angels do is protect. Keep using that."

The Raiff hissed.

"Your powers are weak. Your body is weak," he said, taunting the Stopper. "You could never be as strong as me."

"You will not hurt our town or these children again!" Miss Cornelia commanded, arms raised up and toward him.

The Raiff lifted his finger. A tiny ball of ice exploded out of it, flew up into the sky. He moved sideways. The ice ball did as well. It took the shape of a woman that looked remarkably like Annie.

"Remember her?" he jeered. "Your precious daughter? You couldn't protect her either. Your time is over, you old waste of a witch."

The ice woman exploded. Shards flew in every direction. One long, thin blade of ice struck Miss Cornelia in the stomach. Cornelia collapsed. Gramma Doris and Helena screeched, rushing up to catch her, but they were too late.

Helena stood, hands outstretched toward the Raiff. "You killed my best friend many years ago. It's time you pay, demon."

A swirling tornado of sugar sprang from Helena's hands.

"And you just tried to kill *my* best friend! No pie for you!" Doris roared.

Doris shook a giant frying pan, and sent it soaring,

lofting it through the sugar, toward the Raiff. It knocked him on the side of the head, but he didn't fall over.

"Now, Annie! While he's distracted!" Jamie yelled. "Make him a man again."

"But how?"

Behind them, many trolls had already broken through the ranks of fairies, dwarfs, good vampires, and werewolves that had been trying to keep them from getting to the Stoppers. The trolls sped across the beach; screams echoed up on the cliffs; trees fell in the forest. Blasts of magic echoed across the air. A werewolf plummeted off the cliff as Jamie propped Annie up against him again. His arm held her arm outstretched, his fingers circling her wrist.

Coldness engulfed her anyway. She was so weak. She thought she heard someone calling her name. She couldn't tell who it was. Everything was focused on what Miss Cornelia said, warmth, love. She had to fight the Raiff's badness. She had to.

But how?

Miss Cornelia had already been overcome.

Looking around, quickly, so as not to be distracted the way her mother once was, Annie searched for Bloom. He was there on the shore's edge, bow out, rushing toward her, sprinting alongside the trolls, trying to get to her and Jamie. Then a million bats and feathers tumbled from the sky, swooping around him.

"No!" Annie yelled. "No! Don't hurt him!"

She forgot the Raiff. She forgot how weak she was and instead, tried to sprint toward Bloom and the darkness surrounding him. Jamie lost his hold and she tumbled to the ground, crawling forward, scuttling through hundreds of crabs who were all trying to join in on the action.

"Annie!" Jamie lunged after her, but he wasn't quick enough. She lifted into the sky, just a few feet and dangled there, caught up in a swirl of dark Raiff magic. He peeled back to stare at the Raiff. The demon's arms were outstretched and he was completely focused on Annie. He tossed her to the ground and lifted her back up, slamming her down again and again.

"No!" The bellow came low and to the right. Eva sprang forward, and rushed at the demon's left side, knocking him over for a moment. Annie tumbled to the ground again and Jamie wasn't sure which way to go, which friend to help. Grady O'Grady stomped on the ground, helpless and unable to fire or fly.

They all needed to help one another.

"SalGoud!" Jamie ordered. "Free Bloom from the bats. I'll get Annie. Once Bloom is free, help Eva."

The Raiff roared, trying to toss off the dwarf who was clinging to his back.

The distraction was enough for Jamie to get to Annie. There was blood coming from her ear and he screamed inside. She looked . . . dead.

"Annie!" He gasped, lifting her trunk up off the sand.

Her eyes fluttered and she whispered his name, "Jamie. Did we win?"

"Um . . . No . . . not yet." He couldn't lie even as her eyes fluttered shut again.

"We need to use our power together," she whispered.

"But how? You're so weak . . ."

"With her friends she is strong," Bloom said. There were crow feathers stuck in his hair and some pieces of bat wings on his cloak. He helped Jamie to lift her and the two of them supported her enough so that she could stand in between them.

The Woman in White materialized behind them and said, "I have your backs, children. Keep the ladies protecting Corny."

Gramma Doris and Helena both stood on either side of Miss Cornelia. They had their hands outstretched and dangerous looks on their faces as they tried to ward off any bad monsters and the Raiff's magic blasts of ice shards and balls. Sugar and flour and doughnuts flew everywhere, all at crazy angles. Loaves of bread clobbered trolls in their heads. Pies smacked them in the face, both blinding them and distracting them with the delightful taste. It was enough for the moment, but it wouldn't last.

"Now!" Eva yelled as the Raiff tried to buck her off his back. "Do something now!"

Jamie and Bloom both stood up straighter, each lifting one of Annie's arms.

"We do this together," Bloom shouted.

And Annie's eyes opened.

"I love you," she said.

Nobody knew who she was saying it to. Jamie? Bloom? Tala? The world?

Awake and moving again, Tala bounded toward them and the Raiff. Tala. He was her father. Her dad turned dog by all his sorrow. No. That wasn't fair. None of this was fair or right. She had to fix it. How horrible it must be to be Tala. How horrible it must be to be the Raiff.

"I love you," she mumbled again, a bit louder. "You poor, poor demon. You are so sad inside, aren't you? So full of hate."

The world blurred around her.

Eva yelled and tumbled from the Raiff's back, landing with a heavy "oomph" on the beach stones.

The Raiff stood up even taller and straighter than normal. He seemed energized and bursting with hate.

"How dare you?" He pointed at Annie and the boys, but then turned to Eva. "How dare you?"

Behind him, SalGoud freed Grady's wings.

The dragon took a step forward, closer to the Raiff. And knocked him over with a wing.

"I am powerful and mighty." The Raiff lay on the ground,

the dragon stepping just hard enough on his chest to keep him from standing up. Eva rushed forward and sat on the demon's free arm, keeping him from casting any ice. "This town, these people. They are mine. They will always be mine!"

"People don't belong to other people," SalGoud announced over the hubbub. "This is not a quote. This is me. People don't belong to other people. People's greatest gift is love."

"It is," Annie said, feeling loved, finally, truly, as the still-injured Tala stood in front of her howling, as Jamie and Bloom held her hands. "That's what winning is. It isn't about being mighty or being the boss of everything. It's about love."

"Together!" Bloom shouted and the three of them glowed, beautiful and warm. Happiness. What they had to focus on was happiness. Not fear. Not anger or hate, but the victory song of friendship and goodness. The glowing light of them grew bigger, but it wasn't enough.

"Eva! SalGoud! Canin! Everyone!" Bloom hollered. "Come. Come quickly. We need to work together."

The grogans took charge of keeping the Raiff's arm down and SalGoud and Eva rushed to them, quickly followed by Helena, Canin, and Mr. Nate. Doris stayed in front of Miss Cornelia's still form, protecting her.

"What do we do?" Eva yelled, stashing her ax in her belt.

"Think happy thoughts full of love," Jamie said, which quickly made Eva throw her hands up in the air, disgusted.

"Really, Eva. Do it," Jamie insisted just as another girl rushed to them.

Megan.

"Let me hold Annie," she said, perfect hair blowing perfectly in the wind. "Think of your teddy bear, Eva."

"I don't have—" Eva started to protest.

"We all know you do," Megan snapped, adjusting her grip on Annie. "We all have things we love. Focus on them. Now. Like Jamie said."

Somewhere in the distance, a dwarf screamed.

"Love and happiness," Jamie said quietly, even as the Raiff's hand whipped up into the air, throwing off the grogans. His fingers formed more deadly shards of ice. They launched.

"Stand steady!" Eva roared and then started muttering, "Love and happiness. Teddy. Love and happiness."

Something moved through Annie's body, resonating and glorious. It was like she was one of the strings, perfect, powerful, and good—oh so good. Did the others feel it, too? Rainbows and moonbeams appeared all around them. The beach had become some sort of golden fairytale. Even the most obliterated flowers sprang back to life. The lobsters, crabs, and spiders, the bats and jellyfish started to return to where they came from. But the flowers . . . the people left fighting . . . they glowed like perfect images of themselves.

Everything was beautiful.

The Raiff's ice shards exploded into a hundred flower petals and drifted harmlessly to the sand and the sea-buffed rocks.

"I love you," Annie whispered as Jamie, Megan, and Bloom held her up. "Really, I love everything in this beautiful world."

"No! Not me! I am not loved. I am winning. I am . . ." The Raiff fell to the ground. A man. His horns were gone.

"Not my horns!" He bent at the waist and the knees, shivering, his skin a ghastly color.

"What's happening?" Eva bellowed. "How are we defeating him?"

"Love. Goodness. The usual things." SalGoud smiled.

But Annie . . . Annie was still focusing all of her emotion on the Raiff. That was part of the Tullgren magic—emotions, the ability to love, the ability to feel so much for others that you transform yourself into a dog, the ability to understand why people and demons do the things they do.

The Raiff shuddered. "Do not love me! I don't deserve it."

"I have to love you," Annie said, standing her ground. "There is no other choice I want. I never want my heart to hurt like yours, to fill with hate. So I choose love. I love you, great-grandfather. I love you."

As she said this, the Raiff seemed to shrink into himself. He smalled down. The power that had been so monstrous lessened into something you could barely perceive. He seemed . . . He seemed . . . ordinary. He collapsed on a pile of mussel shells.

Annie gasped. "Is he . . . ?"

"No," Bloom whispered, still holding her steady. "He's just . . . He has no magic."

The Woman in White squealed and appeared by Miss Cornelia's side even as the old Time Stopper began to sit up. "My Captain! It's my Captain!"

She abandoned Miss Cornelia to Gramma Doris and Helena and flew straight to the Raiff, picking his limp body up in her arms. "You have returned to me! I knew you would! Silly demon, keeping you away like that." She began to plant enthusiastic kisses on his nose and forehead, and tweaked his ear with her finger. "I thought you'd never come home."

Her expression took a stern turn. "You have been so naughty! SO NAUGHTY! If I were living, I would just . . . Oh . . . You have put this family through a lot, mister, and you are not going to get off easily, let me tell you. I died waiting for you to come back and bring me some of that tropical fruit you always talked about! And then when you finally return, I'm dead and you're this . . . this . . . demon. That's pretty unforgivable even for the best of wives, mister. You are just . . . Oh. You are in so much trouble."

She twirled around, a frenzy of angry ghost and betrayed wife. Her face turned solid white and then green with rage before it softened again.

"Woman in White!" Miss Cornelia's hands went to her sides. "You are to bring him right to Plutarch, the scorpion man, and keep him in the oubliette. Do you hear me?"

The Woman in White whirled around. "But he isn't dangerous anymore."

"I mean it!" Miss Cornelia shouted. "Grady O'Grady, go with her."

Thomas Fylbrigg, the once-headless ghost and co-founder of Aurora, appeared, smiling. He gave Jamie a wave and hopped on Grady's back. "We'll make sure he gets there."

And with that, the Woman in White lifted the motionless Raiff up into the air with him and flew straight up, over the cliffs, not even looking back.

SalGoud unsnapped Grady O'Grady's muzzle and the dragon roared, quickly following the ghost and the former demon. *We shall see that they get there. And that he stays there.*

The ghosts of Alexander and Hephaistion appeared in the air next to the Woman in White and Alexander said solemnly, "As will we."

Jamie's head whipped up. "I see you now. How do I only see you now?"

"Because you finally believe, sweet boy." Hephaistion cast a blessing upon Jamie.

Jamie's face was puzzled. "In ghosts? I've always believed in ghosts. Well, I mean I have since I've been here."

"No, Jamie. Hephaistion meant in yourself. You finally believe in yourself and your destiny and since we are part of that, you can see us." And with that, Alexander and Hephaistion whisked after the Woman in White and her prisoner. "And we are angel ghosts. Not just ghosts. There's a difference!"

Grady O'Grady flapped his wings and began tossing fireballs at the remains of the Raiff's troops even as he followed the Woman in White. The Raiff's troops screamed and cowered and glared, shaking fists and wings and paws as they ran.

Eva wiped her ax on her pants. "Purcee! Grogans! Join me! Let's rid this town of the remaining pestilence."

"But of course!" the cat man declared as the grogans materialized in his fur, waving knives and forks and possibly a spoon.

Meanwhile, Mr. Nate helped Miss Cornelia into a standing position.

"Annie?" She stared over at Annie who was trying to remain standing with Bloom and Jamie's help. Megan was tending to SalGoud's wounds.

Annie gave a tiny wave and fell forward, landing on top of Tala, who had come loping back.

"Daddy?" she whispered.

He gave a tired woof and nuzzled her face before wrapping a paw around her.

She wasn't sure what had happened. She just knew she

wasn't cold. She wondered if the Raiff really *was* just a man now, and what that meant. Was it finally all over? Were they safe? The town? Her friends? Her . . . her . . . family? She needed to know, but she was so tired. She closed her eyes and surrendered to sleep.

29

A New Day Dawns

Something wispy brushed against Annie's cheek. A mosquito? A fairy? She reached up to swat it away, but her hand touched absolutely nothing except her own skin. The air shimmered cold and light. Someone outside was laughing. No. Singing. Children were singing and it sounded ... happy?

She groaned, rolled over, and pulled something soft over her head. It smelled lightly of rosewater and freshly laundered sheets. A pillow. Where did she get a pillow?

Rolling onto her back again, Annie clutched the pillow against her for another moment. Slowly she pulled the soft cloth bundle off her face. She opened her eyes and then squeezed them shut again because sleep still blurred her vision. She opened them once more. The glowing face of the Woman in White floated above her.

"Go-od mor-ning," the ghost sang in her wispy voice.

Annie peered at her while her brain tried to catch up to reality. Light flowed in through the curtains. Curtains? She wasn't on a beach. She was in her bedroom at Miss Cornelia's. The side of her stomach hurt. The wound. Memories flooded back into her brain and she shivered. "It's over."

The Woman in White nodded and smiled, twirling about in a pirouette. "Yes, it is day. It is day. It is a beautiful day! And it is over."

Annie wanted to smile back. The ghost was so silly, but Annie had so many questions, worries tumbling around inside her head that she couldn't allow herself to be happy yet. "The portal! Is the portal still open? Are there still monsters? Is everyone safe? Miss Cornelia? Is she okay? And Canin? And Lichen and the elves? Is Jamie still an angel?"

She tried to remember if Miss Cornelia had sat up at the beach and regained consciousness. She couldn't remember. Worry overwhelmed her and she shivered.

"QUESTIONS!" The Woman in White clasped her hands over her ears and spun down through the floorboards and away, hooting indignantly while she disappeared. She was absolutely no use sometimes. Some things never changed.

"Annie." It was Miss Cornelia, moving toward Annie's bed from the doorway. "Canin is already being looked after."

Joy filled Annie, warming her heart. Miss Cornelia was here, really here, alive and moving and looking pretty spritely in her rainbow skirts and bird sweater.

Cornelia placed her hand on Annie's forehead, looking down at her kindly. "Canin will mend. So will you, if you simmer down. I am fine. The portal is currently still open. There is a sentinel of Ancient Macedonian Angel Bodyguards named Hephaistion and Alexander who are extricating any stray monster that pops through, which they assure me, is much more fun than drifting around the Elysian Fields. They are Jamie's spiritual great-grandfathers, five hundred times removed, thus his name and Plutarch's interest in him. Let's see. The more important question's answer is that the Raiff is a man now, whisked away to Plutarch's prison by the Woman in White who has finally found her Captain. As you can tell, it's best not to ask her about it."

Miss Cornelia wiggled her eyebrows conspiratorially.

Annie had been struggling to sit up and failing miserably. She slumped back onto her pillows again. Miss Cornelia plumped them up behind her back so she could be in more of a sitting position.

"But, Miss Cornelia, what about Jamie and SalGoud and Eva and Bloom and Megan and Lichen and Gran Pie and the werecats and wolves and fairies and the vampire that the Raiff attacked? And what about the Raiff? I know he's a man but is he—"

"Annie, you have to take a deep breath and calm down, or else I won't be able to tell you anything." She smiled. "But Jamie has been constantly at your side. I only just made him leave so he could get a bit of rest. Breathe, Annie. All is well."

The Woman in White returned through the ceiling, and stopped twirling so that she could nod severely. She sat next to Annie and began taking elaborate exaggerated breaths with both her hands on her chest. "Now take a deep breath and count with me. One and a two werecats flirting on a cold aluminum roof and four. Breathe out. Two and seven and porker pigtails. Breathe in."

"Enough, Woman in White, but thank you." Miss Cornelia shooed her away smiling, and the ghost retreated to the window where she pretended to look out at sea, but really she was listening. Ghosts are great eavesdroppers. Miss Cornelia put her hand on Annie's forehead and smoothed her hair. "Bloom is quite fine. Tala, you see, is fine as well."

The great dog plopped his head by Annie's waist. Annie stretched out her arms to hug him and murmured, "I was so worried about you."

Annie stared curiously at the large white dog and his intelligent brown eyes. "Is he really my father?"

The Raiff's voice drifted back into her memory and she stroked the dog's head. Tala's tail wagged.

"He is," Cornelia said. "We're still trying to work out if we can make him human again. His parents, your grandparents, are here from Ireland working on it nonstop."

"The Tullgrens?" Annie's heart soared. "I thought I'd never see them again."

As if by magic, and perhaps by actual magic, the Tullgrens appeared in the doorway. Mrs. Tullgren clutched her husband's arm as they tottered into the bedroom. Purple Magic Marker stained Mr. Tullgren's cheek and fingertips. He anxiously cleared his throat and Mrs. Tullgren left him to saunter over to the bed where she gave both Annie and Tala a kiss on the nose.

Mrs. Tullgren perched on the edge of the bed. "We were worried about you, too. I think, though, that you are through most of the healing hardness and well on the recovery road."

"How long was I asleep?" Annie wasn't sure who to ask. There were so many people to look at, and they were her relatives, her actual biological family. She'd never thought that was even possible.

"Three days. Jamie and the other children will be very happy you are awake. I'm afraid there's no one who is as much fun to get into adventures with as you are." Miss Cornelia beckoned for Mr. Tullgren to come closer. He drifted to the window and opened the shade and curtains.

"The dwarfs are putting skis on Johann's pig car." He sighed and shook his head as he watched the young Irish dwarf working with the Americans, but a slight smile played upon his lips. "I'm so glad to see dwarfs acting like dwarfs." He turned to Annie and finally approached her, tears leaking out the corners of his eyes. "You were so brave, Annie. So brave . . . You are everything I could have ever dreamed to write, to draw. I am so proud to be your grandfather. And I am so incredibly glad that my stories were wrong and . . ." He got all choked up and dabbed at the corners of his eyes with a spotted handkerchief that kept shifting into a butterfly. ". . . And you survived. I am so terribly glad that you survived."

Annie smiled back at him, but she couldn't stop worrying. "But, Miss Cornelia, the Raiff—"

"Is defeated. The demon is gone and only the man remains. Falling off the cliff was foolhardy, Annie, and an unnecessary risk, but it seemed to have worked out, thanks to Jamie. And Bloom. And Doris and SalGoud and Eva. And Red Nose and Megan and the hags . . . Well, it was quite the community effort, really."

Annie swallowed, remembering the horrible fall, the Raiff's changed face, his horns, the cold-cold feel of him. "Is he gone for good?"

His blood was in her. She would never think of it again, she vowed, crossing her fingers.

"He is captured; we have you to thank, and he can't leave Plutarch's prison." Miss Cornelia patted her cheek. "We have also rounded up a good number of his wee little cronies. We used his own trick on him."

Miss Cornelia laughed, and Annie thought she might be gloating. She deserved to gloat. She looked so vibrant again. Annie hated to remember how she'd looked in the Raiff's fortress, so shaken and old. She had a beautiful new rainbow unicorn skirt on and seemed so healthy and strong.

"What did you do?" Annie asked, anxious to know.

"Well, we all went outside to the beach the morning after the Battle of the Fae, and everyone from Aurora who was well, and all the merpeople, touched hands. Then I put out a stop and we all went searching, rounding up the trolls and the werewolves and the vampires. We have given them to Plutarch. He has imprisoned them all. He has been—he's been busy, poor man."

"Were they mad?"

Miss Cornelia chuckled. "Furious. Luckily, Plutarch has been expanding his prisons since the Purge, so we have room now to hold them all, unlike the last time when we had to resort to the Badlands."

"But can they get back through? Any that may still be in the Badlands? They can't just come over?"

"Well, there is this amazing thing about angels, Annie . . ." Mr. Tullgren laughed again; a bird flitted out of his hair and alighted on Annie's bedpost. "Actually, there are many amazing things about angels. Once Jamie is a bit more trained and grows into his powers with Alexander and Hephaistion's tutelage, he'll be able to close that portal or any portal.

Angels also can protect those they love. And Jamie? Even after all he has been through, he loves a lot, you know. That boy's heart is enormous. He's quite special, just like you. Both of you are proof that the human heart can withstand trolls and demons, lack of food, lack of love, all sorts of horrors, and still shine brightly. That is a triumph and the greatest magic of all."

Annie smiled to see her grandfather so obviously gleeful, but her mind was on other things and she had to know. "Miss Cornelia, er, the Raiff said he knew things . . ."

"The Raiff may know things. He may not. You have to understand, Annie, that evil will lie or sin to get its way. It will bend truth to break friendships. It will place greed in front of loyalty." Mrs. Tullgren shook her fist at the walls, almost as if the Raiff was there. Tala licked her wrist and she calmed down immediately, sighing over her poor boy.

Miss Cornelia glanced over at the Tullgrens. "He does not take defeat well, and few have ever handed it to him the way you did, Annie." She closed her eyes for a moment before continuing. "If I had realized that he had the elves, that he had been degrading the strings to suit his wishes, I would have realized why I was losing my magic so rapidly, and that it had nothing whatsoever to do with my age. But that is over and done. My magic and Aurora are blossoming again. The Raiff is just a man now, a trapped man, no longer a demon. And it will not always be up to you to shoulder the burden of making evil go away. We have Jamie. We have the elves. We even have the Tullgrens visiting from Ireland! Mrs. Tullgren is already at work making a new Gnome of Protection. It's her forte. Well, one of her many . . ."

Miss Cornelia pointed at the bed, and it hovered in the air and then glided effortlessly toward the window so that Annie could see outside. People were working on the carnival setup and the pig car. Behind them was the sea and the portal to the Badlands. Two gigantic transparent warriors armed with daggers and dressed in chitons guarded it, but seemed bored at the moment and were playing cards.

Miss Cornelia cleared her throat and continued, "You have friends out there to help you now, you know. And you have me."

"And us!" Mr. Tullgren exclaimed.

"She bloody better know she has us." Mrs. Tullgren shook her head. "Have you been making any bunnies magically appear lately? That's Tullgren magic, you know."

Annie didn't know what to say. She stared at the carnival workers, putting up a gigantic yellow slide. She stared at Eva and Johann arguing about the length of the skis they were attaching to the pig car's tires. How had they even gotten that here from Ireland? Tala jumped back onto the bed, jostling her. He lay across her lap and whined. She rubbed behind his ears.

"The Raiff said 'woof,'" Annie whispered.

Miss Cornelia cocked her head. "What?"

"When I asked about my father, he said his own magic had transformed him, something about the Tullgren magic always being a bit different or weird or something and then he said, 'woof.'" Annie's hand stilled on Tala's fur. He was her dad, her real dad, and the realization once again hit her full force.

Annie threw her arms around the dog and sobbed. It didn't matter that he was furry. It didn't matter that he drooled. She had found her dad, or he had found her. Between him and Miss Cornelia and the Tullgrens in Ireland, she had a family. A real family. And so did Bloom. It was only Jamie who didn't, which she explained in gasping sobs to Miss Cornelia.

"But he does, Annie," Cornelia said. "He has us. You and me and this entire town. Plus, Heppie and Alexander. For all our good parts, all our less-than-good parts, we are his family. Always. Just like you promised. Let's go find him, all right?"

Miss Cornelia pointed at the bed again and then the door, which shot open. A dwarf waited outside. He gave a little wave and bowed.

"You ready to see some friends?" Miss Cornelia asked.

"Oh, yes," Annie said, and as soon as she spoke the words her bed glided over her mossy carpet and out the door, levitating above the floor and swiftly moving down the hall. It stopped at the top of the stairs. A great noise rushed up from the front room and Annie blinked her eyes, arm solidly around Tala's furry bulk. It seemed as if all the residents of Aurora had crowded into the house's front room. In their hands they held signs that reminded her of the signs they'd held when she entered town, and when she, Jamie, Bloom, and Eva had defeated the crow monster.

HOORAY FOR ANNIE! one said.

ANNIE NOBODY IS A SOMEBODY, read another.

YIPPEE FOR ANNIE!!

Another, held up by twenty struggling pixies, read, JAMIE IS CUTE.

"Three cheers for our Annie!" yelled Purcee. He had his arm in a sling and looked quite heroic. He blew Annie a kiss with his good arm. She blushed.

"Yes, three cheers," said Miss Cornelia, waving her arms about to direct them.

"Hip hip, hooray!" they yelled. "Hip hip, hooray!"

Annie found her favorite elf in the front of the group. A bandage covered his forehead but he looked healthy. The bunny sat on Bloom's shoulder and he didn't hold a sign in his paws. He clapped them instead and gave a big whistle. Next to Bloom was the most beautiful woman ever. Aster. His mother.

"We did it, Annie!" Bloom yelled above the crowd's roar. "We did it!"

They began to cheer for him, too, chanting his name. He

waved them off and shrugged. Eva ran inside and roared, "CHANT MY NAME!" and SalGoud, standing next to her, started laughing, doubled over at his waist.

"Outside, everyone outside!" Gramma Doris called. "We need room for celebration cakes."

"And pies," Helena added.

Mr. Nate already had lemon meringue on his face. "And scones and doughnuts and macaroons and cupcakes . . ."

Everyone hustled to the front lawn, and Annie's bed floated out behind them. She searched for Jamie. The world wasn't as cold as she expected it to be and Mrs. Tullgren explained she had created a nice "BE WARM" spell. Plus, Grady O'Grady had used his breath to start a gigantic bonfire that the pixies and fairies frolicked around happily.

As she headed toward the side yard, Megan hopped on Annie's bed. "I don't hate you, you know."

"I don't hate you either," Annie admitted.

"I have crushes on the elves. All the elves." Megan showed Annie her phone which was full of elf pictures.

"Oh . . ." Annie didn't know what to say. "Does that get confusing?"

"Only in a good way." Megan preened. "Lichen's my favorite, though. He calls me his Healing Hag." Megan flopped back against the pillows. "Best nickname ever. He's even cuter now that he isn't dying. He's almost as cute as Bloom."

There was a flurry of motion and Gramma Doris snapped her fingers and started running around in circles. "She's here! She's here! Everyone try to look not magical. Hurry! Hurry! Pixies, fairies, and all Big Feet, please hide. There is no disguising your magic. The rest of you just try to act like quirky humans! Hurry!"

A small car thundered up the hill and Annie gasped. Fear filled her. She knew that car . . . It was Mrs. Betsey's car, her social worker, the one who'd brought her to the Wiegles and abandoned her there. If she was here then that meant she'd take Annie away again.

"Oh no!" Annie gasped.

Megan touched Annie's hair and then snapped her fingers to make it look more coiffed. "Don't worry, Annie. It's okay."

"You don't understand . . ." Annie began, but before she could finish Mrs. Betsey was out of her car and teetering over to her, unsteady in the snow thanks to her high-heeled shoes. Mr. Nate and Miss Cornelia were actually helping her over toward Annie's bed, which was no longer floating and now safely on the ground like an un-magical bed.

"Oh, no . . ." Annie panicked and tried to hide under the covers before Mrs. Betsey reached her.

"You're messing up your hair!" Megan scolded, snapping her fingers and fixing Annie's unruly hair into a really tall beehive while simultaneously pulling her out from beneath the covers.

Miss Cornelia rushed forward and met Mrs. Betsey. The two women chatted happily as if they were old friends as Miss Cornelia ushered the other woman toward Annie.

Panic made Annie's heart race. She grabbed Megan's hand and tried her best to not hide back under the covers. How could this be happening?

And then she finally saw Jamie standing by the edge of the house. He glowed. He seemed a tiny bit taller, and a little bit more filled in, as if Helena had been feeding him baked goods by the box, but still 100 percent Jamie. He smiled and walked over. His wings were completely hidden away somehow.

She grabbed his hand with her free one and whispered, "I can't go back, Jamie. I can't."

"You aren't."

"I'm not?"

"No. Miss Cornelia would never let that happen." He squeezed her hand gently, entwining their fingers. "I would never let that happen. None of us would, right, Megan?"

"So right," Megan said. "I mean I used to think you were a super pain, but I just read the prophecy wrong and—"

"SO FREAKING RIGHT!" Eva thundered over and hopped on the end of the bed.

Everyone hushed her because saying "freaking" in front

of Mrs. Betsey probably wasn't the best way to make a good impression.

They couldn't say any more because the two women had arrived at the side of her bed.

"Oh, sit up straight, Annie," Mrs. Betsey scolded. "You look like something the cat dragged in. Except your hair, which looks lovely."

Speaking of cats, Purcee jumped on the bed and landed on Annie's lap, purring. Everyone seemed happy. Her grandparents. Tala. Jamie. Miss Cornelia. Eva. Bloom. SalGoud. Canin. Even Megan and the hags. Johann gave her an enthusiastic thumbs-up and an ax wave before Helena scurried over and made him hide his ax behind his back.

"Look like a quirky human," Helena admonished as she spritzed cinnamon spray, filling the air around them.

"Axes are quirky," Johann sputtered. "Cinnamon clouds, not so much."

Mrs. Betsey's mouth dropped open and then she regained her composure and cleared her throat. "Miss Cornelia, since you have submitted all the appropriate paperwork, let me quickly say that you have now on what was a bitter cold, late winter day that has suddenly turned warm, surrounded by all these . . ." She quickly surveyed the peculiar and unusual residents of Aurora, the small, the furred, the giant, the strangely dressed, the covered in sugar. ". . . witnesses . . . for lack of a better word." She faltered in her speech and whipped out two pieces of paper. "Yes. Um. Anyway, since you prove to want what nobody else would want, I hereby declare that Annie Nobody and James Hephaistion Alexander are officially adopted. You and Mr. and Mrs. Tullgren are their legal guardians. Their lives and upbringing rest solely on you."

"And me," Doris grumped, crossing her arms in front of her chest.

"And me," said Ned the Doctor.

"And us," said Helena, pulling Mr. Nate to her side with an expert lashing of cheesecloth.

"And me," said Canin, smiling.

"And me," said Gran Pie, emerging from behind a large shrub.

Mrs. Betsey stepped backward. "My, that's a hairy one. And to think all of you, this whole town, right here on the island, and I never even knew it existed. It's almost as if you'd been hidden away by magic."

She coughed nervously and pushed the papers into an astonished Annie and Jamie's hands.

"So, yes, congratulations. Good luck to you, Miss Cornelia. I hope you know you'll have your hands full with that—that—girl." Mrs. Betsey pointed at Annie dismissively and with great loathing. This, of course, caused both Tala and Canin to growl threateningly even though Canin was in human form. Eva grumbled something about her ax. Mrs. Betsey cleared her throat and seemed suddenly quite eager to leave. She gave an awkward little wave and rushed back toward her car as dozens of pixies flitted after her. She paused and looked behind her. The pixies vanished. "I do like your hair, Annie."

Annie stared after her, openmouthed. Mrs. Betsey had never actually complimented her before.

Mrs. Betsey blinked hard, staring toward Johann and the dwarfs. "Is that a pig car over there?"

"Yes," Miss Cornelia said. "It's decorated for a parade."

"Ah . . . yes . . . right . . ." Mrs. Betsey unlocked her car and scrambled inside, backing away and out of the driveway without another word. The people of Aurora, the furry ones and cranky ones, the very magic ones, and the barely magic ones, all watched her descend the hill.

"Does . . . does . . . What does this mean?" Annie asked quietly even as Mrs. Betsey managed to turn the car the right way and motor down the road toward the town of Mount Desert and village of Northeast Harbor.

"It means that we're adopted, Annie. That this is our forever home, here, in Aurora, with Miss Cornelia," Jamie said, smiling.

"With the Tullgrens having visitation rights, of course," SalGoud said.

Leodora unrolled a giant parchment and flicked her hand. The parchment hovered in midair and expanded.

The Aurora town council hereby declares that James Hephaistion Alexander and Annie ~~Nobody~~ Aquarius-Tullgren are forever residents of Aurora, Maine, and are granted full citizenship now and always.

Thanks to these children and the heroic actions of their forever friends, Eva, Bloom, SalGoud, and Megan, we can be at magical peace. Their names will be inscribed in the town hall as forever heroes.

We are indebted to them always and proud to call them our own.

Signed, the Council

Tears sprang to Annie's eyes. She sat up fully, much to the dismay of Helena and Mrs. Tullgren, and grabbed Miss Cornelia in a huge hug. Then she yanked Jamie into the hug, too. A forever home. Here in Aurora.

"They can't ever take us away?" Annie asked, voice breaking.

"No," Miss Cornelia whispered into her hair. "Not ever."

The townspeople began to chant Annie's name.

"Let the tales of exaltation, brilliance, and triumph begin!" yelled the grogans, all suddenly appearing on Annie's bed.

"And barbeque! It's time for a good barbeque!" added Bench of John.

Everyone started chanting Jamie's name, too. And then Eva demanded songs be sung of her own specific glory, and a bunch of stone giants complied while the fairies danced around the bonfire and the elves sang songs and looked glorious in their new clothes. Grady O'Grady landed back on the lawn and they slid down his spine while he pontificated about the Red Sox taking the American League Championship next season. Farkey and the other merpeople floated out of Aquarius House in water bubbles and joined in the celebration, which was quite an honor.

That afternoon, Annie was strong enough to get out of bed and meet all her friends outside by the carnival, standing beneath the giant Ferris wheel, bundled up in parkas and winter coats to battle the winter cold, since the BE WARM spell wore off.

Eva was still hopping up and down, excited, swaying her ax through the air. "I'm a freaking superstar. We all are. We totally kicked butt. They'll be singing about us forever."

"I would prefer poetic odes and good quotes," SalGoud said, staring up at the Ferris wheel's golden carriages.

"Life better not get boring. That's all I have to say," Eva said, tucking her ax into her belt and making a big bulge in her parka.

Bloom smiled. "I don't think it'll get boring, Eva."

"That's because you're an elf. All you people do is sit around and stare at trees all day and smell herbs." Eva winked at Annie, but Bloom caught it, too.

"Better than fighting all day," Bloom countered. Eva started to do her normal blustering talk, but Bloom continued. "Thank you all. Really. I never would have had my mother again if it weren't for you."

"I wouldn't know that Tala was my dad," Annie said.

"That's so weird." Eva squatted down and Tala trotted over to her and licked her face. She petted her other cheek. "That one has Nutella on it. It probably tastes better."

Tala licked the other cheek.

"I'm just glad that you guys liked me and stood by me even when you thought I might turn troll," Jamie said. He smiled at all of them. "So what now?"

Annie met Jamie's eyes and knew what he was thinking. He was thinking about trying to find his biological parents, getting skilled enough to close that portal, being the best angel he could be.

"I think we should go back to the Badlands," Bloom said. "Eventually. Maybe we could make it into someplace safe."

"A Not So Badlands?" Eva scoffed.

"Why not?" SalGoud said. He clapped Bloom on the back. "I think this is a fantastic idea. As Bo Jackson said, 'Set your goals high and don't stop till you get there.' Also, I would like to finish *SalGoud's Book of Self-Created Quotations*."

"I'd like to win everything at the carnival," Eva announced.

"And hunt down any wayward trolls that might not have been caught yet. I want more adventures with or without Johann and the grogans. They are kind of showboats."

"Takes one to know one." Bloom laughed.

She kicked him and missed.

"How about you, Jamie?"

"Maybe we could check on everyone in Scot's Land and make sure they are okay now that the Queen is gone." He tucked Annie's hair inside her hat. "I was just thinking about what else we could do and the adventures we could have and how we should always stay friends forever."

So was Annie.

And she already knew where they'd start. They'd figure out what it meant for Jamie to be an angel. They'd go to the carnival and win all sorts of prizes.

"We only succeeded because we worked together," Annie said quietly, looking at each of them in turn. "It's because we never gave up on one another that we won. You guys know that, right?"

"Blah . . . blah . . . blah . . . ," Eva muttered, but then before anyone could scold her, she looked up and said softly, "You guys are the best friends a dwarf could ever have. Let's bring it in for a hug. Come on. You aren't going to get this chance again."

Nobody moved for a second.

"Come on!" Eva roared, opening her arms wide and motioning with her hands. "Hug a dwarf!"

Laughing, the children rushed in, wrapping their arms around one another.

"Friends forever!" Jamie yelled, glowing as his wings accidentally burst through his shirt and coat, tearing the fabric.

"And longer!" Bloom yelled. "And to wing-proof new coats for Jamie. And quotes for SalGoud and battles for Eva and . . . and . . . what for you, Annie?"

"Friendship," Annie said, holding on to her friends as tightly as she could. "Friendship and family forever. We'll do everything and anything and we'll do it all together!"

And they would.

Acknowledgments

Thank you to Emily Ciciotte of the Glory-Filled Land of Wisdom and Super Stardom, who like most brilliant and amazing people wanted a certain kind of story. I am so lucky to be able to give it to her. Her heart and gumption and mind inspired so many of the characters in these stories and are what made me a writer. You can see pieces of her everywhere.

Thanks to Shaun Farrar of the Awesomest Man Ever, who somehow always manages to love me and save me, over and over again. There is no better man for me than you. There is no better love. I am so sorry you are the second paragraph.

Thank you to my agent, Ammi-Joan Paquette.

Thanks to the dynamic editorial team of Hali Baumstein

and Cindy Loh. They are brilliant, kind, quirky, and full of so much magic. This book and series would not have existed without their wisdom.

The amazing, passionate Bloomsbury team makes everything magical. Thank you to Donna Mark, John Candell, and Owen Richardson, who made this into such a beautiful book. Thank you to Linda Minton, Diane Aronson, Liz Byer, Amanda Bartlett, and Melissa Kavonic, the managing editor. They all are unsung heroes. As are Courtney Griffin and Lizzy Mason in publicity as well as Cristina Gilbert, Erica Barmash, Emily Ritter, Ellen Whitaker, Shae McDaniel, Beth Eller, and Brittany Mitchell in marketing.

Many thanks to the people who inspired the grogans. You know who you are. A special shout-out to Mike and Lynn Staggs as well as Steven and Jenna Boucher.

Thank you to the readers, librarians, teachers, writers, kids, and other humans. I still can't quite believe how awesome you are and that you read my books and support them. It means everything to me.